Murder
at the
Arlington

Murder
at the
Arlington

Kathleen Kaska

SALVO PRESS
Portland, Oregon

This is a work of fiction. All characters and events portrayed in this novel are fictitious and not intended to represent real people or places.

Although the locale where this story takes place is a real one, various liberties have been taken, and this book does not purport to offer an exact depiction of any particular place or location.

Murder at the Arlington
Copyright © 2009 by Kathleen Kaska

Salvo Press
Portland, Oregon
www.salvopress.com

Vintage cover image of Arlington Hotel provided courtesy of The Arlington Hotel, and based on an old post card.

Cover istockphoto Image of woman by Anna Bryukhanova of Moscow, Russia
Cover istockphoto image of blood by Renee Lee of Salt Lake City

Library of Congress Control Number: 2008938958

ISBN: 9781930486898
1-930486-89-8

Printed in U.S.A.
First Edition

For my San Juan Island writers' group,
Mary Kalbert, and Pam and Mike Herber,
and their ongoing encouragement and belief in Sydney.

With special thanks to the following individuals: For reviewing the manuscript and their very helpful suggestions, my three bright and funny sisters, Karen Stanford, Karla Klyng, and Krisann Price; Jo Virgil of Austin, Texas; Mike Starring of Oak Harbor, Washington; Jim Devaney of Friday Harbor, Washington; and my long-time friend, Ruth Bilbo of Dallas, Texas; and for their warmth and friendly hospitality, the entire staff of the Arlington Hotel.

Chapter 1

Red Newsome had warned me not to enter his joint unescorted. He'd said he wouldn't stop me, but he couldn't be held responsible for my white ass if things got nasty. I tucked my unruly hair under a shabby fedora. I'd picked up the hat at Goodwill, along with a full suit of men's clothes, complete with shiny wing tips. My scheme, which earlier in the day seemed brilliant, now teetered on idiotic. Other than my makeshift costume, the only thing that allowed me to pass as a man was my height. And once inside the Crooked J, my chances were slim-to-none that I'd get an interview with Hound Dog Jackson anyway.

Those obstacles, however, had not crossed my mind when Ernest, my editor, at the *Austin American Statesman* assigned me to get an interview with the elusive Jackson who was performing right here in Austin. Having come aboard only a few weeks ago, I'd jumped at the chance to get the story even though the Crooked J was on the east side of town, even if few whites frequented the establishment, even if any woman going there alone was asking for trouble. Trouble seemed to follow me, so what did it matter? Besides, knowing Ernest, I'm sure he didn't care how I got the interview.

My name is Sydney Jean Lockhart. I'm a reporter, working my way from Travel and Entertainment to hardcore reporting. I like to think of myself as a woman ahead of her time—a time that in my opinion is still archaic. Despite Queen Elizabeth's coronation and Lucy's domination of television airwaves, society still frowns on single women working in a man's world, even in 1952. So, when Newsome warned me not to walk into the Crooked J alone, I took it as a direct challenge.

I gave myself a pep talk and glued on a red mustache. Confidence in my disguise returned. Besides, Newsome and I had only spoken over the phone; he had no idea what I looked liked.

Soon after slapping Old Spice on my cheeks, I elbowed my way up to the Crooked J's bar and ordered a gin on the rocks. The band was on break and to keep the crowd in a frenzy, the bartender had fed the juke-box a pocket of dimes. The walls throbbed to the beat of Glenn Miller's 'In the Mood.' Through the thick blue haze, the sparkle of glitter and glint flashed across the dance floor as rotating spotlights reflected off shimmering clothing and slicked-back pompadours. Women twirled through the arms of their lithe dance partners and slid under their legs with such ease and fluidity they looked like paper streamers whirling in the breeze.

I sipped my drink and lit up. So far so good. No one paid me the least bit of attention. My plan was to listen to the next set and be at the stage door when Jackson took another break. I swayed with the melody when someone bumped my arm and sloshed gin onto my sleeve and cufflink.

"Hmmm. Don't you smell nice." A young woman sidled up to me. If it weren't for her glimmering emerald dress, she would have been invisible in the darkness. "Not many white boys come in here. But you just buy me a drink like we're old friends and everything'll be fine. Call me Vivian."

Trying to deepen my voice would have given me away in an instant. I tapped my cigarette pack on the bar and offered Vivian a smoke, then nodded to the bartender to pour her a drink.

"Vodka martini," Vivian called out. "Wanna dance?" She nuzzled my arm.

My insides burned and it wasn't from the gin. My plan hadn't included being picked up. What the hell; I figured dancing was better than talking. My mother had taught me to jitterbug, which meant I'd learned by leading (probably the reason I couldn't keep a boyfriend). Vivian downed half her martini and seconds later we were rollicking with the rest of the crowd. The top of her head reached to my shoulder. Twirling her was easy. She was light on her feet and I was beginning to feel pretty sassy myself.

Out of the corner of my eye, I noticed the band milling around, preparing for their second set. I danced Vivian toward the stage, but before I could jitterbug closer, a huge presence parted the crowd and glided toward us. Accompanying the figure was a booming voice, which shouted over the music, freezing the dancers in mid-step.

"Vivian! I thought you was home with that bag-of-bones grandmother of yours."

"Gerald, honey. This here's my cousin from Biloxi," Vivian stammered.

"Like hell, Vi. You ain't got no white kin."

Next thing I knew, my feet left the dance floor and seconds later I slid across the stage. My fedora flew off and my hair sprang free as if anxious to announce to the crowd that a transvestite, now entangled in mike stands and electric wires, was in the house. The place went silent. Vivian picked herself up from the floor, took one look at me, squealed, and disappeared into the crowd. Much to my relief, Gerald disappeared as well. From behind the bar, a guy whom I'd assumed was Red Newsome, sauntered up to the stage.

"Miss Lockhart?" he said.

"How could you tell?" I spit the mustache from my mouth and disentangled myself from the drum set.

Red Newsome whisked me off the stage and out of the public's eye, since the blood that trickled from my forehead and slid down the side of my face caused two women to pass out. And since setting up for the next set took longer than anticipated, I had the opportunity to meet Jackson backstage. Anyone who'd gone to the trouble I had, he said, deserved a few minutes of his time. So, with my necktie wrapped around my head, I got my interview quick and was gone.

I arrived back at my apartment around one after a stop at the emergency room. I was confident that once the stitches were removed, the scar near my hairline wouldn't be noticeable. Regardless of the risks involved in my job, and I wouldn't change it for the world. My current profession is a breeze compared to what I used to do. For two years, I taught life science at Limestone Ridge Junior High. Staring down thirty adolescents every morning for the rest of my working life was unthinkable. Writing for a living was a cinch.

I exchanged my man clothes for pink and white striped PJs, pushed my poodle Monroe and my cat Mealworm over to the side, and crawled into bed. My alarm was set for five, but I needn't have bothered. I spent a fitful night listening to the hall clock chime every hour. As sheep number 482 leapt over the fence with a smirk on her face and a cigarette dangling from her lips, I finally gave up on the sandman. Instead, I lay there listening to Monroe's rhythmic breathing. Her warm poodle-body, butt side up, was plastered against me. Mealworm, curled up like a huge cinnamon roll, purred contentedly on my head. At four I slipped out of bed and plugged in my percolator.

While coffee stimulated my brain, I put the final touches on the Hound Dog Jackson article, then dropped it off at the paper. This afternoon I was leaving for Hot Springs, Arkansas on my next assignment, a travel article, not my idea of reporting, but I was low woman on the totem pole. All I had left to do was pack and drive my girls over to my brother Scott's house. I stuffed the last bit of a cold cheese sandwich in my mouth and was rinsing my coffee pot when the phone rang.

"Ready to go?"

"Almost. What's up, Dad?"

"I'm glad you're staying at the Arlington. It's the best hotel in Hot Springs."

"So you've said many times."

"You're booked in 1119, right?"

"You know I am."

"That's where it happened. Thirty years ago last November 15th."

"Shut up, George," my mother called from the kitchen. Old habits die hard. When my mother lived at home, no matter where she was when the phone rang, she'd hurry into the kitchen to attend to something. From that location she could eavesdrop.

"Mom's there?"

"Came this morning to remind me to trim the oleanders. Now she's making my lunch."

After my father retired from Houston Power and Light, they moved back to Galveston where they had both grown up. Having Dad home all the time caused Mom to become really flighty. She'd always had one foot out the door on her way back to Hollywood, where, in her younger days, she dabbled in acting, hoping to make it as a silent-film actress. The closest she'd ever come to stardom was an audition. She lost out to Clara Bow who went on to become the It Girl and Hollywood's new star. But then something happened a few weeks ago after my parents began planning their thirtieth anniversary celebration. The happy moment grew to a heated frenzy, and my mom moved into a friend's beach house on the west end of the island, coming home on occasion to tend to various tasks she'd never bothered with before, like fixing Dad a meal. But live under the same roof with him again, "Never!" she professed.

"What's she saying?" Mom called.

"With you yammering in my ear, Mary Lou, how in the hell can I hear what she's saying?" He lowered his voice, "You're sure there was no problem with you getting that room?"

"It's all set, Dad. The room's reserved. I'm flying to Dallas to stay with Ruth tonight. Tomorrow I'll be in Hot Springs."

"George, stop with that room already." Mary Lou Lockhart could hear a fly sneeze from across town. "Tell her I don't like her traveling alone. Bad things happen to women who travel alone."

"She's a big girl."

"What if she has car trouble?"

"Sydney can take care of herself."

"What if she gets a flat tire?"

"She won't—"

"She could run out of gas."

"For Christ sake, Mary Lou, she knows how to read a gas gauge."

"Tell her not to pick up hitchhikers."

I was no longer part of the conversation so I hung up and left them to their bickering. I pulled out my suitcase and selected a few appropriate outfits. I narrowed my choice of shoes down to eight. When my suitcase wouldn't close, I decided to go with only one pair of sandals. The stroll to the hotel's mineral pool would require a low heel, unless I wanted to look like a tart, and sometimes I did. I was contemplating my black, leather slings or my favorite jade-green Roman-style sandals that laced up over the ankles. The phone rang again.

"Don't take those green shoes. They make you look—"

"Like a tart?"

"I didn't say that."

"Mom, is that bathtub story really true?"

"Your father's such a fool."

"Well, is it?"

"I don't remember."

"How could you not remember something like that?"

"You're not going to talk about that at the hotel are you?"

"You mean in my interviews? No, I don't think that information will be needed for my travel article."

"Mom, is there any chance that maybe you and Dad . . . well, can talk about what—"

"Promise me you won't mention the bathtub."

"I promise. But, Mom—"

She hung up; her way of having the last word. Only family members received the abrupt disconnect. Once, after a ten-minute conversation with a wrong-number caller, I heard her tell the guy not to worry so much that everything would be fine and to call back anytime. Unlike my mother's tightlipped behavior, my father told me everything. Whatever had caused my parents to separate after thirty years was a mystery to both of us. In the meantime, I would not let it get to me. They were adults; it was their problem. I had a job to do.

With a fresh bandage covering my throbbing wound and a few ringlets covering the bandage, all evidence of last night's encounter with Gerald was well hidden. I tucked my undies in my overnight kit, threw in my Chicago Cubs cap, and my jade sandals. I snapped my suitcase shut and sat it by the door. Monroe began to mope, and Mealworm's tail twitch with excitement. I understood my poodle's anxiety, but I wasn't sure why Mealworm got so happy. I suspected she knew where she was going, because she lives to torture Scott. He refers to her as the Vixen. Last time he kept the girls, Mealworm spent the afternoon stalking him and when he dozed off on the sofa, she sunk her teeth into his ear.

I left my quaint West Austin neighborhood and as soon as I hit the Lamar Bridge, heading south, my fourteen-year old Ford, sputtered and popped. Thankfully, it responded to my prayers and minutes later I squealed to a stop in Scott's driveway. I tooted the horn. My feelings of being a bad mother disappeared immediately when my brother's room-mate, Jeremiah, skipped out of the house and down the front porch. In his long, white terry-cloth robe with red roses sewn on the lapels and red felt slippers adorning his feet, he was a joyous sight.

"When did you come back?" I said.

"Well, honey, to tell the truth, I was never coming back." He lifted Mealworm out of her carrier and showered her with kisses. "But when Scott called yesterday, complaining about having to take care of your pets, well what could I do? I can always split again after you get back." He looked around as if to make sure the neighbors weren't at their screen doors listening, as if the robe wasn't a dead giveaway.

"Jeremiah, do you ever get the feeling that you're being used?"

"Oh, my yes. That's what I live for, honey. Hey, what happened to your head?"

"You don't want to know."

We walked inside and Monroe went straight for the sofa, rearranged the pillows to her liking, and settled in. I looked around.

"Scott's working late. He sends his love and hopes you have a fantastic trip. Coffee?" Jeremiah loves playing peacemaker as well as homemaker.

"He's avoiding me. But that's okay."

"Scott's just upset with your father about the . . . incident."

"He always takes Mom's side. We don't even know what the incident is. It may not be Dad's fault. Never mind. I'm not going to worry about it. No thanks on the coffee, I'm running late."

"Don't worry about the girls. I have your feeding instructions from last time. I promise not to give Mealworm any cream, at least not without donning a gas mask first, and I promise I'll stay until you return, no matter how horrible your brother treats me." He wiped away make-believe tears.

"By the way, have you been in that robe all day?"

"It's for effect, honey."

I kissed the girls, and before I made it to the front door, Mealworm retched on the Navajo rug I had brought Scott from New Mexico.

Chapter 2

My car coughed up a plume of black smoke and died just as I turned into a parking space. I rolled to a stop, left the heap to rest in peace, grabbed my bags, and sprinted to the Pioneer Airline gate with five minutes to spare. Less than an hour later I was at Love Field. I threw my bags in the trunk of the sporty, little number I'd rented, and was on my way to my cousin's house as the sun said goodbye to the Texas prairie.

Before I could ring the doorbell, the door flew open. "You're late, as usual." Ruth rose up on her toes, giving me a peck on the cheek. She stood five one in pumps. Standing next to one another, we looked like Mutt and Jeff.

"I'm not late."

"Let's go. I have dinner reservations at the Adolphus. What happened to you? You look like you've been in a fight." She eyed my causal slacks and saddle shoes with disapproval. Ruth was dressed in a white Chanel suit trimmed in something that had one time kept a small animal warm.

"Gerald caught me dancing with his girlfriend."

"Well, you should know better. Where's your Ford?"

"I flew. My Ford is at the airport, near death. I'm afraid it's done for."

"Let's take your rental. My car is on the blink, too. I had to put it in the shop today."

Twenty minutes later we were seated in the Adolphus Hotel bar, enjoying a round of martinis.

"I cleared my calendar and I can go to Hot Springs with you."

"What calendar?"

"Don't be funny. Besides, I don't like you driving across country alone. You could get kidnapped."

"You sound like Mom. And I'm not going cross country, just to a neighboring state."

"I won't be in the way."

"Yes, you would. I'm working. This isn't a vacation. Didn't anyone ever tell you it's gauche to wear white after Labor Day?"

"I'm a trendsetter. A toast." She held up her glass. "I want to celebrate."

"Celebrate what?"

"My new foundation."

"Who are you saving this time?"

"It's a program for divorced women between the ages of twenty and twenty-five from Highland Park and whose parents have disowned them. These poor women have no place to go."

"Aren't those parameters a bit narrow?"

"I don't want an overflow of candidates right from the start."

"Candidates?"

"Well, victims, then."

Ruth's heart was in the right place, but she had not quite gotten the hang of philanthropy. My cousin is a wealthy young woman. Her father, my mother's brother, owned a huge cattle ranch in South Texas. Uncle Martin had a fatal heart attack a couple of years ago while visiting a neighboring ranch—the infamous Chicken Ranch—a brothel in LaGrange. Ruth and her mother Francie sold the cattle ranch the day after the funeral. Ruth probably has more money than Howard Hughes and a newfound freedom that both she and her mother enjoy. In fact, Aunt Francie has been vacationing in Europe for the last six months.

"Speaking of victims, how's your dad?"

"He'll survive."

"Any idea what's bothering your mother?"

"Nope."

"That's a real shame. Maybe I should call."

"Don't waste your time.

Ruth motioned for the waiter to bring another round.

"Hey, I have to get up early."

"I'll have you in bed before midnight," Ruth laughed. "Who's Gerald? Do I know him? Does he have a brother?"

The next morning I awoke up, with only a slight hangover, to the smell of coffee, and by the time I emerged from the shower, Ruth announced that breakfast was ready. I walked into her state-of-the-art kitchen and my

stomach rolled over and played dead at the sight of Vanilla Wafers and
something green jelled in a bowl.

"Don't be picky," Ruth said. "It's Sophia's day off. I hope this coffee's
not too strong."

Le—mug

She handed me a Limoges cup and saucer. The tea-colored brew was-
n't even dark enough to cover the flower pattern in the bottom of the cup.
I passed on breakfast and coffee, and listened once more to Ruth's pleading to come along. She has a one-track mind; derailing it is like trying to
stop a locomotive with a feather. I stood firm. I knew what would happen.
She'd become a nuisance after the first ten minutes, and I wouldn't get
any work done.

I grabbed a handful of Vanilla Wafers. "Gotta go. I want to miss—"

"You might decide you need me. I can proof your work."

"—the rush-hour traffic."

Ruth followed me outside to the curb and froze. The sunlight sparkled
on the fender of my blood-red rental and ricocheted off the hood orna-
ment. Seeing the flashy car in broad daylight rendered my cousin speechless. I took advantage of the rare opportunity, hopped in the car, waved
her a heartfelt goodbye, and left.

As I drove through the tony Highland Park neighborhood, I fiddled
with the radio and found Doris Day singing 'When I Fall in Love.' It was
a cool, crisp morning, but I didn't care. My hair was tied back with a
green ribbon and I was ready to feel the wind in my face. I lit a cigarette
and stepped on the gas. Soon the opulent mansions gave way to open
fields, and before I knew it, I was heading east down Highway 30 in my
rented Plymouth Coup convertible.

Seven hours later, I exited at Caddo Valley onto Route 7 and in no time
I was in downtown Hot Springs turning onto Central Avenue, otherwise
known as Bathhouse Row. A string of magnolia trees lined the east side
of the street shading the eight bathhouses. I slowly cruised by, taking in
the scenery. Relaxed-looking men and women, wearing white robes
lounged on the front porches of the Buckstaff Bathhouse. Many of these
old spas now sat quiet like dressed-up dowagers resting after decades of
entertaining the country's elite. Across the street, were gifts shops, restau-
rants, and bars, including the infamous Ohio Club where Al Capone and
Bugsy Seigel once held court.

After I'd accepted the assignment, I'd spent a couple of days in the
library, combing through periodicals to get a feel for Arkansas' second

largest town. Up until the early forties, people flocked to Hot Springs to "take the waters," a sure cure for everything from rheumatism to premature balding. After World War II, the health craze began to fade, and a new attraction, one more exciting and lucrative, moved to town. Illegal gambling drew a new kind of tourist, and although the town had been cleaned up a few years ago and had settled into a period of cautious tranquility, the fallout of gangsterdom still lingered.

Just past the bathhouses, the avenue formed a Y and the historic Arlington Hotel came into view like a sentinel from the past. The eleven-story hotel is an architectural wonder with spires reaching above the trees and swimming pools and hot minerals tubs built into the mountainside. The Arlington's publicity packet boasted of soothing mineral water piped from the aquifer directly into the guest rooms. The hotel's own spa rivals those on Bathhouse Row. In the thirties and forties, the hotel played host to presidents and dignitaries. The formality had long disappeared, but the elegance remained. The folks at the Arlington, learning of my assignment, were delighted to have some free publicity thrown their way.

I pulled into the parking garage and was swarmed by a flurry of attendants. I pitched my keys to a valet and minutes later, I was standing in the lobby. Two sweeping staircases framed the room. Overstuffed lounge chairs and deep sofas were tastefully mingled with modern and antique furnishings. Soft chandelier lighting spread a welcoming glow across the room. Plumes of cigarette smoke rose above open newspapers. A piano tinkled in the background.

Unfortunately, there was a long line at the front desk, waiting to check in. I was tired after my long journey and soon grew impatient. My grumbling stomach caused the woman in front of me to turn around and shoot me a disapproving look. All I had eaten were the Vanilla Wafers. I wanted nothing more than to throw my bags on the bed, order room service, don my bathing suit, and head for the outdoor-mineral pool. In my thousands of miles of traveling, I'd also learned never to expect things to work out as planned.

Finally, it was my turn at the front desk. "I'm Sydney Lockhart. I had room 1119 reserved."

"That room's not quite ready, ma'am." A tall, morose woman with tightly curled, gray hair tried unsuccessfully to smile. Her name tag read "Mrs. Willis."

"But it's four o'clock," I said.

"I understand. I can put you in another room immediately; it's just that 1119 isn't ready."

Acid started to boil in the pit of my empty stomach. My feet suddenly throbbed. The image of myself soaking in the mineral pool evaporated. This was not good.

"Check in time is at three." I tapped the crystal on my watch.

"I understand, but we had a late check-out and the housemaid has not yet cleaned that room."

"How long of a wait are we talking about?" It was hot in the lobby.

"I'm not sure," Mrs. Willis said.

"Could you check, please. After all, I am here to write an article about this hotel."

"I'll see what I can do."

"Thank you."

She ordered a bellboy to ride up to the eleventh floor and check on the room. Mrs. Willis finally smiled. I fumed.

A second elevator slid open and a family tumbled out. Three kids, all under the age of five, were dressed for the pool and chattering in a foreign language I didn't recognize. Looking bemused, the mother walked up to the front desk. "Miner-a-pool?"

"Seventh floor, ma'am."

"Seven?"

"Seventh floor, down the hall to the right when you get off the elevator, then out the back exit. Children under twelve are not allowed in the mineral pool, but the upper-level swimming pool is heated."

"Seven? Exit?"

Mrs. Willis muttered something about foreigners and rolled her eyes. Finally, she raised seven fingers and pointed up. Having understood, the family got back into the elevator, leaving the middle child behind.

It was comforting to know that Mrs. Willis' rudeness was not discriminatory.

I smiled at the little boy who began entertaining himself by digging in the dirt of a huge rubber plant, which stood near the entrance to the restaurant. A few seconds later the elevator door opened and Dad ran out to collect his son who now had a mouth full of potting soil.

The bellboy returned. "Five more minutes," he said to Mrs. Willis, frowning as he noticed the mess on the floor.

"Great," I said. "Check me in and by the time I get to the eleventh floor, it'll be ready."

Mrs. Willis hesitated, but couldn't come up with a viable argument as to why she couldn't accommodate me. Taking her time, she diligently informed me of the hotel's amenities: the bathhouse on the west wing of the third floor, the gymnasium with the latest equipment, and the beauty salon and women's boutique downstairs. Then, the bossy woman eyed my slacks and saddle shoes and added, "If you plan to dine in the hotel, reservations are necessary, along with proper attire."

I filled out my check-in card. As I handed it to her, I saw her glance at the check mark I made in the small box indicating my single status. She raised her eyebrows. Finally, she handed me a brass key with the number 1119 engraved on it. It felt cold in my hand.

Okay, what's the hurry? I had my room. I'd unpack, get my bearings, and by the time I dipped my toe into the mineral pool, I figured the foreign family should be pruned enough to have called it an afternoon.

The elevator operator slid the door open. I stepped in with my entire luggage in tow (the bellboy was too busy cleaning the dirt off the floor to help me with my bags).

"Welcome, ma'am. What floor please?" The operator was an old man held up by a foldout stool. Mahogany skin stretched tight over a thin frame. Deep veins edged into the papery-thin surface of his face. He reminded me of a dry maple leaf. His warm, welcoming smile softened the effects of Mrs. Willis' uppity attitude.

"Eleven, please."

A few seconds later, the elevator bumped to a stop.

"Room number?"

"Eleven nineteen."

"West wing," he pointed to the left. "Enjoy your stay ma'am."

I tipped him and stepped into the hall. A huge mirror hung on the wall and I got a good look at myself. My wild red hair sprang from my head like a mass of overgrown weeds. I pictured my green ribbon tangled in brush alongside the highway. No wonder Mrs. Willis told me about the salon. I tucked in a few strands, but the effort was hopeless. I picked up my suitcase, turned toward the west wing, when a fleeing figure careened into me. My overnight kit fell to the floor and sprang open. Without stopping to see who she had a-bombed, a shrieking housemaid ran down the hall, and disappeared into the service stairwell. I stuffed my underwear back into the case and found my room. I stood for a moment outside of

1119, rubbing my biceps. By tomorrow, I'd have a nice bruise.

A few years before, my father had told me the story. Of all the stories he had in his repertoire, I think this was the one of which he was most proud. I'd heard about this room so many times, I could almost picture it, not the room itself, but the bathroom, more to the point, the bathtub.

I opened the door and walked in. My foul mood instantly lifted. Two windows, reaching up to the ceiling, brought in spectacular views. From the front window I could see Bathhouse Row and Central Avenue. The rest of the city sprawled for miles toward Lake Hamilton. The side window framed a view of Music Mountain and the mountain tower perched high above the trees. A movement to the left caught my eye and I saw a wave of steam rising upward, and there, carved in the hillside and nestled in a grove of trees, was the mineral pool.

I dropped my bags, kicked off my shoes, hopped on the bed, and leaned back on a mass of pillows propped up against the headboard. I don't know which was more colorful, the landscape or my room. Splashed across the drapes and bedspread were swirls of reds, greens, and golds, forming magnolia flowers in various stages of bloom. The walls were painted in a soft cream, providing a nice contrast to the colorful decor. On the wall over the bed hung a modest painting of a bowl of magnolia flowers. A small settee and a writing desk and chair made up a quaint work area on the other side of the room.

All of a sudden, I felt as if I shouldn't be here, like I was intruding. I opened the windows to let in some fresh air. Okay, too long on the road, too long without food. I called room service and ordered a ham sandwich and chopped salad. Before I hung up, I added a bottle of red wine. Hey, all work and no play makes me cranky. I unpacked my clothes and writing supplies and headed for the bathroom with my cosmetic bag.

I pushed open the door. Two damp towels rested in the sink. A bar of soap, wet and slimy, floated in the soap dish. Tiny, black hairs were sprinkled across the white hexagonal floor-tiles. I couldn't believe my eyes. With all the extra time, the damn housemaid had forgotten to clean the bathroom. Then I noticed one end of the shower curtain was ripped from its rings. A leg, hairy and white, was draped over the edge of the tub. I jerked the curtain aside. I've been accused of being too picky. But what could I say? Having a dead body in the very bathtub where I was conceived really pissed me off.

Chapter 3

Before I could pick up the phone and report my discovery, someone pounded on my door. The shrieking maid must have found Mr. Hairy Legs before she slammed into me when I stepped off the elevator because when I opened the door, the house detective pushed past me and rushed into the bathroom.

"Don't touch anything," he shouted. "The cops are on their way."

A tall man with a respectable paunch and glistening black hair raced in behind the house detective. Lingering over him like a putrid fog was the lime scent of cheap hair tonic.

"Miss Lockhart, please come out here. Are you okay?"

"I'm fine. Who are you?"

"Hamston Charles, hotel manger."

Probably thinking I was one of those weak females who swoon at the sight of blood, he grabbed me by my elbow and dragged me into the hall. I jerked free and stepped back inside. "I guess this means I can't stay in this room," I said.

"Miss Roberts, my secretary, is arranging another room for you right now. Same view, just one floor below. Listen, I must insist you—"

He sidled in front of me as my elbow made contact with his solar plexus, a little harder than I had intended.

"—come out into the hall," he gasped. "I'll have the bellboy bring your things. Your room-service order is being delivered there right now."

If Mr. Charles had ideas about whisking me away before I learned anything about the murder, he had another thing coming. Besides, this was my chance to write a real story, one that could prove my worth as a reporter. I had no intention of writing fluff the rest of my career.

The man in my bathtub had obviously died from loss of blood—his jugular was slit from his right ear down to his throat.

"It's Ellison James," the house detective said. "He disappeared three days ago and now here he is. How do you like that?"

"Shut up, Grady." Mr. Charles tried to grab my arm again, but I dodged him.

"Who's Ellison James?" I asked.

"Our bookkeeper," Grady said. "He took off with last week's deposit and no one has seen him until now."

"Grady, keep your damn mouth shut." Mr. Charles stepped between us again, but jumped away when my elbow started to rise. "This is a police matter. Miss Lockhart's a guest in this hotel. She doesn't need to hear this."

I looked over Grady's shoulder, which was easy since he was short. Ellison James appeared to have been about thirty-five, a handsome man with a lean muscular physique, all too apparent since he was totally naked. His Frank Sinatra hair cut was a class act. In fact, except for the look of terror on his face, he resembled Blue Eyes.

Judging by the amount of blood that had pooled in the tub, it was obvious he was killed right there. The absence of clothes was perplexing, however.

"Someone must have stripped him after they slit his throat," I said. "Unless he was wandering around naked."

"My thoughts exactly," Grady cackled. "Ellison was a card, but he usually kept his clothes on in public."

"He's quite handsome."

"Was."

"Right."

Mr. Charles threw his arms in the air and walked back into the hall. "I must be speaking Greek," he shouted. "No one's listening to me."

"No one ever listens to him," Grady whispered. "He's a boob." Grady pulled a Lucky Strike from his shirt pocket, offered me one, and we lit up.

Before Grady and I could assess the situation any further, three police officers walked in acting as if this were an everyday occurrence. "Everybody out in the hall, now," the overweight, tired-looking officer said.

"That's what I've been telling them," Mr. Charles said. He reached into his coat pocket for what I assumed was a handkerchief and not finding one, mopped the sweat from his brow with his tie. "Miss Lockhart, you must go down to room 1019." Looking startled at his now sweat-stained tie, he smoothed it out and tucked it into his shirt.

"If this is the woman who found the body," a silky voice behind me spoke, "she's not going anywhere."

I turned and my breath lodged like a gumball stuck in my windpipe.

"Lieutenant Ralph Dixon, Hot Springs Police Department." He flashed a badge.

Mr. Charles let out an exasperated sigh. "This is Miss Sydney Lockhart. She just checked in."

"You're the one who found the body?" he asked.

Mr. Charles answered for me. "One of my housemaids found Mr. James first."

Lieutenant Ralph Dixon was gorgeous. In my stocking feet, we came eye-to-eye, one of the rare times I wished I wasn't a tall woman. A lone curl from his dark brown hair lolled gently on his forehead. His eyes were the color of bonbons. I stole a glance at his left hand, in particular his third finger—no ring. Just as I imagined our first date, he shattered my illusion with his first question.

"Where's your husband, Mrs. Lockhart?" he reached for a small note-book inside the breast pocket of his jacket.

"That's Miss Lockhart. I'm here on business."

"Business?" His left eyebrow rose slightly.

"I'm a reporter."

"You're here alone?"

"I wanted to bring my cat and dog, but the hotel has a no-pet policy. My cousin wanted to join me, but she's busy taking care of rich, divorced women whose parents don't want them." I blew smoke in his face and scanned for flaws in his flawless appearance. His charcoal-colored jack-et was tailor-made and fit him like a skin. His blindingly white shirt was starched, pressed—impeccable. Two-tone, black and white wing tips stuck out from the cuffs of his creased tweed trousers.

"How long were you in the room before you noticed the body?"

"No more than five minutes. I unpacked, admired the scenery, and ordered room service. I went into the bathroom to arrange my things when I discovered Mr. James in my tub."

"Your tub? Stay here often on . . . business?"

"Miss Lockhart insisted on this room." Mr. Charles jabbed his finger at 1119. "In fact, she got huffy when the room wasn't ready. My desk clerk offered her another room, but Miss Lockhart became . . . threatening."

"Threatening?" I said. "How was I threatening?"

"Why did you insist on this room?" Lieutenant Dixon eyes traveled slowly from the top of my head down to my feet.

It wasn't a lustful look. I felt he was searching for signs of Ellison James' blood on my person. I wasn't about to tell him about my conception in this bathtub. In fact, the tub in room 1119 was beginning to give me the willies.

"My parents honeymooned in this room," I said.

"I see, and when you found out the room wasn't immediately available, you threatened the desk clerk." He glanced up at my bandaged forehead as if my recent wound told him all he wanted to know. The brawling, intimidating, redhead from Texas was also a throat-slasher.

"I did no such thing. I just told her—"

Lieutenant Dixon was clearly not interested in excuses since he interrupted me with, "Did you know the dead man, Miss Lockhart? Did you have an appointment to meet him here? Is that why you threatened the desk clerk when your room wasn't ready?"

"How could I have known him? I just got here."

"From before maybe?"

"When before? I've never been here!" Trickles of sweat dripped between my breasts, but I kept my outward demeanor calm and cool and stared back at this arrogant man. That's it! There's the flaw I was looking for. Arrogant! How could I even think of dating an arrogant, stuck-up man, no matter how well he dressed?

"Don't leave town, Miss Lockhart."

The same bellboy who had cleaned up the rubber-plant mess in the lobby arrived with his cart. I repacked and handed him my luggage.

"Take her down to 1019," Mr. Charles stole another look in the bathroom as if to make sure the nightmare was real, then stormed down the hall. The scent of lime hair tonic remained.

The elevator operator was instructed not to let anyone on the eleventh floor. All people staying on the top floor were told to wait in the lobby until further notice. I followed the bellboy downstairs to my new room. "What happened up there, Miss? I heard someone was murdered."

"The bookkeeper."

"Mr. James? Elsa will be heartbroken."

"Who's Elsa?"

He looked down to see if anyone was in the stairwell before answering. "Elsa, a housemaid, and Mr. James were . . . friends. You know."

"What's your name?"

"Mickey. Mickey Saunders. I work here everyday after school and on weekends."

"Nice to meet you, Mickey. I'm Sydney Lockhart. So, Elsa and Mr. James were an item?"

"Huh? Oh, right." He winked. "An item."

He unlocked 1019 and placed my bags on the bed. I gave him a dollar. A bit generous, but if I was going to find out why Ellison James was murdered in my room, I'd need some allies. "Thanks, Mickey. Is Elsa working today?"

"Oh, yes, ma'am. She's the one who found the body. I mean before you did."

My meal was waiting and the wine I had ordered had been replaced with a bottle of champagne. I wondered if it was a mistake, or a way of compensating me for having a dead body as a one-person welcoming committee. I read the card on the cart. "Complements of the house. Enjoy your stay, Miss Lockhart."

I washed down my ham sandwich with a glass of champagne. Then I changed into my bathing suit, wrapped a bathrobe around me, donned my green tart sandals, and grabbed the bottle. Dead body or not, I was going to enjoy myself. On the way to the pool, I tried to imagine what Lieutenant Ralph Dixon looked like under his snappy suit and starched shirt. Then I reminded myself that arrogant men were bad news, especially cops; especially cops who might add my name to their list of murder suspects.

Hoping to avoid hotel people as well as the police, I scurried down the stairs to the seventh floor. The only people I saw were the foreign family, now pink and wet, coming in from the pool. The father was trying to remove what looked like a pine cone from the mouth of his son—the same little boy who had dug up the potted plant. The child must lack some sort of mineral, causing him to crave earthy snacks.

I removed my sandals, stuck my toe in the mineral pool, and sighed. Perfect. I shed my robe and slid the rest of my body into the soothing water. I had the entire place to myself. With my towel rolled into a pillow on the lip of the pool, I leaned my head back and closed my eyes. As soon as I did, I saw flashes of Ellison James, his hairy leg hanging over the tub, the look of horror in his stark blue eyes, his head resting in a pool of blood. Lieutenant Dixon couldn't have been serious about me being a suspect in James' murder. He was just covering all the bases, I told myself. Why in the hell did I have to be so damn pushy when I checked in? A little patience and the desk clerk would not have given me another thought.

Instead of dwelling on my troublesome start at the Arlington, I tried to concentrate on what I'd do on my first full day in Hot Springs. I'd order coffee at five a.m. and start working on my article. I had enough information to describe the ambiance of the hotel, what the traveler will experience as soon as they walk up the stone steps leading to the front door. At seven I'd have my first massage at the hotel spa, and then breakfast in the Venetian room. I had an interview scheduled at ten with the hotel's public relations person, a Miss Fredricks, then I'd have the rest of the day to hike some of the trails up Music Mountain. Good plan. I reached over for my glass of champagne. I was well on my way to putting the afternoon out of my mind.

"I wouldn't be smiling if I were you."

My eyes flew open. Squatting at the edge of the pool, not two feet away, was Mr. Arrogant. Steam rose between us, and for a moment I thought he had materialized from the vapor.

"Didn't bring your swimsuit?" I said. "Your jacket will wilt in this steam."

"I'm fine." He picked up my bottle of champagne and studied the label. "Expensive."

"A gift from the hotel."

He refilled my glass.

"I'd offer you some, but I know you're on duty."

"Right."

I heard slight regret in his voice, but didn't feel sorry for him. "Why shouldn't I?" I said.

"Shouldn't you what?"

"Be smiling."

"Because I was serious about you not leaving town. James' body was still warm. He couldn't have been dead more than a few minutes."

"Do I look like a killer?"

"I've seen all kinds."

"Okay, then. What's my motive? Where's the murder weapon?"

"Give me time."

"But Elsa found the body before I did. So you must have other suspects."

"I do."

"Good," I scoffed. "I like being part of a group."

"Nice shoes." He nodded toward my sandals, which sat on the bench by the towel cabinet.

I ignored the compliment and closed my eyes, pretending to enjoy my soak. When I opened them a few seconds later, he was gone.

Chapter 4

"I knew that room was bad luck." I heard my mother shout from the kitchen. My father had just repeated to her what I had reported.

"She's back again?" I said.

"She's after me to trim the crepe myrtles."

"Bad luck? Is she trying to tell me something?"

"Just ignore her," he said.

"I heard that," Mom shouted again.

"They couldn't clean the room and move you back in?"

"Dad, it's a crime scene now. The entire wing is off limits. I did get to see the bathtub though."

"Yeah, with a dead body in it. That's not what I'd hoped you'd experience."

"I wouldn't have experienced anything special. My first memory was when I was two and Emil Soukup's pet squirrel bit me on the ankle. I don't think I could recall anything of my conception, inspired by the sight of the bathtub or not."

"I just wanted the moment to be special. Now, I can never tell that story again with the same sentiment."

"Thank God," I heard Mom say. "After almost thirty years, that story's a bit old." Then I heard the kitchen door slam.

It was my parent's honeymoon, too much champagne and a squeaky bed. My mother, despite being tipsy, didn't want the people staying in the next room to hear. My father suggested the bathtub, and so goes history.

"Are you all right, then?" Dad sighed.

I didn't want to tell him about my conversation with Dixon. No need to worry him further. "I'm fine. I had a nice soak in the mineral pool, and room 1019 is identical to 1119."

"What a shame," Dad said. "Your mother just stormed out."

"I heard."

"Lattie LaVelle came over last night."

"Lattie the Lush? Mom's friend?"

"Yeah. The old sot said she was heart-stricken over your mom's leaving. But I really think she was on the prowl for another husband. I got her drunk."

"Dad!"

"She was two-sheets-to-the-wind when she got here, so it wasn't hard to do. Listen. I figured if anyone knew what upset your mother, it'd be Lattie."

"Learn anything?"

"Sure did. Once that woman's tongue gets loose, she's a tidal wave of information. Whoops. Your mom's coming back. I'll tell you later."

And there I was again, standing with a dead phone receiver in my hand and a thousand questions assaulting my brain. Since I was in a family frame of mind, I called Scott to check on Monroe and Mealworm. I had to listen to five minutes of whining before I had a chance to speak. Whining is Scott's favorite pastime, but this was on my dime and I had to call a halt to it.

"Are the girls okay?"

"What do you think? Jeremiah is in domestic bliss. He's been referring to himself as mommy. He's promised Monroe that tomorrow he'd paint her toenails red."

"Love you." I hung up. I didn't tell him about the murder. I'd let Mom do that. She could pay for the call. It would give her and Scott something to do tonight.

Tired, but too strung out to call it a night, I got dressed and went to the lounge. Lou Holly and the Intones were doing a great job sounding like Benny Goodman, so I ordered a martini and pulled out my cigarettes. I rarely smoke—except when I drink, or find a dead body in my room. When I'm with Ruth we use her ebony cigarette holders she ordered from some African import catalogue. Sitting there alone, I almost wished Ruth were with me. Before I ate my first olive, Mickey, the bellboy, sidled up to my table.

"Things are really hopping around here," he whispered. "Mr. Charles has been running all over the hotel like a madman. Cops are still swarming the place."

"How's Elsa?" I opened my cigarette case and offered Mickey a smoke. He plucked one and tucked it in his vest pocket.

"Thanks, I'll save it for break. She's a mess. After that dick finished with her, she looked like a ghost afraid of death. Mrs. Lindstrom, the head of housekeeping, wanted to send Elsa home, but the girl insisted on staying. Her shift ends soon."

"Mickey, could you tell Elsa to stop by my room before she leaves? I'd like to speak to her, you know, compare notes. Tell her to use the stairs."

"So no one will see her?"

"Right. The cops might get the wrong idea."

"Gotcha."

It was a little before ten when I heard a soft knock on my door. I opened it, but left the chain on.

"Miss Lockhart? I'm Elsa Dubois. Mickey said you wanted to talk to me."

I unchained the door. "Please come in. Did anyone see you?"

"No, ma'am."

Elsa slipped in and hovered in the doorway, ringing her hands in her green and white striped pinafore. She couldn't have weighed more than ninety pounds. Her dark brown hair was cut in a pageboy, giving her heart-shaped face a gaunt look. Even red and swollen, her enormous violet eyes were stunning. She had a look of whimsical gaiety, which her grief and maid's uniform couldn't hide. Her black-seamed stockings disappeared under a lacy slip that showed at the hem of her skirt. Elsa Dubois looked like she'd just stepped out of a Toulouse Lautrec painting and was ready for the chorus line.

"Mickey told me you were the one booked in 1119."

"That's right. We crashed into one another right outside the elevator. You must have just left the room."

Tears started rolling down Elsa's cheeks.

"Sit down here." I brought her to the sofa and poured her the last of the champagne.

"I'm afraid it's a bit flat."

Elsa drained the glass in one gulp. "Thanks, ma'am. That awful detective thinks I killed Ellison."

"Did you?"

"Oh, no ma'am! I couldn't, but he thinks I did."

"Join the club. That's his job—intimidation. Tell me what happened,

Elsa. Let's try and figure this out."

"Mr. Charles told me that I shouldn't talk to anyone."

"Mr. Charles won't find out. Trust me."

She hugged her arms tight around her narrow shoulders and shook her head.

"Listen, Elsa. You and I found the body. That makes us both look bad. We need to help each other. Now tell me what happened."

Elsa took a deep breath. "I hadn't seen Ellison for three days. They said he stole some money from the hotel, but that's not true. Ellison would never steal. The day he disappeared he and Mr. Charles had a big fight— a lot of yelling in Mr. Charles' office. At least that's what I heard. I was so worried about him. I thought I'd never see him again." Elsa leaned back on the sofa and seemed to meld into the pillows.

"Go on."

"This afternoon I was in the linen room on the eleventh floor."

"What time?"

"Around four. I'm assigned to that floor. Anyway, while I was folding sheets, Ellison slipped in. He told me that he had to see me. It was important, and that he'd pick me up outside the employees' entrance when I got off tonight at eleven. He said not to tell anyone. Then he left again. Less than twenty minutes later he was dead."

"You didn't go to 1119 to clean it when you found his body?"

"No, I cleaned that room earlier today, right after lunch."

"After lunch? I tried to check in around four and the room wasn't ready. I was told that there was a late check out."

"No. That's not true."

"Then why did you go to 1119?"

"Ellison called about ten minutes after he'd left the linen room and told me to meet him in that room right way."

"Did you often meet in the hotel rooms?"

"Oh, no, ma'am! If we were ever caught fooling around in a room, we'd be fired on the spot."

"So why did he want to meet there? What did he say when he called?"

"He just whispered. He said, 'It's me. Something terrible has just happened. I need to see you right away. It can't wait. I'm in 1119.' Then he hung up."

"And you went there immediately."

"Well . . . I brushed my hair and checked my lipstick. But I wasn't more than a couple of minutes."

I took a moment to run the sequence of events through my brain, and then let out a sigh. "Elsa, that wasn't Ellison who called you."

"It wasn't?"

It's a good thing Elsa had her looks, because her pea brain wasn't going to get her very far. "No, it wasn't. Ellison was already dead."

Elsa turned white, and I was afraid she'd pass out.

"In the short time you primped, Ellison was murdered and his clothes were removed. The call probably came from the killer. Was the door locked?"

"It was wide open. Since that room is at the end of the hall, I thought that Ellison wasn't too worried about anyone seeing us. I walked in and the room was empty. I started to leave when I saw a leg through the crack in the bathroom door. At first I didn't know it was him, and then I went in and peeked around the shower curtain, and . . ." She buried her face in a pillow.

"Can you think of anyone who would want him dead?"

"Ellison was so sweet. He wouldn't hurt anyone." Her tears gushed. I handed her a box of tissues. "What am I going to do now? We . . . we had plans." She blew her nose and swallowed. "Ellison was taking me to Little Rock in the morning."

"Why Little Rock?" I said, imagining wedding bells, eloping, wild weekend in the big city.

Elsa, startled at my question, was silent for a moment. "Well . . . I've never been to the state capitol. It was going to be just a fun day. You know . . . see something new." Elsa burst into tears again. "Now I'll never get there."

I was about to offer to take the girl to Little Rock just to get her to stop crying. I began to think that Elsa was more heartbroken over the missed trip than the murder of her lover. "Any idea why he and Mr. Charles were arguing?"

"Probably the missing money. But I'm not sure. Mr. Charles is a real jerk. No one likes him. He treats the staff like dirt."

"Did he and Ellison argue often?"

"No . . . not that I know of."

I knew Elsa was lying. Her left eye twitched and her throat closed, emitting a squeak. But I let it pass. It had been a long day. This morning while I was in Dallas getting ready to leave, Elsa was probably at home getting ready for work, and Ellison James was alive. I wondered what Lieutenant Ralph Dixon was doing, probably polishing his gun.

I told Elsa to go home and try not to worry. I knew my encouragement sounded weak, but I had nothing else to offer. As she left the room she turned back and said, "Maybe I could take an early bus in the morning."

I watched her walk down the hall with my box of tissues. Either Arkansas' capital was a hot spot on the Arkansas must-see list, or Elsa's reason for wanting to go to Little Rock was a lie.

After she left, I started to unpack for the second time since I'd arrived at the Arlington. I slipped on my PJs and started the task of arranging the rest of my clothes in the dresser. I opened the top left drawer, and damn if it wasn't already full of clothes—Mr. Ellison James' clothes, no doubt, judging by the amount of blood they'd soaked up.

Chapter 5

I wanted nothing more than to close the drawer, crawl into bed, and pull the covers over this crazy day. Ellison James' clothes would be there in the morning. I could say that I had just discovered them. If I called now, Dixon would be here in a flash, questioning me again.

I picked up the phone and made the call. I'm innocent; I have nothing to hide. Five minutes later there was a hard, urgent knock on my door. I'd barely had time to, as Elsa had said, brush my hair and check my lipstick.

I threw open the door. "It took you long enou . . . Oh. Hi, Grady." Standing behind the house detective was a uniformed police officer, the hefty one who had accompanied Lieutenant Dixon earlier. Grady spoke first.

"Hey, Miss Lockhart. You look nice." He eyed my PJs. "Officer O'Riley," Grady pointed his thumb over his shoulder.

Officer O'Riley tipped his cap. "What's the problem, Miss Lockhart?"

"There's something here you need to see. I let the two men in and glanced down the hall to make sure there was no higher ranking official coming to investigate. I mean, we're talking murder here.

I had left the drawer opened. The officer was looking over the clothes. "I'll call the boss. Probably belonged to the dead man," he said.

"No shit, O'Riley." Grady said, then mumbled to me, "I thought about working for the Hot Springs Police Department, but since I can read and write, I was over qualified."

"Speaking of the boss," I said. "Where's Dixon anyway? Don't tell me he's already gone home for the evening."

"Are you kidding? He's interviewing every hotel employee who worked today," O'Riley said. "Got 'em lined up outside Charles' office. No one goes home until after he's talked to everyone. It's a zoo on the third floor."

While Officer O'Riley made the call, Grady and I shared another cigarette and listened to the one-sided phone conversation.

"Right. Right. Got it." O'Riley moved the receiver away from his mouth. "Lieutenant Dixon wants us to fingerprint this room. He said it would be best if Miss Lockhart moved into another room."

"No way!" I shouted. "I'm not moving again. Tell Dixon I'm wearing my PJs and I'm not moving."

"She wearing her PJs . . . What? Pink and white stripe, I think. What? Oh, the dead man's jacket. Brown. Why? Got it. Right." He hung up. "He said you can stay, but don't get in the way while we're fingerprinting. There's a sofa in the sitting area near the elevator. You can wait there."

My PJs were the type that covered me from neck to ankles, but I grabbed my robe anyway. Grady and I walked out as three other officers arrived.

"How many cops does it take to check a room for fingerprints?" he said.

"I give up. How many?"

"Four. One to dust the chalk and three to search for the fingers."

"That's the worst punch line I've ever heard."

"Stick around, they get better."

Grady and I made ourselves comfortable on an overstuffed sofa. The house detective was a small, wiry man about fifty. He wore a fedora and a rumpled gray jacket with black slacks. His face had once been handsome, but the deep folds around his eyes and mouth spoke of a hard life.

"What do you know about this Ellison James?" I asked.

"Quiet guy. Kept to himself most of the time. Liked to wear flashy clothes—expensive, flashy clothes. Clothes that couldn't be bought on a bookkeeper's salary."

"So you think he had his hand in the hotel's till?"

"I didn't say that. It's just that his tastes were highbrow. Who knows, maybe he has . . . had a rich momma."

"I heard that he and Elsa had a thing going."

"Yeah. I heard that, too. But . . ."

"But what? You think she killed him?"

"Nah. How could a little spit of a girl slash a man's throat? He'd have to be unconscious. But for a girl with a new beau, she's been moping around like she's at death's door. And not just since James' disappearance, days before that."

"Maybe it was a troubled relationship. Who knows?"

"Right. Who knows?"

"Elsa said that she and James were planning a trip to Little Rock in the morning. Know anything about that?"

"Little Rock? No idea."

An hour later the officers were finished and I returned to a dusty room. At this point, another room seemed like a good idea. I was too antsy to sleep, so I cleaned up the mess. Then I noticed a gaping hole in the dresser. The drawer containing Mr. James' clothes had been removed, leaving a blatant reminder of what had been there.

I pulled out my notebook and made notes about the murder. I didn't believe Elsa was guilty, either. She didn't seem smart enough to carry off the well-planned crime. The killer was trying to point his dirty deed in someone else's direction—Elsa's and mine. Surely Lieutenant Dixon realized that. If he spent too much time following the wrong trails, the trail to the killer would become cold. I'd point that out to him as soon as I could.

In the few minutes after Ellison James had left Elsa in the linen room, he ended up in room 1119 where someone slit his throat and removed his clothes. The killer then called Elsa, pretending he was Ellison, and told her to come to 1119. He then ran down the stairs and stashed the bloody clothes in 1019. It had to be someone who worked at the Arlington. Eleven nineteen was at the end of the hall, tucked away in the corner, very private, almost hidden. All I needed to do was find out who killed him and why. I hoped to get a feel for what was going on around the hotel during my interview with Miss Fredricks.

The sunrise was spreading its orange glow out of my window when room service delivered my coffee. It was going to be a glorious day. The yellow and gold leaves on the trees were catching the early light and appeared as soft beacons in the haze across the mountains. I wrote for a couple of hours and went down to the third floor for my massage. My attendant was a chatty woman named Myra, and she proudly informed me that she'd worked at the spa for thirty years. She gave me a tour and I took notes. Then it was time for my own treatment. Myra showed my to my whirlpool and handed me two cups of warm mineral water to drink. Steam clouded the room and even though my hair was wrapped in a towel, I knew my ringlets would be tighter than a pig's tail when I left.

"Slowly drink both cups of mineral water, honey," Myra said. "It flushes your kidneys and makes you perspire. I'll be back in a few minutes, just relax."

I wasn't sure if my kidneys needed flushing, and I had started to perspire as soon as I walked into the steamy room, but who was I to argue with thirty years of experience in the rejuvenation business. Just as I was starting to doze, Myra gently nudged my shoulder and, noticing my comfort, reluctantly pulled the plug, explaining that twenty minutes was the maximum time allowed in the pool. She wrapped me in a sheet, escorted me to a wet sauna, and said that I could sweat for up to five minutes, or as soon as I'd had enough. She'd be standing by with a dry sheet. I left the sauna feeling five pounds lighter. Myra led me to the massage table and placed steaming hot towels on my shoulders and lower back, areas that held most of my tension. Then she returned, and using warm oil that smelled like eucalyptus, massaged the rest of the tension out of my body.

"Do you like it quiet, or do you like a little talk?" Myra asked.

Normally I like my massage without conversation, but considering the murder, I opted for chatting. Besides, I could tell Myra's tongue was anxious to do some wagging.

"Talk's fine with me, Myra."

"I heard that you were the one who found Mr. James. That must have been a real shocker."

That's not what I'd call "a little talk," but I welcomed the topic.

"Yeah. I was about to set up my things in the bathroom when I noticed a naked leg hanging out of the tub."

Myra giggled. "Oh, I don't mean no disrespect, but picturing that just made me laugh. Mr. James was always so prim and proper. The idea of him dead in a tub without his clothes seems queer. There used to be a time, not many years back, when all sorts of wild things happened in Hot Springs."

"What do you mean?"

"Boisterous parties that went on for days on end, gamblers, gangsters, Hollywood people . . . you know the type. We had 'em by the droves. One time there was a shoot-out right outside the hotel entrance. When it was all over, four thugs and two cops were sprawled dead. There was so much blood; the janitors couldn't get it out of the sidewalk. They had to sandblast."

"That must have been bad for business."

"Are you kidding? Bing Crosby was playing in town that night. Folks just walked around the police and all the mess, crossed the street, and went to the show. This was a tough town 'til it got cleaned up. Those were some fast-moving times."

The wistfulness in Myra's voice sounded as though she missed all the grizzly excitement.

"All finished," she said and pointed to my head. "Your bandage has wilted in the steam. I can replace it for you?"

"Do you have one of those small ones that isn't so noticeable?

Myra rifled through a first-aid kit and pulled out a smaller version of the strip that had covered my gash. "This should do it— barely notice-able. If I were you, Miss Lockhart, I'd be careful. It hasn't been that long ago since we had bad guys running around here like rats."

"I just happened to be in the wrong place at the wrong time."

"No such thing," she said.

"Thanks for not asking about my stitches."

"None of my business. You can go ahead and get dressed."

I suddenly had dozens of questions, but Myra fled before I could open my mouth.

When I climbed down from the table, I felt as limber as a wet noodle, hungry, too. I went back to my room, showered, and was heading out for breakfast when the phone rang.

"Your mother's bought a one-way bus ticket to Los Angeles."

"Jeez."

"I don't want her to leave," Dad said. "She may be wacky, but she's the only wife I have."

I sat down on the sofa. The lightness I felt after my massage was gone. I didn't want my mother to leave, either, but this time I was afraid it would happen.

"You said you found out from Lattie what was bothering Mom. Tell me."

"Your mother doesn't remember getting married."

"Say that again."

"We eloped."

"I know that."

"But you don't know the details."

I lit up. "Go ahead."

"Her parents didn't want us to get married. They said I was too old for her. Anyway, I got a head of steam one day and went by the Peacock Cafe where your mother was waiting tables. I gave her the ultimatum, now or never. She asked if I'd wait until she served Mr. Drake his scrambled eggs and toast. I said to hell with Mr. Drake. Your mother threw off her apron and tossed her order pad. We were in Hot Springs and married before the sunset."

"And she doesn't remember that?"

"Well, we started celebrating the moment we left the cafe."

Things were as clear as the glass of a gin bottle—the elopement, the ceremony, my conception—my parent's wedding was one big drunk.

"But surely you have the marriage certificate," I said.

"I put it in my luggage, I think. Anyway, when we got home, that certain piece of luggage didn't make it back to Texas. I must have left it in the hotel."

"Why didn't you call the Arlington?"

"When we returned to Houston, we set up house and never looked back. It wasn't until your mother started planning the anniversary party and began digging through her trunk and asking questions. Since she couldn't remember the ceremony—to give your mother credit, it was rather quick, five minutes at the most—and there was no certificate, she assumed that we skipped that part and just started on the honeymoon."

"That's ridiculous."

"That's your mother, my wife, soon to be my ex-wife."

"The courthouse would have the record."

"I checked. A fire in '48 took care of that."

"Witnesses?"

"A bartender and restaurant hostess. They're probably dead by now. This wouldn't be much of an issue if your mother wasn't going through the change."

"Maybe Lattie can talk some sense into Mom."

"Sure, one wacky woman trying to talk sense to another. They'd probably both end up running off to California."

"I should come home."

"Nothing doing. You stay there and do your job. I can handle your mother."

"Call if she gets on the bus."

"Will do."

•

The breakfast crowd had thinned and the Venetian Room was quiet. I heard a piano tinkling and turned to see an elderly black man playing the ivories.

"Sounds nice," I said.

"Thanks, Miss. Just something I'm working on. I don't go on the clock until later, but I usually comes in early and plays. Don't have no piano at home. Plays wherever I find one. You Miss Lockhart?"

My popularity was becoming an annoyance.

"That's me," I said.

"I heard a tall redheaded white lady found Mr. James. Sad. Real sad."

"Did you know Ellison James well?"

"Everybody knows everybody well here at the Arlington, like it or not." He smiled and turned his attention back to his composition.

The maitre d' showed me to a nice, sunny table next to the window. I'd planned to read the morning paper. Despite the murder headlines, I couldn't get past page one. Maybe Dad should let Mom go to Los Angeles so she can get it out of her system. Who knows? My parents would have to work this out themselves. I had my own problems here.

A waiter came over and I half expected him to know who I was and ask my involvement in the murder. Instead, he poured my coffee and took my order for Eggs Benedict, fried potatoes, fruit, orange juice, and a basket of fresh-baked rolls and orange marmalade.

Moments later, as I was smearing a roll with butter, Mr. Arrogant slipped into the chair across from me.

"Is that how you stay so slim?" he said eyeing my table of food.

His remark sounded too smug to be a compliment so I ignored it. "Catch any killers lately?"

"In Hot Springs? Are you kidding? This town is a criminal Mecca."

He looked as if he'd been awake all night. I almost felt sorry for him.

"So I heard. Why did you want to know the color of Ellison James' jacket?"

"You don't miss a beat do you?"

"I'm a reporter. I pay attention." I added marmalade to my roll and took a bite.

"We had a witness. A guest in the hotel saw a man in a brown jacket running up the stairs shortly before James was killed. He was muttering obscenities under his breath. That's why the man remembered him." The lieutenant motioned at the waiter to bring coffee. "Mind if I join you?"

"Looks like you already have. Am I still a suspect?"

His brown eyes bore a hole through me. Time seemed to stop. He finally spoke. "I've moved you to the bottom of the list."

"Why's that?"

"You're too smart to hide the clothes in the room where you're staying. Besides, I made some phone calls. Seems you're who you say you are."

My second course arrived and I had yet to offer my guest a roll. I can be difficult, but not rude.

"Hungry?" I asked.

"No, but thanks anyway." He pulled his jacket sleeve back and glanced at his watch. "Gotta go." He gulped down his coffee and started to leave, then turned back. "Hey, what happened to your head by the way?"

"Someone mistook me for a man and picked a fight."

His eyes locked with mine. "Mistook you for a man? That's hard to believe. Be good."

"Always."

The waiter came and refilled my coffee cup. "Are you okay, ma'am?"

"Sure." I swallowed. "Why?"

"You look a bit . . . flushed."

Chapter 6

Rita Fredricks sat straight-backed in her office chair. Her black hair was swept up into a French twist and pulled so tight it made her eyes slant. A pencil protruded from her twist, and her rhinestone-framed glasses sat pertly on her sharp nose. She was clicking away on her typewriter with the speed of a freight train. She spoke of efficiency without saying a word.

I cleared my throat. She peered over the top of her glasses, and continued typing. "You must be Miss Lockhart." She finished typing with a final tap on the key, and extended a long, slender hand with well-manicured nails. "Right on time. Please sit down. Can I get you some coffee?"

"No, thank you, Miss Fredricks. I just finished breakfast."

"Call me Rita."

"Sydney. And thanks for the welcome gift. The champagne was wonderful."

"Glad you enjoyed it. Sorry to hear about your unfortunate incident yesterday afternoon. I hope things have smoothed out for you."

"Things are just fine. Myra massaged my troubles away."

Rita laughed. "Myra's an institution here. We have guests that request her services when they make reservations. She even has a regular clientele of Hot Springs folks." Rita pulled the cover over her typewriter and stood up. "Except for the west wing of the eleventh floor, the hotel is at your disposal. I'll show you all the nooks and crannies and tell you about our lively history. Shall we go?"

We started in the mezzanine, which in less sophisticated terms was the basement. Two dress shops, a jewelry store, millinery, barbershop, ladies' salon, furrier, and drug store were just opening for the day. A dark bar, called the Central Avenue Pub, was tucked away in the corner, but didn't open until later.

"We have some of the finest wares in Hot Springs. Our milliner has a store in New York City and she's able to bring the latest styles to our little town." Rita opened the door and we went in.

"Oh, my," was all I could utter. "I could spend an entire day here as well as a fortune."

"Told you," Rita said. "I can't walk in myself without buying something. Hello, Ellen."

The woman behind the counter smiled.

"Here. How about this one?" Rita plucked a cute little soft-green velvet cap with rhinestones in the veil from the rack, and handed it to me. "This would look great with your beautiful red hair. Try it on."

She didn't have to ask twice. With my black dress and my jade sandals I'd knock 'em dead. I looked in the mirror and slanted the cap slightly over my right eye, casting a shadow over my face. The woman looking out at me was none other than a redheaded Lauren Bacall.

"It brightens your green eyes," Rita said. "And covers up that little bandage.

My battle wound was becoming an annoyance. I was trying to decide how I could surreptitiously look at the price tag when Rita gently lifted the cap off my head and told Ellen to wrap it up and send it to my room. I gasped at the thought of adding this pricey little item to my hotel bill when Rita whispered in my ear. "Don't worry. I'll comp it. I can do that. Let's go. I want you to see the dress shop."

I hadn't planned on spending what was left of the morning shopping, but Rita seemed to be having fun, and it was only a matter of time before I could worm some good gossip out of her. We toured the rest of the shops and ended the mezzanine portion of the tour in the gymnasium. Some of the workout equipment looked lethal. Pulleys, levers, wood-planked platforms made for Lord knows what. Rita went over to help a frightened woman remove her sleeve from a rowing machine that was about to squeeze her arm and transform it into a flat appendage.

"We have instructions on how to use the equipment. Unfortunately most folks don't bother to read them," Rita said, slightly out of breath.

As we were leaving the torture chamber, I noticed a door about four feet high locked with an iron bar and various padlocks. Steam seeped from under the door.

"Don't tell me," I said, "the steam room."

Rita laughed. "You could say that. We call it the pit. The hot-springs water that flows up from the aquifer is 143 degrees. A dip in that water would scald the skin off the bone. To cool it to a safe temperature, the water is filtered through a holding tank before it's piped into the mineral pool at about 106 degrees. The pit used to be part of the tour until three frat boys decided to sneak down here one night and play 'I dare you.' The idiot who took the dare ended up in the hospital with one big blister from his waist down." She looked at me and winked. "Rendered the boy useless in the romance department."

"Ouch," I said.

"It was a big joke until the hotel ended up in litigation."

"Hence the padlocks."

"Hence the padlocks. Mr. Charles is the only one with the key. It's a good thing, too; otherwise, one of his loyal subjects might just decide to boil the boss."

We left the mezzanine and went to the third-floor ballrooms. The first one we entered was crowded with people decorating for a wedding. We strolled by as blue and white paper streamers were being draped across the stage. The wedding cake was already in the center of a round table and a woman, obviously the mother of the bride, was arguing with a pastry chef over the placement of little blue flowers on the icing.

"This won't do," the woman whined. "These flowers are too small, and the bride and groom on top look dumpy. My daughter is definitely not dumpy."

"I'll change out the bride and groom, but as far as the flowers, I copied your picture exactly, ma'am," the chef said.

"They simply have to be redone," Mom chided.

The chef threw his hands in the air. He noticed Rita for the first time and made a gesture as if to say, "What am I to do?"

Rita nodded and he removed the cake from the table and whisked it away.

"Weddings are a headache sometimes," Rita said. "But the Arlington has a reputation for providing a great reception. We average about seventy-five a year. Not many facilities can provide a huge ballroom, dinner, photographer, flowers, and music. We do it all."

I thought of my parents and wondered what their wedding was like. An elopement doesn't warrant all the big to-dos. Was that the problem with my mother? After thirty years, she all of a sudden felt cheated out of a grand wedding? Like my father said, "Who the hell knows?"

We left the busy ballroom and entered another. This one was quiet and peaceful. As we strolled across the cavernous room, our heels echoed loudly on the parquet floor. More than two-dozen chandeliers threw daggerlike shadows across the walls. The floor-to-ceiling windows were covered with heavy, forest green drapes that flared toward the bottom and spread across the floor at the window's base like the skirt of a woman's evening gown.

"How long have you been a reporter?" Rita asked.

"Just a few weeks. Does it show?"

"Not a bit. I like seeing women out in the work force, doing jobs that are usually done by men. And before that what did you do?"

"I used to teach. After two years on the front line, I found myself rushing home every afternoon to a filled martini shaker I kept in the icebox. It was time for a change."

Rita laughed. "I know what you mean. The stress of this job can be overwhelming at times, but I wouldn't change it for the world. It gives me a feeling of independence, of accomplishment. Despite the difficulties, I'd rather do this than be caught up in someone else's life, worried over minute details on a daughter's wedding cake, a daughter who probably wouldn't notice anyway."

"Maybe it's the daughter who's the particular one."

"It's not. I've met the family. The girl's focus is clearly on her husband-to-be. She wouldn't know if the flowers on the cake were blue or black."

"How long have you been with the hotel?"

"A little more than a year. You wouldn't believe how hard it was to land this job. It came down to two guys and me. I had to show I was smarter and more efficient. I pulled it off." The look of triumph in her eyes was startling, like she'd finally won a long, hard-fought battle. I could empathize.

"Public relations gets me out and about," Rita continued. "I get to visit with movie stars, politicians, and the people who come in for the horseracing season."

"That must be an exciting time of year."

"You said it. Actually, it's the busiest time of the year. Rooms are booked months in advance, and some people have standing reservations for the same room every year."

"I heard Hot Springs used to be a hot bed for illegal gambling."

"You don't know the half of it. We finally got a DA that wasn't scared of the bad boys. There were times when walking down Central Avenue wasn't safe. But that's all changed now."

"Are you sure about that?"

"I know what you're getting at. Ellison James. Well, now, you might have a point there. I can't believe he was murdered like that. How awful."

"Was he a friend of yours?"

"Friend? Did Ellison James have friends?" She shrugged. "His office was next to mine. And since he was the bookkeeper, I worked with him often on the budget. But I can't say I knew him well. Kept to himself most of the time. He was a bit odd, and I always felt suspicious of him."

"You think he stole the money?"

"I'm not saying that. I'm just saying that he . . ." Rita stopped, turned, and gave me a stern look. "This is off the record. This won't show up in any article?"

"Off the record. But I am interested. After all, his body was in my bathtub and . . ." I stopped before I said anything about the bloody clothes in my second room. That may not be good for my reputation. ". . . and I feel sorry for Elsa. She must be heartbroken."

"Ha! Elsa's a conniving, little twit. She comes across as a bit on the slow side, but that's just a cover. She's looking for a sugar daddy and she'll play whatever role necessary."

"What role was she playing with Mr. James?"

"The wrong one, since you asked. Like I said, Ellison was shady."

"Any idea why he'd take Elsa to Little Rock?"

"Little Rock. Those two were going to Little Rock?"

We'd strolled around the perimeter of the ballroom and were back at the entrance. Before Rita could say anymore, Mr. Charles poked his head in the door. "How's the article coming, Miss Lockhart?"

"Great. Rita has given me some attractive tidbits about the hotel and Hot Springs. When the article comes out, your switchboard will light up like a Christmas tree."

"Just what I want to hear. Keep up the good work, Rita," he said and then disappeared down the hall.

"I hate that man," Rita said. "Off the record of course." Rita took her handkerchief from her skirt pocket and waved it in the air. "He must pour on the sickly lime stuff. You can tell he's in a room, just from the scent."

"I noticed."

"Are you afraid of heights?"

"No, why?"

"I'll take you up to the roof cupolas. The view is incredible. But we have to walk a sort of gangplank to get there. I often sneak up there for my coffee break."

It was breezy standing on the roof, but Rita was right. I had a panoramic view of the town, until the wind blew my hair over my face. Rita's twist, however, remained in place. We walked around and Rita noted some points of interest. Directly across the street from the hotel, standing twenty-three stories, was the Medical Arts Building, the town's only skyscraper. I'd read somewhere that the top two floors had once been home to a gangster until an angry business associate tossed him from the balcony. Maybe it was my imagination, but I swore I could see bloodstains on the street below.

A few blocks from the Garland County Courthouse, the twin spires of Saint John the Baptist Catholic Church poked up through the trees—a testament that not all of Hot Springs' edifices housed lawless characters. Four blocks past the hotel, where Central Avenue forks and becomes Whittington Avenue and Highway 7, The Majestic Hotel, the Arlington's rival, spread across the Y intersection.

"The Majestic is a classy hotel," Rita said, "but it doesn't hold a candle to the Arlington." She looked over and noticed me battling with my unruly hair. "Here, turn around." She removed the scarf from around her neck and tied my hair back in a ponytail. "It's always windy up here. I should have told you. There, that's better."

We walked to the front where two prominent cupolas stood at each end. I remembered seeing them from far away when I drove into town. Close up they looked like twin Rapunzel's castles with narrow slits for windows. They extended from the roof, but were connected by a steel-grated footbridge, about eight feet long and two feet wide. As I imagined my heel getting stuck in the grate, I saw Rita remove her shoes. "There's a solid plank down the center," Rita said. "If we walk on that, we won't tear our stockings. I'll go first. Wait until I step off the walkway before you start across."

I watched as Rita rushed to the other end and disappeared inside. When it was my turn, I stepped up and the wind whipped my skirt around my knees and Rita's scarf across my face. I was beginning to wonder if the scarf was such a good idea when the walkway started to shudder. I gasped and tightened my hold on the rails. I took another step when suddenly, without warning, a blast from a fire truck's siren almost sent me over the edge. Too nervous to let go of the rail and pull the scarf from my face, I continued to edge my way across like a blind person walking a tight rope. Rita's cigarette smoke told me how slow my progress really was. When I finally reached the other side, Rita held out her hand.

"It's okay," she said. "The walkway's a bit shaky, but it's safe. Watch your step. It's kind of dark and hard to see the floor."

Forget the floor, I couldn't see a damn thing where I was. Rita stepped back to give me room. She lost her footing and stumbled, caught herself, and let out a scream. She grabbed my arm, and for a brief moment, I thought she was about to shove me off. Instead she pulled me close to her. I stepped down into the cupola and jerked the scarf from my face.

Lying at our feet was a body. As my eyes adjusted, I realized it was Elsa. I bent over and touched the side of her neck, but had no hope of finding a pulse. Just like her lover, her throat had been slit. Rita stepped behind me and looked over my shoulder. She swayed and suddenly I had two bodies at my feet.

"Rita!" I squatted next to her and slapped her face to try and bring her around. "Rita, wake up." I shook her shoulders and her head bobbed like a rag doll. Just as I was about to leave her and go for help, her eyes fluttered and she raised up on her elbows.

"What?" She swallowed hard. "What happened?"

"It's okay. You just fainted."

"Elsa. Is she . . ."

"I'm afraid so. Can you stand?"

She sat up, rubbed the back of her head, and then looked down at her fingers. "I'm bleeding!"

I turned her head around and looked for myself. The good news was that she had not cracked her skull when she fell. The bad news was that she'd landed in Elsa's blood. Not wanting to upset her further, I said the stupidest thing. "It's just a scratch."

She stared at me as if I were an idiot. Then realization of my lame attempt to reassure her must have dawned on Rita, because after a moment, she burst out laughing.

Hysterics, no doubt. And just as quickly, she stifled her laughter and pulled herself together. "Let's get the hell out of here."

Chapter 7

I waited in Rita's office for Detective Dixon. He was next door talking to Rita and Mr. Charles. Too anxious to sit, I paced. After fifteen minutes, claustrophobia settled around me like a straight jacket. I wanted to flee the room, the hotel, even the city. Instead, I settled for the door next to Rita's desk. I expected a closet, but found a dark and musty-smelling room. A few pieces of furniture, pushed against the walls, were covered with sheets. I walked over and pulled open the drapes, causing dust to frolic in the sun's rays. I opened the window to let in some fresh air and a breeze set something to tinkling. I found the light switch, and half a dozen chandeliers, gently dancing in the breeze, threw a ghostly light over what once had been an elegant dining room. The wall opposite the windows was covered with framed photographs. There must have been more than a hundred of them. I walked over for a closer look and was amazed. Wedding photos. In some, I recognized the ballrooms Rita had shown me. There were happy couples photographed in the lounge, others outside on the front staircase. Some were taken soon after the turn of the century; some during the War showed proud grooms dressed in their military best beside their brides. So, other events besides murder did go on in the Arlington.

The photos were mesmerizing and I quickly became lost in the wedded bliss of the past. I began to make up stories. One sweet looking couple now had twelve grand kids and lived on a farm in Mississippi. One bride looked like she'd made the biggest mistake of her life. I imagined the newlyweds now divorced and living on opposite sides of the country. One groom had an ear-to-ear smile that pierced my heart. His wife had a half-grin that told me she probably had a couple of belts before she said "I do." Then my breath caught. I lifted the picture from the wall. My parents.

Tears puddled in my eyes.

"Another warm body, Miss Lockhart?"

I almost dropped the picture, but had enough wherewithal to shove it under my sweater. I folded my arms across my midsection and stepped into the shadows as I turned around. "Call me Sydney. We have to stop meeting like this."

"How do you manage to show up only minutes after a murder?"

"Lucky I guess. You can't pin this one on me, Lieutenant Dixon. I'd been with Rita for the past hour."

"What were you and Miss Fredricks doing on the roof?"

"Sightseeing, as I'm sure Rita told you. How is she anyway?"

"Shaken up, but fine."

"I can't believe this is happening!" Mr. Charles shouted from the outer office. "I have nothing to say. Get out of here." Flashbulbs went off and a door slammed.

Dixon grabbed my arm and pulled me across the room to another door. "Come on, let's go before Charles comes in and lights into you. The press is lined up in the hall and he's madder than a warthog." Dixon led me down a hallway to the stairwell. "Go on up to your room and stay put. I want to talk to you again before I leave. Right now I have my hands full."

His left eye was flecked with specks of gold, a detail I hadn't notice before. Not wanting to seem rude for staring, I turned away and started up the stairs, my knees a bit weak. It must have been from all the excitement. I had no intention of going to my room. He watched me climb the stairs. I could feel his eyes on my back as if he knew I couldn't be trusted. By the time I reached the fifth floor, he'd gone back into the hall. I opened the stairwell door and ran across the fifth floor to the other side of the hotel where another stairwell took me back down to the lobby. Come hell or high water, I was going to get information for my story.

A nagging thought kept tugging at my brain. Elsa had said that she'd cleaned 1119 right after lunch, but rude Mrs. Willis at the front desk said that there had been a late check-out. My hotel informant should be able to help me clear things up. I scanned the lobby for Mickey, instead I found Ruth sitting at a table in the bar, drinking a martini and smoking a cigarette from her black ebony holder. She was wearing white gloves.

I rushed over and sat down at her table. "What the hell are you doing here?"

"Actually, I had planned to spend my day at Neiman Marcus. The fall shipment of lingerie has just arrived and I wanted to get a jump on the crowd. There's a new girdle on the market that comfortably slims the thighs and tucks the tummy. But then I read about the murder at the Arlington Hotel in the evening edition of the *Dallas Morning News*. I left before the sun came up."

I reached over and finished her martini in one gulp. "You still haven't answered my question."

"I couldn't have you wandering around this place with a murderer loose! I checked in about ten minutes ago and was lucky enough to get a room right next to yours. How about that?"

"Was it luck or a hefty bribe?"

"It doesn't matter."

"How did you get here? I thought you put your car in the shop?"

"I did. They didn't have the blinker thing in stock."

"The blinker? That's all?"

"I couldn't very well drive around without a left blinker. The mechanic said he'd have to order one and it wouldn't arrive for an entire week. What's this world coming to? So I bought a new one."

"A mechanic?"

"No, silly. A car—a Chevy Syline Deluxe. It was time for a change."

"This doesn't have anything to do with the car I'm driving, does it?"

"What if it does?" Now fill me in on what's been happening. Don't leave a thing out."

Ruth changed cars like I changed hotel rooms. I tried not to think about my Ford and what I'd do when I returned to Austin. If I came out ahead on this assignment maybe I could afford a new coat of paint and a shiny new bell for my Schwinn bicycle.

A waiter came by and Ruth ordered two more martinis. I realized that I hadn't eaten since breakfast and the olives weren't going to do it for me. When the martinis arrived I ordered a little something to tide us over until dinner. "Bring us two tunas on rye, cut the onions, two bowls of tomato soup, and two orders of deviled eggs." Then I said to my cousin, "I assume you haven't eaten since you've been on the road all day."

Ruth's mouth fell open, but nothing came out. Finally she said, "What, no dessert?"

"Don't be a smart ass. Murder investigations make me hungry and I have a high metabolism."

"Well, I don't. I can't eat all that. You know me, I eat like a bird."

"A bird—sure—a ravenous vulture, maybe. Listen, we have to eat fast. I'm supposed to be in my room right now."

"Why?" Her eyes widened. "You have a date!" She shoved another cigarette into its holder. "You make me sick. You haven't been here more than two days and you have a date."

"Ruth, you should get a job. Something that obligates you to a schedule. Better yet, you should get married. It'd give you something to do."

"Maybe your date has a brother. Now tell me about the murder."

"Which one?"

Ruth choked on her olive.

Our meal came and I sent the waiter back with instructions to send it up to my room. "If I'm going to tell you everything that's happened, we'll need a little privacy."

"Great. And be sure to tell me what you have under your sweater. You look like you're wearing armor."

The food arrived at 1019 at the same time we did. I let Ruth take care of tipping the waiter while I stepped into my closet to tuck the photo away in my luggage. I was about to stick it in the bottom of my cosmetic bag when I noticed something had been slid in behind the photo. I removed the backing and found my parents' marriage license. With a little luck my Mom might get her money back on that bus ticket.

Between the soup and sandwich course, I told my cousin all about Ellison James and Elsa Dubois.

"Since Elsa's dead, who's the main suspect now?" Ruth asked. She eyed my unfinished sandwich.

"Good question. Grady and I didn't believe Elsa capable of murder, but Rita Fredricks seemed to think Ellison's lover was guilty."

"Grady?"

"The house detective."

"Rita Fredricks?"

"The woman in charge of PR."

A loud knock on the door caused both of us to jump.

"Your date?" Ruth asked.

"Not exactly."

I answered the door and Detective Dixon walked in before I could say hello.

This time Ruth choked on her deviled egg.

"I thought I told you to come straight to your room. I came by about fifteen minutes ago and you weren't here."

I walked over and slapped Ruth on the back. "My cousin, Ruth Echland, from Dallas." I said. "She decided to join me."

He nodded a hello. "Fine," he said.

I wasn't sure what he meant by that. Everything he said came across as sarcasm.

"She's staying next door."

"Fine."

This time he sounded a bit relieved.

"Excuse me, Miss Echland. I need to speak to your cousin in private." He grabbed my hand and we went into the hall.

"Listen. Things are getting ugly. Are you sure you want to stay in this hotel?"

My stomach fluttered and I felt another flush rise from somewhere deep down inside up to my slightly freckled face. I wanted to spit out a curt statement to show how cool I was, but all I could do was choke on my words. It must run in the family. "U . . . ugly?"

"Two people have been murdered in less than twenty-four hours, both right under your nose. Until I can get a handle on this, I've got to believe that you're in danger."

Then he squeezed hard and I realized that he had not let go of my hand.

I finally found my voice, "You mean, like someone thinks I may be a witness?"

"Right. Maybe the Park Hotel. It's just down the street."

"I'll stay here. I have a job to do." The gold flecks in his eyes started to shimmer. "Does that mean you don't suspect me anymore?"

"It means you need to be careful. I'm glad your cousin's here." He let go of my hand and disappeared down the hall before the slight pressure on my fingers disappeared.

I knew that if I went back into my room, Ruth would notice my flushed face immediately. Instead I raised the hall window, and stuck my face out to cool off.

I walked into the room a few minutes later just in time to see Ruth leap back on the bed. No doubt she'd heard the entire conversation through the keyhole. I let her stew for a moment. "Dessert?"

"What?"

"You wanted dessert." I noticed the remnants of both our sandwiches had disappeared. "They have a great Devil's Food cake on the menu."

Ruth threw her napkin at me.

"Let's go to the mineral pool," I said. "You did bring your bathing suit?"

"What do you think, Miss Murder Suspect?"

We had to share the pool with a guy whose body hair was thick enough to weave a sweater. Nestled in his chest hair, and barely visible, was a St. Christopher's medal, which dangled from a chain around his thick neck. He spread his beefy arms along the edge of the pool, commandeering nearly half the area. His arm span must have been ten feet wide. Ruth and I sat huddled together on the other side. I knew Ruth was anxious for information and I was anxious to talk, but we sat there like two mute bimbos, staring at the big man. He was smoking a cigar and, judging by the sweet aroma wafting over, drinking something potent.

"You two gals here alone?" he said.

Ruth and I looked at one another. She moved a closer to me.

"Not that I'm trying to pick you up," he continued, "but I hear there's a madman loose, slit two throats already." He rattled the ice in his glass. "Marine Staff Sergeant Muldoon, retired." He saluted and took a swallow.

"We don't know anything. Nothing," Ruth said, sounding as if she were pleading the Fifth.

I poked my elbow into her side. "What she means is that we've only heard rumors."

"Rumors, haw! This is still a rough town, ladies. I'd watch my backs if I were you."

"What have you heard?" I asked.

He stuck the cigar back into his mouth. "Everybody thinks he's dead, but he ain't. I got information that proves it."

"Who's dead?" Ruth said.

"Harry Metzner. He runs this town. Things don't go his way and . . ." He ran his finger across his throat. "He has a room on the top floor of the Majestic Hotel. No one ever sees him. He has a private elevator—goes right to his suite. Has his henchmen do his dirty work."

He downed the last of his cocktail and stood up, causing a tidal wave to undulate in our direction. I rose just in time, but Ruth was too slow and the surge washed over her head. He stepped out and put on his robe.

"Hey, you two gals want some action just ring my room," he said. "Muldoon in 809. There're a few casinos still around if you know where to look." He winked and was gone.

"My hair!" Ruth sputtered. "I'll have to reset it. It takes hours to dry."

"Don't worry. There's a salon downstairs. You'll be as good as new in no time."

However, the situation put a damper, so to speak, on our afternoon gab session. We left the spa and Ruth headed to the salon. I changed into my pencil skirt and white mohair sweater. I opted for my seamed stockings. I tried to get my hair to sweep over my left eye like Rita Hayworth's, but ringlets won't sweep no matter what. Maybe I should have joined Ruth at the salon.

Ruth and I agreed to meet at 5:00 in the hotel bar. In the meantime, I went in search of Rita. I hadn't expected to find her. I had assumed she'd gone home. Fainting in a pool of someone else's blood has a tendency to ruin a person's day. My assumption was wrong. Rita was back at her desk. Her French twist a bit worse for the wear, but otherwise she looked as professional as ever.

I stuck my head in the doorway. "How's it going?"

"Sydney. Sorry our tour was cut short."

"Murder has a way of altering plans. I'm surprised you didn't go home."

"I could have, but keeping busy helps. It's just me at home. I'd rather be at work. I do need a break though. Do you have time for a drink? We can go to the Ohio Club across the street. I really need to talk to you."

"I'm free for a while."

"Great. Meet me in the lobby in half an hour."

On my way to the elevator, I ran into Mr. Charles who was mumbling to himself and fiddling with his tie. He looked as if he'd aged ten years since this morning. Seeing me seemed to put him in a worse mood.

"Finished your interviews, Miss Lockhart?"

"Almost. There's another person I'd like to talk to." I pushed the elevator button.

"And who's that?"

"Mr. Metzner. Do you think you can arrange an interview?" I wasn't really serious, but something about Mr. Charles made me want to see him sweat. I guess it's kind of like kicking someone when they're down, although that doesn't say much for my character.

The elevator arrived. I stepped inside and said. "Just leave a message at the front desk. Any time's fine with me. I turned to the operator, "Down, please."

Mr. Charles muttered a string of naughty words, one of which sounded like witch.

Since I had a few minutes before I was to meet Rita, I headed to the mezzanine where the employees' room was located. I wanted to find out when Mickey was working again. As luck would have it, he was just punching his time card.

"I need to ask you a question," I said.

"I'm sort of late," he smiled. He pulled a black vest from a closet. "Come on. We can talk while I work.

"New uniform?"

"Naw. I'm waiting tables tonight in the Fountain Room. It doesn't open until 6:00. I'll be setting the room up by myself. It'll be nice and private."

We took the service stairs to the Fountain Room. While Mickey pushed a cart stacked high with various glass and tableware, I followed him from table to table. "Remember when I checked in?"

"Sure. I had to move you to another room."

"I mean before that. While I was at the front desk, Mrs. Willis said that my room was not ready because of a late check-out."

"Oh, right. I remember."

"You went to check on it," I handed him a wine glass. "Who did you ask?"

"Mrs. Lindstrum, the head of housekeeping, has a list with rooms that have been cleaned and the times they were cleared for check-in. I checked with her and she said the room was ready at 12:30."

"Does she check each room herself to make sure?"

"I don't really know how that works."

"Do you think Mrs. Lindstrum would talk to me about it?"

Mickey checked his watch. "She gets off work soon. But I heard she's pretty upset over Elsa's murd . . ." He stopped in the middle of straightening a salad fork. "Hey, you found her body, too. Man, what bad luck. You'll never forget your stay at this hotel."

"Right. Where do I find Mrs. Lindstrum?"

"She works out of a little room next to the laundry room. Take the service elevator to the basement. The room's down the right hall. Last door on the left."

"Thanks, Mickey. Have a good night."

I didn't need Mickey's directions to find Mrs. Lindstrum. Once I stepped off the elevator, I followed the sound of her sobs. Her door was open. "Excuse me, Mrs. Lindstrum?" She let out a scream. "Sorry, I didn't mean to scare you. Do you have a minute?"

"Who are you?"

I wasn't expecting that question since everyone working at the hotel seemed to know who I was. "My name's Sydney Lockhart. I was with Rita Fredricks today when we found Elsa."

"Poor girl. I hope when they find her killer they send him straight to the gallows. I know that's not a Christian thing to say, but Elsa had her whole life ahead of her."

"I'm sorry, Mrs. Lindstrum. She was a nice girl. I had the chance to talk with her last night. Seems we had something in common."

"What's that?"

"We both found Ellison James' body."

"I keep thinking who's going to be next. I should probably keep my door locked." She blew her nose. "I'm leaving soon. What do you want?"

"When I checked into 1119 yesterday, the front desk said it wasn't ready."

"That detective was here asking me about that. Like I told him, that room was ready. Elsa cleaned it and called at 12:30 to say she was finished."

"Do you check each room to make sure?"

"No. That would take too long. Usually, around 2:30 I send the front desk a list of rooms ready for check-in. But if we're busy, like on the weekends, I just call the front desk."

"You called the front desk yesterday, rather than sending down the list."

"That's right."

"Who did you talk to?"

"Jesse Willis."

"Well, Mrs. Willis had the wrong information. Do you remember what you told her?"

"Same thing I always say. "Such and such room is ready. Maybe she was in a hurry and marked it down wrong."

"Maybe. Did you have any late check-outs yesterday?"

"A couple, around two o'clock, but nothing later."

"Thanks, Mrs. Lindstrum. I'm really sorry about Elsa."

"Such a sweet girl."

I left the head of housekeeping to her tears and went back to the lobby to find Rita.

Chapter 8

Rita was on time. We walked across the street to the Ohio Club and found two seats at the bar. Since it was a bit early for cocktail hour, we ordered Bloody Marys. Something about tomato juice and celery seems to diminish the alcohol aspect of the drink, making it more like a late afternoon snack.

"You've made an enemy, Syd." Rita stirred her drink with the celery.

"You mean your boss?"

"He stormed into the office in a tizzy fit. Something about that red-headed, nosy . . . bitch. Before I could hear more, he slammed the door behind him. What did you do?"

"I asked him to get me an interview with Mr. Metzner. I heard that—"

Rita's Bloody Mary didn't make it all the way down, and without warning it came back up. She grabbed a cocktail napkin and covered her mouth and nose before the liquid spewed. I waited while her coughing fit subsided.

"How . . ." She coughed again. ". . . did you find out about . . . him? He's supposed to be dead." She looked around to make sure no one was within earshot.

"But he's not. I heard he runs the Majestic Hotel and some other establishments. Could he be connected to the murders?"

"You're asking the wrong person." Rita stiffened.

"Whom should I ask?"

"Listen, Syd. You don't want to talk to Metzner. No one talks to Metzner, if he's still around, and I'm not sure he is."

Rita looked more terrified than she had when she found Elsa's body, so I decided to drop the subject, for the moment.

"You said you had something to tell me."

I thought I'd blown it with Rita. She sat for a moment without saying a word. I guessed she was trying to decide whether or not to trust me. After my blunder with Metzner, I wouldn't blame her if she didn't. I was in luck.

"Funny things have been happening at the hotel the past few weeks. Money's been stolen; files have gone missing from file cabinets; Ellison James disappeared for a few days; and now Ellison and Elsa are dead. All the employees are strung as tight as piano wire. We used to be a fun group. And now . . . it's like no one trusts anyone. And we're all thinking, who will be next?"

"Any ideas why he was murdered? I figure Elsa was killed because she knew too much, or saw something she shouldn't have."

"Ellison was involved in something he shouldn't have been involved in, but I have no idea what that could have been."

"What makes you say that?"

"Intuition."

"Grady seemed to think that Mr. James was living high above his means."

"I don't know where he got his money, but buying those expensive suits on a bookkeeper's salary was impossible. Hey, maybe he was blackmailing someone."

"How long had he worked for the hotel?"

"He was here when I was hired. I'd say about two years before me."

"Did he always appear to have money?"

"Oh, I see what you mean. As long as I've been here Ellison James had deep pockets."

"So maybe it's something as simple as family money."

"Could be. But I don't think so. He could have been skimming the books for years."

"But if someone found out, why slit Mr. James' throat, why not just turn him into the police?"

"Old habits are hard to break."

"What do you mean?"

"I mean for years, matters like this were settled a lot faster and a lot easier. Going through the proper channels just took too long. Listen, Sydney." Rita pushed her empty glass aside and laid her hand on my arm. "You need to be careful. I mean it. You saw what happened to Elsa. I don't want that to happen to you."

Neither did I. After another Bloody Mary, we walked back toward the hotel.

"My car is in the back lot. I'm going home, put an ice pack on my head, and try to forget this day happened."

I felt bad for Rita. I'm here just to get a story, but this is her job, her life. Maybe I shouldn't be so pushy.

"I never had a chance to thank you for the velvet cap. That was very nice of you."

"Don't mention it. Every girl needs a special little something to spiff up her wardrobe."

She walked down the street a ways, then stopped and turned. "Grady would know."

"Know what?"

"How to find Metzner. Remember, be careful."

It was twenty past five, but since Ruth is always late, I wasn't worried about keeping her waiting. However, when I walked into the hotel my cousin was in the lounge and the look on her face told me she was not happy. One glance at her hairdo and I knew my tardiness was not the cause of her consternation. I had only a few seconds to find soothing words for the disaster that sat on top of her head.

"Don't cry," was what came out of my mouth. The suggestion was too powerful. Tears started to trickle down Ruth's face.

"I look like a poodle."

"Hey, poodles are cute. I have one, remember." Wrong words. The trickle turned into a gush.

"It's a little-old-lady salon. There wasn't a woman in there under seventy. It looked like a geriatrics ward. Those who hadn't fallen asleep sitting under the dryer were gossiping like termites."

"At least you didn't come out with purple hair. Come on. Let's go back to your room. I'll see what I can do. Maybe I can fix it."

"You! The only thing you can do is put that mop of yours up in a ponytail."

"No need to get nasty. Anyway, ponytails are cute, too."

Before we left the lounge, I asked Ruth to wait a moment while I went back to the Fountain Room. I needed Mickey's help again. He was setting small vases of fresh flowers in the center of each table. "Find Mrs. Lindstrum?"

"Right where you said she'd be. But I'm afraid I didn't learn much. I need a favor."

"Name it."

"I want to find out why Jesse Willis had the wrong information about room 1119 when I checked in yesterday, but I'm afraid I made a bad impression on her. She probably won't speak to me."

"Mrs. Willis is a sour puss."

"Think you can find out?"

"You mean like snoop?"

"Exactly."

"I'm your fella. I'm not sure how to do that just yet. I need some time to make a plan."

"Thanks, Mickey. I'll check back with you later."

Forty-five minutes, two dozen bobby pins, and half a can of hairspray later, Ruth's hair was tucked nicely into a twist, not quite as spiffy as Rita's but considering Ruth's short hair, the 'do was not bad.

"I've an idea. Let's get out of the hotel. There's a great restaurant right off Malvern Avenue called Coy's Steak and Seafood. We'll have a nice meal and talk."

"I might be too upset to eat."

Ruth was never too upset to eat, but because of her experience at the salon I went easy on her and let her kid herself.

"We'll have martinis in the restaurant bar until you get hungry."

We slipped on our shoes and grabbed our purses, but before I reached the door someone knocked.

"Who is it?"

No response. I went to open the door.

"Don't!" Ruth cried. "It could be the killer."

"Don't be silly." I turned the doorknob and before I could open the door, an ugly bald man shoved his way in. Following him was another thug-looking guy who smelled strongly of salami. One grabbed me and the other grabbed Ruth.

"Let's go, ladies. Boss don't like to be kept waiting."

I didn't say anything, but I'd no doubt that word had gotten out and I had my appointment with the still-living Mr. Harry Metzner.

Chapter 9

My eyes blinked to the sudden explosion of light and the first thing I saw was a nest of straw right under my nose. As my eyes adjusted I realized that the nest was actually part of my cousin. The hasty application of Ruth's blindfold pulled several bobby pins from her hair and her French twist now looked like a plate of French fries—hair spikes and pins sticking out in all direction.

The salami-smelling guy removed Ruth's blindfold, causing her to squeak like a tiny mouse.

"Shut up," Salami said. "Sit down. Boss's on his way." He shoved us down onto a red brocade sofa. Ruth landed on top of me and said something about her hair. I kept quiet. What she didn't know wouldn't hurt her.

A short, overweight man wearing a red dressing gown waddled in and wedged himself into the armchair across from us.

"I thought you were dead," I said.

"Thinking has gotten you in trouble. You shouldn't do that."

"Thinking or getting into trouble?"

He reached inside his jacket and Ruth squealed again. He pulled out a cigar, bit off the tip, and spat it into the fireplace. Salami scurried over and flicked his lighter.

"If I was you, I'd check out of that hotel and go back to Texas before it's too late."

"Yes, sir," Ruth said. "We're on our way."

Boss and I ignored Ruth. "I'm not finished with my research."

"You're finished all right. I'll make sure of it. Understand?"

"In case you've been living under a rock, it's been a free country for almost two hundred years."

"Let me take care of them, Boss." Salami made a move as if to grab

Ruth and me by our necks.

Metzner stopped him by raising a hand. "Not yet, Chester. Miss Lockhart talks tough, but she ain't stupid." He leaned forward as if to make sure I heard, "I want you gone before the sun comes up."

The guy had seen *High Noon* one too many times. Before I could raise another objection, he rose and waddled out. Chester Salami pulled the blindfolds from his pocket and smiled. I felt a heavy weight on my shoulder. Ruth had passed out.

"I told you not to come here." I pressed a wet cloth across Ruth's forehead. She didn't remember how she had gotten back to the hotel. When I told her that she'd been carried in like a sack of potatoes over the shoulder of our escort, I thought she'd pass out again.

"Well, it doesn't really matter now since we're leaving."

"You're leaving. I'm booked here until the end of the week, and an old, fat man wearing a red robe isn't going to run me out of town."

"Syd, those guys mean business."

"So do I. I'm staying."

"I'm staying, too. Aunt Mary Lou would never forgive me if I left you here alone and you got your throat cut."

I gave Ruth a hug. My cousin could be a pain in the butt, but she's been known to rise to the occasion.

"Okay. We'll just have to be careful. You were right. I should not have opened the door like that."

"I won't let you out of my sight. I promise."

I wasn't sure if we needed to be that careful. "As I recall, we were on our way to dinner when we were abducted."

Ruth smiled. The mention of food always perked her up. Me, too.

Our waiter brought over a narrow pan filled with warm saltine crackers and a cruet of French dressing—the complimentary appetizer for which Coy's was famous. I ordered the baked salmon and Ruth opted for prime rib. Half way through our salads, my knees began to shake. It must have been a delayed reaction from our kidnapping of only an hour ago. I suddenly realized how lucky we were. We could have easily ended up at the bottom of Lake Hamilton, wearing matching concrete blocks instead of tart shoes. I tried to hide my fear for Ruth's sake. Metzner really did scare the crap out of me. I held no illusion as to my tough-girl facade. If Metzner wanted us dead, Chester Salami would have had no qualms about carrying out his boss' orders.

"Are you okay?" Ruth said.

"I'm fine. I think this is the first time I've relaxed since I left Austin two days ago," I lied.

"So tell me everything. I've gotten bits and pieces. Who do you think the killer is? Do you think the same person killed both people? Is that detective married?"

I filled Ruth in, giving little insight to Lieutenant Dixon. I needed to keep my head clear if I was to figure this out and keep both my cousin and myself alive.

By the time our meal arrived, I was feeling better.

"What if Metzner finds out that we're still at the hotel in the morning?"

"I've no doubt that he'll know. In fact, he probably knows where we are now and what we're eating."

Ruth looked around the restaurant. "You think he's the killer?"

"No. That would be too obvious. I think he did just what he meant to do. Scare us. I just can't figure out why." I told Ruth about my comments to Mr. Charles. "I sort of asked for it. I've been a pain in Charles' butt and he saw another opportunity to get back at me."

"That means this Mr. Charles is connected to Metzner."

"That's no surprise. Eat up. I just got my second wind and the night's young. I want to talk to Grady and maybe Rita if I can get her home number."

"You haven't told me what you had hidden under your sweater."

"You don't forget anything do you?"

"Nope. If we're going to work late we need extra fuel." The waiter walked by and Ruth ordered two pieces of chocolate cake a-la-mode and two coffees.

When we returned to the Arlington we had to wait to talk to Grady. We were told he was in the process of persuading some drunks to leave the mineral pool. Feeling that the crowded lobby was safer than our hotel rooms, we waited there. Ruth had just pulled out her ebony cigarette holders when Mr. Muldoon sauntered over and joined us. Remembering that he was the one who dropped Metzner's name, which eventually led to our later-than-desired dinner arrangement, I was not too happy to see him.

"Buy you chicks a drink?"

"No, thank you," Ruth said.

"Hey," he snapped his fingers at a passing waiter. "Three Manhattans, and make 'em sweet, extra cherries." Then he turned his attention back to us. "It's the least I could do. Glad you're okay."

"What do you mean?" I asked.

"My big mouth got you two gals in trouble."

"Is there anyone here who doesn't know every move we make?" I said in exasperation.

"I just happened to be leaving the parking garage when I saw you two escorted into the limo. I had a feeling you were, maybe, in trouble."

"What clued you in? Could it have been the blindfolds?" Now I was pissed. "Why the hell didn't you help us? Or maybe you set it up. Maybe you have connections with Metzner."

"Don't curl you hair, honey. Told you this was a rough town. I was just making small talk. Didn't know you'd go running your mouth off. I figured if you weren't back by morning, I'd call the cops." Something across the room caught his attention and he quickly got up and left. Probably some chick he'd promised to meet at the bar and forgotten he'd made the date.

I looked around and saw Grady coming our way. The waiter arrived with the three Manhattans.

"Bring me a coffee, Johnny." Grady sat down. "Thanks for the drink. I'll have to hide mine. Still on duty. Those yahoos in the pool were a bit ornery." He took off his drenched jacket and hung it on the back of his chair. "Who's your friend?"

"Grady, this is my cousin Ruth. Ruth, Grady, the house detective."

"Bringing in reinforcements?"

"Rita said I should ask you about Metzner," I said wasting no time. "But before I had a chance, I had the opportunity to meet the man in person."

Grady's coffee arrived and he surreptitiously poured the hot liquid into a potted plant, then filled his cup with one of the Manhattans.

"Do you think Metzner's the killer?" I said.

"Metzner's a has-been. Had his wings clipped when the attorney general cleaned up the town a few years back. Metzner copped state's evidence and managed to stay out of jail. Rumor has it that he has enough money hidden in his mattress to keep living the good life."

"So, he's not running this hotel?"

"Who knows who's running this hotel? Metzner probably still has his sticky fingers in the operation, but he's pretty much kept a low profile."

"He threatened us with an 'or else' if we didn't leave town by sunrise." Ruth scoffed.

"I wouldn't worry about it," Grady said.

"That's easy for you to say. You weren't blindfolded and kidnapped." Ruth took off a glove and felt to make sure her 'do was in place. Most people worried about having a clean pair of undergarments on if they ever met with an accident. Ruth worries about her hair being in place if her body ever ended up in a ditch on the side of the road.

After I got Rita's phone number from Grady, Ruth and I bid him good night. We left him to enjoy his "coffee." Grady's cavalier attitude concerning the town's token mobster didn't leave Ruth and me feeling much better about what could have been our last night in Hot Springs.

Once in my room, Ruth kicked off her shoes and flopped down on my love seat. "Since we've decided to tough it out and stay, maybe, just for tonight, we should stay together in the same room."

"We have an adjoining door. Let's just leave the door open. I'm sure we'll be okay. Don't worry. You go on to bed. I want to call Rita."

"You're right. I am a light sleeper, nothing can get by me." Ruth actually looked appeased and I was beginning to feel fairly serene myself. I still hadn't told Ruth about finding my parent's wedding photograph. I didn't want to bring up the subject as an epilogue to murder. We hugged and parted. I would have held on to Ruth a bit longer had I'd known that I wouldn't be seeing her again for a while.

Chapter 10

As soon as I heard Ruth snoring, I pushed the door without actually closing it, and picked up the phone to call Rita. No answer. No big deal, except I'd been wondering why Rita suggested I talk to Grady about Metzner. I suppose it was to reassure me that Metzner wasn't a threat, but my intuition told me there was more to it.

I changed into my PJs, and decided to put the day's mishaps behind me and write. Writing is not only what I do for a living, it's therapeutic. Once I start clacking the keys or scribbling on my notepad, I'm able to forget my troubles. I enter another world and often lose track of time. Writing the article on Hot Springs was a breeze, so I decided to tackle another story—one that might get the newspaper to take me seriously. Title: "Old Gangsters Don't Die, They Just Become Puppeteers." Maybe not the best title, but you get the idea. For some reason I couldn't get Metzner off my mind. I pictured him sitting in his bawdy apartment on the top floor of the Majestic with strings reaching all over town, not only to the Arlington Hotel, but to the hidden casinos, the state government in Little Rock, and maybe even the local police. But since I had no proof, my suspicions were just that, suspicions.

Maybe I'd work my ideas into a novel instead. Change a few names, set it in Chicago, and promote it as a thriller. Of course I'd have to use a pseudonym. Who'd buy a gangster book written by a woman? But then Sydney is an androgynous name. Still, once I become a famous writer, and I will, people will recognize my name. I could use my initials: S. J. Lockhart, or use the masculine spelling of my middle name: Jean, and I'd become Gene Lockhart. I was losing myself in my literary fantasies when I looked at the clock and realized I'd been curled up on the love seat, scribbling nonsense for two hours.

I stood up and stretched and decided I'd schedule another massage for first thing in the morning. I hadn't yet visited the bathhouses. The Buckstaff was highly recommended.

I walked to the window and gazed out on a sleepy town. A few lights twinkled across Central Avenue and fog rose over Lake Hamilton. I thought of Carl Sandburg's poem "The Fog Came in on Little Cat Feet." It's one of my favorites—short and serene and as I reflected on it, I began to relax.

In the distance, the Oaklawn Race Track, lit up like stars on a faraway horizon, created an oval-like glow. Then something below caught my eye. I noticed a man strolling down Fountain Avenue, the street that branched off Central and ran right in front of my room. He was cloaked in a heavy coat. His hat was pulled down over his head, shading his eyes. Even with the covering I recognized Staff Sergeant Muldoon. He didn't appear to be in a hurry. He walked toward the Park Hotel a block away, turned, and came back in this direction. I turned my lamp off so I couldn't be seen. Once he reached the Arlington, he did something odd. He looked around and sat down on a park bench. I'd assumed he'd come from a night of casino hopping, but I now suspected that he was waiting for someone. I watched a while longer. No one else came by and Muldoon remained where he was.

Okay, maybe he was an insomniac. Maybe he'd lost a bundle at the crap table and needed to lick his wounds before calling it a night. Maybe he was just weird. I was about to put an end to my voyeurism when he glanced up in my direction. I ducked behind the drapes. He stared for a few seconds before turning away. Then he folded his arms across his chest and stayed put. Had I not promised Ruth I'd stay close, I'd have marched down there and offered to keep the man company. After a few minutes, I gave up. If Mr. Muldoon wanted to spend the night on a park bench, that was his prerogative. I was going to bed.

Just as I pulled the covers up to my chin and snuggled my head into my pillow, a woman's scream jolted me up out of bed. I jumped up and ran to the door. Remembering what happened earlier, I resisted opening it. I waited. A few seconds later, a loud thump and another scream more horrifying than the first sent me flying out the door. I'm a pretty smart woman, but even smart women can't resist coming to the rescue of another woman in distress. The hall was clear of domestic abuse. I stepped back to return to my room and bumped into something soft. Before I could turn around, I felt a rag pushed over my mouth. Suddenly everything went dark.

Shivering and achy, I reached down to pull up the covers but there weren't any. Through narrow eye-slits, I hoped to see the Hot Springs mountain tower outside my window. I saw only darkness. My head felt like it was spinning on a Tilt-a-Whirl. My mouth tasted as if I'd been chewing foil. I closed my eyes to make the dizziness stop. A few deep breaths and my brain finally sputtered to life like an old Nash Rambler I used to own. Images began flashing in my mind. I remembered looking out my hotel room window and seeing Muldoon walking along the street. The evening was peaceful. I had tucked myself into bed and had fallen asleep, thinking of Carl Sandburg and little cat feet and wondering if I should present Monroe and Mealworm with a little feline sister. And then things turned ugly. Surely I was dreaming—having a hell of a nightmare was more like it. Surely it was almost dawn—I'd wake myself up, order room service, and sip my coffee.

I rolled over. A spring poked into my back, and I realized that I wasn't in my cozy bed; my sweet cousin Ruth wasn't in the room next door sawing logs; there'd be no room service; there'd be no coffee. And suddenly, me, smart-woman Sydney Lockhart, knew she was in a shit load of trouble.

After a few deep breaths, I opened my eyes again and sat up. My head felt as if hundreds of tiny horses were stampeding my brain. I felt for a lump, and not finding one, I concluded that I'd probably been chloroformed—hence the tinny taste in my mouth. The only light was a glow coming from somewhere above. Once my eyes adjusted to the darkness, I was able to make out my surroundings. The small room was almost empty except for a chair and a cot on which I sat. The place was damp and smelled of mold. One wall contained shelves with rows of jars connected by webs of industrious spiders. I reached over, picked up a jar, and dusted it off. Well at least I wouldn't starve. The jars contained some sort of canned fruits or vegetables. I could always break one and use the glass shard to fight my captor when he returned. And if he never returned I could always slit my wrists.

A faint glow from a narrow window high above was beginning to lighten the room. Wonderful! The dawn of another adventurous day—this one in some old abandoned basement.

Standing up made me woozy. I sat back down and more images began to flash in my mind—a chair flying through the air, a woman screaming, my cousin Ruth sleeping soundly in the next room. I forced my brain out of its stupor and things started to clear up. There was a ruckus in the hall—a staged ruckus for my entertainment no doubt. And I showed up on time just like an idiot. I always thought of Scott as being the impulsive one in the family, rushing ahead into bad situations. Like the time he and Jeremiah had a fight over a ruined soufflé and Scott moved out of their apartment, withdrew all his money out of his savings, and plopped it down as a down payment on a house. He's been struggling with a mortgage ever since. My stupid brother. What would he think if he found out that his sister pulled a Scott? Could I have been wrong all these years? Maybe Scott was the smart one. After all he was at home in bed and I was God-knows-where.

Well, I certainly wasn't going to sit here and wait for my captor to write the next chapter of this saga. I took the chair, placed it in the middle of the cot, and climbed up for a peek. Before I could see anything, the chair wobbled, and I tumbled. Luckily, I landed on the cot. When no one came to investigate the noise, I tried again.

I shoved the cot out of the way, sat the chair under the window, and hoisted myself up again. I tried to push open the window, but it wouldn't budge. I looked around for something to break the glass when I heard what sounded like a lawn mower. Did kidnappers wake up early to mow the lawn before starting their day of malice and mayhem? I counted on that not being true and started shouting. After several minutes and a raw throat, I gave up.

I had to get out of here. I noticed that the shelves were actually a free-standing bookcase. I quickly removed all the jars and muscled the case under the window. It was heavy and I knew it would hold my weight. I climbed each shelf like a rung of a ladder and got high enough to look out. Using the sleeve of my pajama shirt, I cleaned away some of the grime and at first all I saw was water. Then the sound of the lawn mower started again and I looked around and noticed a pier jutting out into a lake. It wasn't a lawn mower after all. An old man sat in a boat, pulling the cord on an outboard motor. I struck at the latch on the window and it gave. Climbing a shelf higher, I shoved the window open and, grateful for my slim figure, wriggled my way out the narrow opening. The morning air was brisk and a thin layer of frost covered the ground. Once I was out, I ran over to the dock.

"Hello," I shouted. I got no response and walked out onto the pier. "Hello."

The guy finally looked around. He cut the outboard motor, climbed from the boat, and walked over. If he noticed my inappropriate attire, he kept mute and instead said, "Mornin', ma'am."

This guy looked as old as Moses. I stood there in my bare feet and PJs, rubbing my arms and shivering.

"Where am I?"

"Highway 27 Fish Camp. We're closed for the season."

The icy ground was beginning to freeze my feet and I started dancing around a bit to keep warm. "Fish Camp?"

"Lake Ouachita."

"Who are you?"

"Milo Small, caretaker. Angelo and Shirley won't be back until March. They spend every winter in Key West. Angelo makes great spaghetti. You should come back then. Hey," he looked at my feet. "Lose your shoes?"

I wanted to say, "What the hell do you think, Milo?" But I held my tongue. I'd done too many stupid things in the last few hours.

"Do you have a phone I could use?"

"Nope. Closest phone is at the Sinclair station in Mount Ida."

"How far is Mount Ida?" I looked around, hoping to see the hustle and bustle of a town nearby. Except for a few cabins and boats moored to the dock, there was nothing.

"'bout five miles down the road.

"Can you take me there?"

"Won't do you no good."

"Why's that?"

"Phone's broke."

"Any other phones around?"

"Nope. It's Sunday and everything is closed."

Realizing I'd have to be the smart one here, I said, "Listen, Mr. Small. My name's Sydney Lockhart and I need your help."

"Sure. What can I do?"

"Okay. First I need to get out of the cold. I'm about to freeze."

"My cabin's around the bend there."

"Great. Let's go." I wasn't thrilled about going into Milo Small's cabin, but if I wanted to keep from losing my toes to frostbite, I'd have to endure. I spotted the cabin among a clump of oak trees and scampered over. Milo took his time. I was about to let myself in when the door opened. A woman no bigger than a child stood there and said, "Oh, my. Sorry dear, we're closed for the season. Angelo and Shirley are in—"

"Key West, I know. You must be Mrs. Small. Your husband invited me over. I'm Sydney Lockhart. May I come in?"

"Excuse my manners. Come on in, dear. We don't get many visitors here in the off-season. She held open the door and the warmth from the wood-burning stove engulfed me like a warm blanket. Before I could explain my presence, Milo joined us.

"She lost her shoes, Mamma."

"So I see. Would you like some coffee?"

Coffee sounded like liquid manna from heaven and I wasn't going to refuse, but I was beginning to wonder about Mr. and Mrs. Small's lack of curiosity about me. A strange woman showing up out of nowhere wearing pajamas and no shoes should surely raise some questions even if Highway 27 Fish Camp was closed for the season.

"I'm lost," was all I could say.

"Poor thing. Make the coffee, Milo, while I get our guest a pair of socks. Don't have shoes big enough for those feet." Mrs. Small laughed and shuffled down the hall.

I looked down at my feet. Size ten isn't that big for a five-ten woman, but if you're as small as Mrs. Small, I guess anything over a size four would seem rather large.

While I waited for my hosts to return, I considered how much I should tell them. Not that it really mattered. They didn't seem very excitable. Then I realized that I didn't know much myself. Someone abducted me last night and locked me in the basement of Angelo and Shirley's Highway 27 Fish Camp near Mt. Ida. I decided on the truth, as much as I knew of it.

Mrs. Small returned with a pair of gray and white socks with red heels, the kind my Aunt Rosie used to fill with cotton and turn into stuffed monkeys. Aunt Rosie had given me one of her homemade-sock monkeys when I was five. The ugly thing scared the hell out of me and my mother had to hide it in the closet. For some reason, that unexplainable fear was returning as Mrs. Small handed me the socks. Maybe I should just hide in the closet like the monkey and hope for the best.

Milo came in from the kitchen carrying a cup of coffee.

"Thank you so much," I said. "Listen, I'm sure you're wondering what I'm doing here. I mean, I said I was lost and I guess I am, but, well—"

"We know why you're here," Milo said.

"You do?"

"Yep. Saw you crawl out of the root cellar. At first I thought you was that ol' fox that's been raiding the place. I almost took my rifle and blew your head off. Then I remembered you were in there."

This made Mrs. Small chuckle. "Oh, Papa, you're so funny."

"You knew I was in the root cellar?"

"Yep. That man brought you in last night. Said he needed a place for you to sleep it off. You'd gotten drunk and passed out. Said he needed to get rid of you before his wife came home. Told me not to let you out because you were . . . what did he say Mamma? You weren't playing with a full deck. He gave me twenty bucks for my trouble.

"What man?"

"See there, Mamma. She ain't playing with a full deck. She can't remember."

I shook my head. "I am playing with a full deck! All fifty-four cards! Fifty-two. I mean fifty-four—I . . . included the jokers." Oh boy. "Listen, that's not what happened. I wasn't drunk. I was kidnapped."

Mr. and Mrs. Small didn't seem impressed by my story. "No matter," Mr. Small said. "Your boyfriend said he'd come back for you this morning." He looked at the clock. "Should be here any minute now."

"He's not my boyfriend. You've got to help me. That man's a killer. I am staying at the Arlington Hotel. Can you take me there? How far away are we?"

"Is that in Hot Springs?"

"Yes."

"That's about forty miles from here."

"I'll pay you. I have to get out of here before that man comes back."

"Don't know," Milo said, rubbing his chin. "He seemed like a pretty nice guy. Didn't he, Mamma?"

"Yeah. But if he was fooling around on his wife with a crazy, drunk woman, he probably wasn't all that nice." She glanced at my forehead. "She looks like she's been in a fight."

"I'm not a crazy drunk woman! And I haven't been in a fight." All of a sudden I realized what I must look like, standing in this cabin in a pair of dirty pajamas, my hair a rat's nest for sure, and wearing a pair of frightful monkey socks. I reached up to make sure my bandage was in place and realized it was gone.

Milo and the Mrs. exchanged glances and whatever Milo said next, I knew would seal my fate. While they communicated telepathically, I thought about running for it. If they decided to stick me back in the root cellar and wait for my kidnapper to return, I was done for. Maybe I could find some Arkansas farmer who would be willing to take me back to Hot Springs. I looked toward the door when Mrs. Small spoke. "She kinda looks like cousin Belle, don't she?"

"She does at that. Well, I guess I better start the truck. I just hope I have enough gas to make the trip."

I wanted to rush over and give them both a kiss. I wanted to know who Belle was so I could send her a thank-you card. But what I really wanted was to get the hell away from Highway 27 Fish Camp before it was too late.

Chapter 11

Before Milo returned with the truck, Mrs. Small came out of the bedroom carrying a jacket and a pair of boots.

"You can't go driving off down the road like that. Here, someone left these in one of the cabins." She handed me the boots. "And this is one of Milo's old jackets. It's cold outside."

"No shit," I wanted to say. But this sweet woman was about to help save my life so I refrained from being sarcastic. I may have been an idiot last night, but not today.

I heard Milo revving the engine, and I headed for the door. Mrs. Small grabbed her coat and followed me out. "Put this on your head, honey." She tossed me a red and black hunter's cap complete with earflaps.

"Thanks. My ears feel like they're frozen solid."

"It ain't your ears that need covering. You need to hide that hair of yours."

I didn't want to imagine what I looked like. To tell the truth, I didn't really care.

"Let's go. I'll ride shotgun," she said. "You can sit in the middle."

As soon as we left Fish Camp and turned onto Highway 27, I began to breathe a little easier. But I worried about driving past my kidnapper and expressed my concern to Milo.

"Thought about that, too. I did. I drained some gas out of the tractor and I figured we'd drive north across the lake. It's a mite bit longer, but that guy would be coming from Mt. Ida. This way we'll miss him."

"Speaking of my kidnapper, what did he look like?"

"Stocky guy. Smelled sort of like a meat locker."

Chester Salami. That's what I suspected. "Had you seen him before?" I was wondering how he knew to hide me in Fish Camp's root cellar.

"Never seen the guy, but Mama and me's just here for three months in the winter. The rest of the time we live in Mena. He could be one of Angelo's regular summertime customers. Lot of city folks come to Lake Ouachita to cool off."

"I wouldn't exactly call Chester Salami a city folk. More like a gangster."

"Coming from Hot Springs, it's the same thing," Mrs. Small said.

We hadn't driven two miles down the bumpy dirt road when Milo said, "Whoops."

"What?"

"Looks like we're being followed."

I instantly hunkered down. "Who is it?"

"The salami guy," Milo said. "I think he seen you. Now I know he seen you."

"Why?"

Before Milo answered my question he jerked the truck sharply to the right and we left the dirt road behind. A shot rang out and Mrs. Small joined me on the floorboard.

"We got trouble, now," Mrs. Small said.

"Hang on. They couldn't capture me in Italy and they ain't gonna capture me now!"

"Uh oh," slipped from Mrs. Small's mouth.

"What's uh oh, Mrs. Small?"

"Papa's back in the war. It happens whenever he hears a gunshot or even a backfire."

We wove and bumped down what I imagined to be no more than a dirt trail through the woods. Mrs. Small and I held on to one another and bounced around like two bundles of laundry. I looked up at Milo and sure enough, his face seemed to have transformed from that of a mild sweet old man to a determined soldier committed to going down fighting. I wasn't sure which Milo I preferred. If he could save us from the clutches of Chester Salami, I didn't really care. I just hoped we'd all come out of this alive. If something bad happened to this sweet old couple, my conscience would haunt me forever. Another shot rang out and the slug pinged into the bed of the pickup followed by another, which shattered the back window and sprayed us with shards of glass.

Visions of a 1939 Packard squealing to a stop in front of a restaurant and gangsters in long black coats jumping out with machine guns, mow-ing down everyone, flashed before me. I think the movie was Jimmy Cagney's *The Roaring Twenties*. Although I was nowhere near a city, and only one gangster with an ordinary gun that fired one round at a time was chasing me, my situation seemed every bit as horrific. Other strange thoughts flicked through my mind—thoughts that had nothing to do with my predicament, thoughts that didn't even constitute my life flashing before my eyes, thoughts that were utterly ridiculous, like how much did Rita pay for that velvet green cap and who would have to pay my hotel bill if I didn't return, like whatever became of the math teacher, Mr. Thomas, who quit the day after my snake escaped from my science room, crawled onto his desk, and tried to swallow his arm, like why did Chester smell like salami?

I should have taken Metzner's warning seriously. What did I do to deserve kidnapping? What did I do to cause Metzner to want to kill me? There was no doubt in my mind he was connected to the murders and that he believed that me, Sweet Syd, Innocent Syd, was a threat to him. I was merely a victim of being in the wrong place at the wrong time.

Another bullet hit somewhere in the bed of the pickup.

Milo's escape plan was not working. At this rate we'd be dead in a manner of minutes. I was about to try and convince Milo that we stood a better chance of surviving if we surrendered. After all, Chester Salami only wanted me, not the Smalls. Just as my sacrificial plea was ready to slide from my lips, the truck suddenly became airborne.

"Yee! Haa!" Milo shouted as we flew over an embankment. "Don't worry girls. I know a short cut through the back of Fuzzy Fitzsimmons' farm. The enemy won't be able to follow us driving that city car." We landed with a jolt that threw my head up under the dash and caused my teeth to come down hard on my unsuspecting tongue. I tasted blood. Mrs. Small was under me so I managed to protect her from the jolting crash. I was sure the tires would blow, but they took the impact better than me. We plowed through the Fitzsimmons' farm like a tractor gone wild. I crawled from underneath the dash and looked up at Milo who was grinning from ear to ear. I stole a glance through the now-open back window in time to see Chester Salami get out of his car at the top of a steep ridge. Milo was right, there was no way Metzner's henchman could follow us down that embankment in his low-to-the-ground Studebaker. Salami stood with his hands on his hips, then he turned and got back into his car. I feared we'd not seen the last of him.

Milo drove into a plucked cotton field, then into the hen yard in back of Fitzsimmons' house. He continued to whoop and holler, scattering chickens, dogs, goats, and any other farm animals in our wake. Within seconds we were on another back road leading away from the farm. Mrs. Small brushed some of the glass away and crawled up on the seat next to me. "We usually just go to church on Sunday morning," she said. "Who would've guessed?"

Who indeed? I almost couldn't wait to get back to the Arlington and tell Ruth.

"We're going to outsmart that goon," Milo said. "I know what he's thinking. He's going to keep going down that back road looking for us to join up somewhere along the way. He thinks we've got to drive up that way sooner or later. But I know a place down here where we can hide out for a while. I used to run liquor back in the twenties. Me and old Fitzsimmons had us a still in a cabin in these woods. That's where we're headed."

Milo seemed to have left World War I and Italy and returned to reality. That didn't give me much comfort, though. We must have traveled only about five miles from Fish Camp. But if we were taking a less than direct route, we could be days from Hot Springs.

I'm sure by now Ruth was awake and hysterical that her cousin was missing. I'm sure she called Detective Dixon to report my absence. And I'm sure he had no clue as to how to find me. Suddenly I felt alone and frightened. Then a horrible thought occurred to me. What if they'd nabbed Ruth as well? I had run from my room, leaving the door wide open. Snatching Ruth from her bed would have been a piece of cake. As Milo, Mrs. Small, and I bounced through the woods, I did something I rarely do. I started to cry.

I thought of the courage and stamina my father had living with my mother all those years and managed to choke back my tears. Milo and Mrs. Small seemed to be having such a good time, and I didn't want to rain on their parade. I was also beginning to wonder if Milo knew where the hell he was going. He'd already turned around and backtracked at least three times. If it weren't for the sun, I'd have no idea which direction we were headed. Then Milo stopped the truck.

"What's wrong?" I asked.

"We're here." Milo said, clambering out.

I looked around and saw only what I'd been seeing for the last half hour, trees, bushes, and more trees and bushes, except for a woodpile about twenty yards away. If worse came to worse, we could always make a campfire, which sounded rather good, since I was starting to shiver again.

"Milo's often told me about this place," Mrs. Small said, "But I've never been out here."

While Mrs. Small and I stood outside the truck absorbing nature, Milo tugged at a large piece of wood from the woodpile.

"Come on, girls. She's leaning a bit, but the stove's still upright and I can have a fire going in no time," Milo shouted. That's when I realized the woodpile was actually the cabin.

"We won't have to worry about snakes this time of year. They're all hibernatin'."

Wonderful. I'm sure Mr. Thomas, the math teacher, would have appreciated Milo's assessment.

I stood outside the cabin listening to Milo bang around inside. He emerged a few minutes later covered with cobwebs. "I got a fire going. We'll warm up and give the salami guy a chance to give up on us. Then we'll head back to the road."

"Don't think we can do that," Mrs. Small said.

"Why?" Milo and I responded in unison.

"Seems a bullet hit the gas tank. I smelled it as soon as I stepped out of the truck. It's a wonder the thing didn't explode."

I slumped down on a splintery piece of wood that was once the cabin step and began to wonder if I'd ever see civilization again. Last night I'd dined in a fancy restaurant, looking like a million bucks. Less than twenty-four hours later, I was wearing filthy pajamas, a red and black hunter's cap, a pair of old work boots, and a jacket that smelled like it had spent the last twenty years in a pig sty. I shuddered to think what my hair looked like. If I made it back to the Arlington, they probably wouldn't even let me in the door.

Mrs. Small sat down beside me. "You got some dirt smeared on your face, honey."

Such a sweet woman. I stuck my hands in the pockets of the jacket so they wouldn't find their way around her throat.

Chapter 12

I could feel the warmth coming from inside the cabin. I turned around. Through the open doorway I saw Milo swallowed by a cloud of thick smoke. He was rooting around, pulling up boards from the floor.

"Come on in. It's nice and toasty in here." The smoke didn't seem to bother him. Mrs. Small followed me inside. That's when I noticed the stovepipe had become detached from the hole in the roof. I gently shoved, and although the pipe shuddered and squeaked, it slid back into place. Within a few minutes the smoke began to clear. In the corner sat a lopsided table and two chairs. I checked for scorpions that may have been homesteading under the seats and once satisfied there were none, moved the chairs closer to the stove. I motioned for Mrs. Small to sit. I occupied the other chair. Milo was still busy dismantling part of the cabin's floor for what I assumed would be more firewood. I was about to tell him that I had no intention of staying here any longer than I had to when he let out another yell.

"Whoo whee." He reached down into a hole in the floor and pulled out a jug. "I knew there had to be some here." He brushed off the dirt and tugged. With a loud plop, the cork came out and the smell of hooch wafted across the room. He sniffed and took a sip. "Damn. Got better with age. More than thirty years old, I'd say." He tilted the jug back, let it rest on his forearm, and took a long, slow swallow. Then he walked over and squatted down between us.

"We seem to be in a pickle," Mrs. Small said. She reached for the jug, sniffed, and took a swallow, mimicking her husband.

"What about Fitzsimmons?" I asked. "His place couldn't be but a couple of miles back. Maybe we could ask him for help."

"Not a good idea," Milo said. "We had a falling out years back. In fact, if he figures out that it was me who plowed through his hen yard, he'd probably be chasing us as well."

"But he doesn't know me," I said. "I could go back, get help, and then send help for you."

"She's got a point there, Papa." The Smalls were now passing the jug back and forth.

"You think he has a phone?"

"Naw. Doesn't even have indoor plumbing." Milo burped.

"But he still might help. I don't see any other way," I said. "I noticed a pickup parked by the house. We can't just sit here, and if we walk back to the road, Chester Salami might find us."

Mrs. Small handed me the jug. I sniffed as proper protocol warranted. The fumes rushed in and paralyzed my trachea. It was a few seconds before I was able to catch my breath. I passed on taking a sip. If my two companions wanted to spend the rest of their Sunday morning tipping the jug, that was their business, but I was going back to Hot Springs no matter what. I stood up to make my pronouncement when buckshot sprayed the side of the cabin. We all hit the floor at once.

"Milo Small, you low-down skunk's ass! I'll see you dead before I let you off my land!"

"That'd be Fuzzy," Milo said.

"Is he serious?" I gasped.

"Reckon so."

Another shot exploded and this time lead actually flew through the cabin wall.

"Seems to be getting closer," Mrs. Small said.

"You two stay down." Milo crawled toward an opening that was probably a back door at one time. "I'm going around the back. Try to sneak up on him."

Before I could tell Milo that the idea was just plain stupid, he was gone and another shot came through, this time hitting the stove pipe and knocking it from the stove. It crashed with a loud clang. A thick cloud of soot filled the room and covered Mrs. Small and me. Fuzzy stomped up onto the front step. "I said come outta there you slimy lizard!"

Feeling like a little pig fleeing the big bad wolf, I grabbed Mrs. Small and we crawled toward the back door. I shoved her outside and then ran over and picked up the jug of hooch. With the pipe gone and the stove now open at the top, I flung the jug into the belly of the fire and fled the cabin. I didn't expect the explosion to rock the ground on which I rolled, but it did. I prayed to God that I hadn't killed the cranky farmer on the front porch. I checked to make sure Mrs. Small was unhurt. Finding her black with soot, but otherwise in good shape, I ran to the front of the cabin. Milo was dragging the unconscious Fuzzy Fitzsimmons away from the burning mass.

"Is he dead?" I yelled.

"Naw, just knocked out. Grab his gun," Milo said. "It's over by the porch. Now'd be the time to take Fuzzy's truck and get the hell out of here before he wakes up."

I handed the shotgun to Mrs. Small. Milo and I dragged Fuzzy away from the flames. Milo pointed in a straight direction to the Fitzsimmons' farm and I took off through the woods. My mission was to get the pick-up, drive it back, and pick up everyone. Backtracking to the farm was easy, I just followed the route, which we'd taken earlier—broken branches and rutted tire tracks led the way.

Fuzzy's truck made Milo's look like a Cadillac. The stuffing spilled from rips in the seat and the clutch and brake pedals were missing, leaving behind two metal spokes on which to place my feet. But at least it started and the gas tank was half full. When I drove up, I was relieved to see that Fuzzy was mumbling, although not yet conscious enough to know what was going on. Milo and I tossed him into the bed of the truck.

"What about this fire?" I said. "What if it spreads?"

"That ain't gonna happen," Milo said. "Not much wind and not a lot of brush around it to catch. It'll just burn itself down."

I trusted Milo's judgment and we left the scene. By the time we arrived at the farm, Fuzzy was sitting up, but still incoherent.

"Hurry! Let's put him in his house and hightail it outta here," Milo said. "You take hold of his feet."

I walked around to the back of the truck and grabbed Fuzzy by his boots. His eyes popped opened and locked on my face.

"Lord save me! The devil's come!" He screamed and passed out again.

We laid Fuzzy on his filthy kitchen floor. Mrs. Small covered him with blanket she'd found, then we left.

I wanted to drop Milo and Mrs. Small off at Fish Camp and drive to Hot Springs alone. I felt they'd done enough and I didn't want to involve them any further. But they insisted on accompanying me to the city. After all, Milo argued, someone had to drive Fuzzy's truck back.

With Chester Salami long gone, we felt safe enough to take Highway 27. This time I drove, Milo rode shotgun, and Mrs. Small sat in the middle with the shotgun in her lap. I glanced at them. We were a fine trio. According to Fuzzy, I resembled the devil with my red mop and black-sooted skin. Milo had a scratch on his forehead where blood had dried and Mrs. Small looked like she was ready for a black-face act in a vaudeville show. They were both smiling. I guess this adventure was more exciting than a Sunday service at the Mount Ida Church.

As we rode in silence, I tried to figure out what had happened. Now that the danger had passed, I realized Metzner wanted to get me out of the Arlington, but I had no idea why. Another murder? Another robbery? Or maybe he just wanted to frighten me into leaving for good. If he'd wanted me dead, I wouldn't have been chloroformed and dumped in the root cellar. And when Chester Salami was chasing us, his aim would have been much better. I had no doubt I'd find out the answer to the puzzle soon enough.

The hour's drive to Hot Springs was uneventful. Milo smoked and Mrs. Small slept. The closer we got to town, the more immediate my worries became, like how was I going to get back into my room without a key, never mind my appearance. I remembered Rita mentioning the employee parking lot in back of the hotel off Fountain Avenue. I could pull in there, take the service stairs up to the tenth floor, and . . . and then what? Maybe Ruth was sitting patiently in her room waiting for word from me. But if I knew my cousin, that was not the case. Ruth didn't sit and wait for much. If she wasn't in her room, I could hole up in the stairwell until I heard her return. Without a better plan, I pulled into the parking lot and left the engine idling.

I thought about keeping the Smalls around and introducing them to Detective Dixon so they could corroborate my story of kidnapping, attempted murder, and the explosion of a still, but I'd put them through so much already. I decided to send them on their way.

Milo walked around to the driver's side of the pickup as I crawled out. "You want us to stick around?"

"No, Milo. Thanks for your help. You saved my life."

"Naw. I haven't had this much fun since the Big War."

"What about your pickup stuck out there on Fuzzy's land with a hole in the gas tank? And what about Fuzzy?"

"I been thinking about that. Fuzzy's fine. It'll take more than an explosion to take him down. I'll just keep Fuzzy's truck 'til he delivers mine."

"What if he calls the police and says that you stole it?"

"Fuzzy don't want nothing to do with the police, and neither do I for that matter. We kind of like to handle things our own way out at Lake Ouachita. You sure you want to go back into this hotel?"

"I am. It'll take more than a kidnapping to take me down."

Milo chuckled.

I started taking off Milo's things; the cap, jacket, boots, and when I got to the monkey socks, Milo told me to keep them as a reminder of my visit to Fish Camp.

Milo smiled, hopped into Fuzzy's truck, and waved. I wanted to say goodbye to Mrs. Small, but she was still asleep. I guess the last few hours were just too much for the old gal, or it might have been the hooch.

I stood there for a moment, watching them drive away. In the background, sirens blared, tires squealed, horns blew, lights flashed. Yes, I was definitely back in the civilized world. I ran up to the employee's entrance and peeked in. The coast was clear. I dashed down the hall to the stairs. Taking the steps two at a time, I rounded the seventh floor landing when I ran smack into Grady, knocking him over. He yelled and started scrambling back the other way.

"Grady, it's me, Miss Lockhart."

He turned around and stared, mouth gaping, eyes fixed. "My Lord! What the hell happened to you? The police have been combing the town trying to find you."

"I heard the sirens. Is that all because of little me?"

He laughed. "Your cousin's caused quite a stir since you disappeared. She threatened to bring in the FBI if you didn't show up by noon, but those sirens are because of a fire in the next county, somewhere near Mount Ida.

"Can you let me into my room? And then call Dixon and tell him I'm back."

"Be glad to. Hey, Miss Lockhart? Knock, knock."

I was in no mood for jokes, but didn't want to be rude. "Who's there?"

"Uneeda?"

"Uneeda who?"

"You need a new pair of PJs."

"Not funny, Grady." We climbed to the tenth floor landing. I walked down the hall ahead of him.

"Knock, knock."

I pretended not to hear him, hoping he'd shut up.

"Knock! Knock!"

No such luck. "Who's there?" I huffed.

"Igotta."

"Igotta who?"

"I gotta good view of your tush through that giant rip in your PJs."

I quickly felt behind me and sure enough I was showing enough flesh to warrant an arrest for indecent exposure.

"Take a picture, Grady. It lasts longer."

Chapter 13

Grady used his key to unlock the door to Ruth's room.

"One room over," I said.

"Your room's a crime scene. It's in shambles."

"Dixon's cops tore up my room?"

"Actually, they were the second team to work it over. Whoever snatched you last night had a go at your room first. Fortunately, they didn't destroy anything."

"So they were looking for something then?"

"Seems so."

I poked my head inside Ruth's room. I didn't know what to expect; bad guys under the bed, Metzner hiding in the closet, Chester Salami behind the shower curtain. I sniffed the air and felt a bit better—Chester wasn't around.

I tried the adjoining door and it was locked. I wanted to have a look at my room regardless. Also I needed some clothes.

"Any idea where my cousin is?"

"Last I saw of her she was down in Charles' office with Dixon. I think she was about to call your parents.""No! Grady, get down there and tell them I'm all right. Don't let her call my parents! Unless you want the entire Lockhart family here, you've got to stop her."

"Dixon will want to see you right away."

"Give me ten minutes. I need to shower first."

"You'll need longer than that to get that soot off your face." Then he looked down and pointed to my feet. "Monkey socks! I used to have a little monk—"

I slammed the door in his face. Grady was becoming an annoyance.

I locked the door and for good measure placed the chair under the door handle. Then I checked the windows. I didn't care if I was on the tenth floor. Sure that I was safe, I picked up the phone and ordered room service—a medium-rare hamburger with French fries and a Cobb salad with French dressing. I'd need strength to tell my story. When I gave my room number there was a pause. Then I heard a faint voice say, "Hey, she's back." I felt like a celebrity.

I walked into the bathroom, took one look in the mirror, and almost passed out. How Grady even recognized me was a wonder. I looked like I'd been dipped head first into a dustbin. My hair was no longer red, but a gray-black—the color of charcoal; my face looked like the face of a miner who'd spent the last thirty years underground; my sweet pink and white PJs were done for. I filled the bathtub, stripped off my grimy clothes, and submerged myself in hot, steamy water, which immediately turned murky. I had to drain and refill the tub three times before the water drained clean. I could have spent the rest of the day soaking my sore, weary body, but I knew Ruth would be back any minute.

The thought hadn't even had a chance to vaporize when I heard, "Sydney! Let me in!" Ruth was beating on the door. "I'm so glad you're alrig . . ." I heard my cousin start to cry.

I jumped out, wrapped my hair in a towel, and donned Ruth's bathrobe, which left my legs below my knees bare. I threw open the door and Ruth threw her arms around me. "I thought . . . I'd never . . . see you . . . again."

"It's okay. I'm fine. I was worried about you, too." Why was it that when I was in trouble, I was the one who ended up comforting Ruth? Once when we were about twelve years old, we tried to start Uncle Martin's tractor, which was sitting in the cornfield. It started with a loud bang and shudder and I fell off, slicing a gash in my arm. While waiting to be stitched up in Doc Montgomery's office, Ruth cried so hard that she fainted, slashing her head on the corner of an end table. Since she was in such a state, I wound up taking care of her and received my stitches later.

Before I could reassure her any further, Dixon walked in. "Good morning, Miss Lockhart."

"Sydney."

"You gave us quite a scare."

If he noticed I was decked out in a too-short bathrobe and terry-cloth turban, he didn't let on. I guess in his line of work, nothing surprised him anymore; or maybe it was me. He sat down and flipped open his notebook. I told him everything—the ruckus in the hall, my kidnapping and internment in the root cellar at Highway 27 Fish Camp, my adventurous escape with the Smalls—well, almost everything. At first he listened without taking notes. I think he thought I was pulling his leg. When I got to the part about Salami shooting at us, Dixon started scribbling fast.

"Are you sure it was him?"

"Positive. But I think he was just trying to scare me. I figured if he wanted me dead, I'd never been dumped in the root cellar to begin with."

"Don't underestimate these guys. Salami botched the job."

"How do you know?"

"We found his body a little while ago. Slumped over the steering wheel—bullet in the back."

The nice, warm feeling I had from my soak in the tub evaporated as quickly as the steam in the bathroom. I looked over at Ruth sitting on the sofa. She was hugging her arms around her body. I moved over and snuggled up to her. She started to cry again.

"I agree with your assessment. I don't think they wanted you dead, at least not right away. They planned to keep you until you talked."

"About what? I don't know anything."

"Well, they think you do. They want something and they believe either you have it or know where it is."

"By they, you're referring to Metzner?"

"That's our most logical guess, but Metzner's been out of action for some time. He rolled over on some big-time gamblers back in the mid-forties. The new attorney general, F. J. Rochester, cut a deal with Metzner and he's pretty much kept his nose clean for the past few years."

"So I heard. But why has he come out of retirement? Isn't that risky for him?"

"You bet. So it must be something big." Dixon turned and gazed out the window—his brow furrowed and eyes squinted. I noticed that he hadn't shaved and his suit was a bit wrinkled. I guess I wasn't the only one who'd had a long night. He turned his attention back to me. "You did a crazy thing last night, rushing into the hall like that."

Here it comes. The lecture I'd been expecting. Instead he closed his notebook and stood up.

"The way I see it," Dixon continued, "is that they think you took something that was left in 1119 when you found the body or you found something in James' clothes later that day. Did you?"

"What do you think?"

"Answer the question."

"No. There was nothing to take. The only item in 1119 that didn't belong there was the naked, bloody body of Ellison James, and I certainly didn't dig around in his bloody clothes when I found them in the drawer."

"Speaking of clothes, most of yours are gone."

"What?! Those goons stole my clothes!"

"Give me a list of what's been taken. I'm finished with the room and housekeeping should be up shortly to clean up the mess. Look around and see if you can tell me what's missing. Let's go."

He unlocked the adjoining door and I walked in to what looked like the aftermath of a tornado. The furniture was upturned and pillows, cushions, and bed linens were tossed. Drawers were pulled from the dresser, and like a couple of days ago, the entire place had been dusted with fingerprinting chalk. Scattered in front of the dresser were most of my undies that I had placed neatly in the dresser drawer. I went to the closet and my heart fell.

"Everything's gone," I cried. "My new pencil skirt, my slacks, blouses, and . . . No!"

Dixon came up beside me and looked for himself. "Your green sandals. Too bad." He sounded like he really meant it. "Looks like you need to go shopping."

"There are some things that can't be replaced." I didn't tell him about my parents' wedding photo and license. Some stories just took too long. And some had unhappy endings, like a despondent wife running back to her glamorous past. Looked like my mother was on her way to LA. I couldn't stand to look any longer. I slammed the closet door, ran back in Ruth's room, and flopped down on her sofa. She started crying again; actually, she hadn't really stopped. I was in no mood to comfort her this time. Let her cry.

Dixon walked back in. "Hey, look. They left this." Twirling on his finger was the green velvet cap Rita had bought me yesterday. I shot him a hateful glare. He tossed the cap onto Ruth's bed, and turned to leave, then paused. "Highway 27 Fish Camp—that's near Mt. Ida, right? Near that fire that brought out fire trucks from every surrounding county. You don't know anything about that do you?"

A flippant answer always works in place of a lie. "Like I had a map of Arkansas!"

"Right. Next time we talk maybe you'll tell me about those charred pajamas you left in a pile on the bathroom floor and how you singed your eyebrows."

So Milo was wrong; the cabin didn't burn itself down. I hoped the Smalls had a fish camp to return to. And despite him trying to shoot me, I hoped Fuzzy wasn't a charred piece of meat.

Dixon finally left. Room service delivered my food and housekeeping started cleaning my room. I was more confused than ever. And for the first time, really frightened.

"Look on the bright side," Ruth said, drying her eyes. "We get to shop. Too bad there isn't a Neiman Marcus in Hot Springs."

"In a bathrobe. You go shopping, Ruth. I'm about to collapse. I didn't exactly sleep last night. After I've eaten, I'm going to bed. Speaking of going to bed, I thought you were a light sleeper. Why didn't you hear anything last night?"

"I guess it was all those martinis. I slept like a brick."

The maid was finishing up when I went back into my room. "I put your private things on the dresser, ma'am. I thought you might want to arrange them yourself."

My private things. That's all I had left, a green cap and some private things. "Thanks. That was nice of you." I turned to give her a tip and realized that my purse was gone, too. Ruth came in, handed the girl a five, and smiled. "Don't worry, Syd. You take a nice little nap, and I'll buy you some clothes. It's the least I can do."

"Today is Sunday. Nothing's open."

"Have no fear. Where there's money, there's a way."

"I wear a size eight. And I don't like anything flashy or flouncy."

"Oh, Syd. Trust me." Ruth skipped out the door.

Nightmares. As soon as I closed my eyes, I'd surely have nightmares.

Chapter 14

I didn't think I'd be able to sleep, but two hours later I was roused from a macabre dream in which I was running through the woods with my hair blazing like an inferno. In the background I heard Irving Berlin's "Cheek to Cheek," floating through the air. I sat up in bed and realized the tune was coming from Ruth's room. She was whistling. I rolled over and smashed my pillow over my head, but her whistling turned to singing and that was intolerable.

"Okay, I'm awake," I called.

"Nice nap?"

"How can you be so cheery?"

"Shopping makes me happy."

As soon as Ruth stepped over the threshold of a department store, she was truly in heaven, instantly levitating down the aisles.

"I found a cute little shop. There was a phone number on the door. Once I explained the situation; the owner was happy to open up. You'll love what I bought you. Now I know you don't like flashy clothes, but . . ."

Shit. I felt like running down to the bar in my—or Ruth's—bathrobe and my velvet cap and ordering a double of anything. I was not ready to view the damage. I pulled the covers over my head.

Undeterred by my grumbling, I heard her open the first box and giggle. I peaked out and saw a bright yellow and blue striped balloon skirt whirl through the air, followed by a blousy yellow top with huge blue buttons down the center and one sewn on the cuff above each elbow. Then came the petticoat. Because of my tall slender figure balloon skirts and petticoats made me look like a walking circus tent. But the crowning glory was the yellow pumps and yellow gloves. There was no way in hell I was leaving this room wearing that outfit.

Ruth came over to the bed and pulled off my protective covering. "Oh, my." She stepped back and cocked her head to the side. "You look like shit."

I began to have fond feelings for the root cellar at Fish Camp. Quick thinking was required and I sprung out of bed. "I feel like shit, too. I don't even want to look in the mirror."

I called down to the bathhouse and luckily Myra had a cancellation. A private elevator led directly to the spa and wearing a robe in route was perfectly acceptable.

"Ruth, you did good," I tried to sound sincere. "Can you keep yourself busy while I let Myra massage some life back into me?"

"No problem. You want me to go back to that dress shop. I could buy you—"

"Please don't. I mean, you've done so much already."

"You can't just wear this one outfit for the rest of the time here."

"We'll go shopping together. Tomorrow."

When I got to the spa, I called Rita's office.

"Syd! I'm so glad you're okay. We were so worried."

"Thanks. I'm fine, well almost. I do need a favor though."

"Anything."

"I don't know if you heard, but my clothes were stolen. My cousin bought me an outfit, but, well, our tastes are very different and after shopping with you yesterday, I thought you'd be able to find—"

"Say no more. I'll call Ellen to open the shop. I'll find something for you in no time and have it sent to your room. Clothes, a size eight, right? And shoes?"

"Right. Shoes size ten. Send everything to the spa. I'm scheduled to have Myra work her magic on me."

Finished with the sweating and the kidney purging, I lay on the table and told Myra that today I'd like my massage without conversation.

"After what you've been through, dear. I don't blame you. You just relax and try not to think about anything."

Myra's advice sounded good, but was impossible to follow. Although Dixon and his boys were working hard on the case and Ruth had proclaimed herself my bodyguard, when she wasn't shopping, or sleeping, or sitting in the salon getting a poodle 'do, I felt I was still in jeopardy. If two people could be murdered so easily in this hotel and two people kidnapped, one twice (that being me), then I could hardly relax. I closed my eyes and tried to release the hold on my brain.

Was Dixon right? Was I supposed to have something that Metzner wanted? Or maybe he feared that Ellison James had uttered a few dying words since I happened upon the body so soon after his throat was cut. Or maybe it wasn't the old retired gangster at all. But since Chester Salami was dead, Metzner's the most likely suspect. If that were true, he wasn't working alone. He'd stick out like a sore thumb here in the hotel. Maybe it was that bald guy who helped with the first kidnapping. But he'd be noticed, too. No, it had to be someone who works here, someone whose movements would not be questioned, and that could be dozens of people.

Rita had mentioned that files were missing from the office, which led me to believe that the housekeeping staff was probably innocent. Mr. Charles popped into my mind. His job, more than anyone's, depended on the success of the hotel. If he wanted to kill Ellison and Elsa, wouldn't he do it elsewhere? Wouldn't he try to avoid bad publicity? Unless something happened that caused him to act immediately—a crime of passion maybe. Speaking of passion, any ideas I had of calling my father with the good news about finding the wedding photo and marriage license were gone. My mother was not a bluffer. If she said she planned to flee to California, she was getting on that bus; you can bet on it.

"All done," Myra said.

I was deep into my ruminations when Myra's voice startled me.

"You got some bad bruises there. Those kidnappers must have really worked you over."

I knew Myra was fishing for details of my encounter, but I was in no mood to rehash the event so I changed the subject. "Did you know Elsa Dubois very well?" I gathered my sheet around me and sat up on the table. Myra walked over to a window and opened it. She pulled out a pack of cigarettes and offered me one, but I declined. Then she glanced at her watch.

"I don't have another client for ten minutes." She clicked her silver lighter shut and inhaled. "I knew Elsa. But she's not what I'd call a friend. Younger generation, you know. She was a party girl, most of the younger girls are. But who can blame them. Hot Springs is a fun town."

"I heard she was looking for a rich husband."

"What girl isn't? She may have found one. Although Ellison wasn't rich, he seemed to have money."

"Elsa told me that she and Ellison were planning a trip to Little Rock. Heard anything about that?"

Myra drew in another lungful of smoke and squinted her eyes. "Little Rock?" She exhaled, watching the smoke snake toward the window. "Except for the capitol, there ain't much in Little Rock that ain't here in Hot Springs."

"I don't follow."

"I mean people leave town so they can do things they can do here, but without being seen."

"But Elsa and Ellison's romance wasn't a big secret. Besides, when I spoke to Elsa she seemed determined to make the trip by herself."

"That's strange. But those two together didn't fit for some reason."

"Grady seemed to think that the romance was in trouble. He said Elsa had been upset recently."

"Donna Jennings would know. She and Elsa were close friends. I'd talk to her. She works in housekeeping."

"Thanks, Myra. And thanks for the overhaul. I feel like I'll live."

"Want some advice?" She stubbed out her cigarette and flicked it out the window. "With everything that's happened to you in the last three days, maybe you should stick to why you came here in the first place."

"Good advice, but someone has gotten me mixed up in these murders and I can't just sit back and wait for something to happen."

"If I were you then, I'd watch my back. Be careful who you trust, and remember things aren't always what they seem."

That last bit of counsel made me think of Ruth. Neither one of us should be wandering around alone. What's it going to take for me to learn that lesson?

Rita was true to her word. She'd delivered a nice pair of gray slacks, a white silk blouse, and a pair of black pumps. There was a lovely green and black scarf as well and a note attached to the box. "I added the scarf for a bit of color. Heard you still had your undies. Lucky girl."

I gathered the boxes and hurried back to my room. I was showered, dressed, and ready when Ruth returned. Her face fell when she walked into my room. I rushed over and gave her a kiss on the cheek, and before she could ask I explained, with much sadness, that the clothes she bought me didn't fit. With any luck when we exchanged them, there wouldn't be other sizes available. Just then there was a knock on the door. Ruth and I jumped.

"We should probably buy a gun," Ruth said.

"Miss Lockhart. It's me, Mickey."

I opened the door, grabbed Mickey by the shirt, and dragged him in.

"This snooping around stuff is fun."

"Find out anything?"

"Sure did. First, I waited until Mrs. Willis left for lunch. Then I went to see Mrs. Lindstrum and told her I wasn't busy and could take the room list down to the front desk for her. When I got there the desk clerk was swamped. Several people wanted to check out at the same time. So, I helped out a bit. I had to get some carbon paper from the drawer and when I opened it, I saw the file of room lists. I looked through it and didn't find the list for the day of Mr. James' murder."

"Dixon probably has it," I said.

"There's another one," Mickey said.

"What do you mean?" Ruth said.

"I took the carbon paper to the desk clerk and asked her what she needed it for. I told her that I planned to run this hotel one day and I wanted to know how things work. She got a big laugh out of that, but gave me my answer. She said that each day's room list had a carbon copy which is kept with Mrs. Lindstrum."

"So Lindstrum sends the original to the front desk and keeps a copy for herself. You're good, Mickey, real good."

"Thanks. I then went back to Mrs. Lindstrum's cubbyhole. As I was walking down the hall, I saw her head out the back door, probably for a smoke. I went through her files."

"And?"

Mickey unbuttoned his jacket and pulled out the carbon-copy list. "I'll have to return it soon before she finds it missing. I'm bell hoppin' today. Just call and I can be up here right away."

"Brilliant, Mickey," I gave him a smack on the cheek.

He peeked out the door, "Coast's clear," then he left.

I took the list over to the desk and turned on the lamp. Whoever made changes on the original, must have been in a hurry because the carbon copy was smudged as if rubbed over by an eraser.

"Look," I showed Ruth. "You can still see the original time. Eleven nineteen was cleaned and ready by 12:30, like Elsa had said. Written over it looks like 4:30."

"Evidence!" Ruth shouted. "We have evidence."

"We have nothing, Ruth, except the confirmation of my suspicion that someone had changed the time on the list. And that someone wanted this room for a few hours that afternoon."

"To kill Ellison James."

"Maybe. My intuition tells me that his murder wasn't planned. I think something was going on in that room. Ellison wasn't expected to be at the hotel. Remember, he'd been missing for three days. And when he surfaced, he sneaked in to see Elsa."

"He asked her to meet him in 1119."

"No. He asked her to meet him after work at the employee's entrance. It was the killer who phoned Elsa, pretending to be Ellison, and told her to come immediately to 1119. In those few minutes after Ellison talked to Elsa, he must have gotten in the way. Otherwise why kill him here? If someone at the hotel wanted him dead, wouldn't it make sense to kill him some place else?"

"Syd! You almost got in their way, too. If you'd been a few minutes earlier, you would've walked in on the murder."

That thought sent chills down my spine.

"But why did the killer want Elsa to come to that room?"

"At first I thought the reason was to pin the murder on her. But since she was murdered, too, that can't be it. I need to call Dixon, and give him the carbon copy."

"But Mickey needs to get it back in the file, and Dixon's going to wonder how you ended up with it. Mickey could get in trouble.

"You're right. I'll have Mickey return it. Then I'll call Dixon and tell him of my suspicions."

"Let me get this straight," Dixon said, making himself comfortable on my sofa and tossing his hat on the desk. "A little bird told you that a carbon copy of the room list is kept by the head lady of housekeeping. And you're not going to tell me the name of that sparrow?"

"Hmmm . . ." I raised my eyes to the ceiling as if deeply contemplating my answer. "That's about right, Lieutenant. I have to protect my sources."

"Sources! Give me a break. And when I look at the carbon copy, I'll probably find something interesting."

"That's for you to decide."

Ruth giggled. We both looked at her, wondering what was so funny.

"Just stay out of trouble." He let out a sigh. "I can't go searching all over the county if you two disappear again." He grabbed his hat and left.

"What was that all about, Ruth?"

"You made his left eye twitch."

Chapter 15

I was about to pick up the phone and call housekeeping to see if Donna Jennings was working, when it rang.

"Hel—"

"Two murders! Syd, what's going on in that hotel?! Wait until your mother finds out."

"Where's Mom?"

"Who the hell knows. She left yesterday morning after cleaning the cabinets. Said she didn't want to leave behind a dirty house."

"She hasn't left for the West coast has she?"

"May have. I'm beyond the point of caring. Don't change the subject. You need to get out of that hotel and now."

"I'm okay, Dad. Things are kind of tense here at the moment. But I'm being careful and Ruth's here watching after me."

"Tell Uncle George hi," Ruth said and waved.

"That's supposed to make me feel better?" Dad sighed.

"Ruth says hi."

"I love Ruth, but that girl was twelve before she could lace her shoes."

"Dad says hi and to tell you he's glad you're here with me."

"When are you coming home? I can't keep this second murder from your mother too long. I clipped the article from the newspaper, but she's going to wonder about that hole in the Sunday paper."

"Tell her you clipped out a coupon."

"From the news section? Listen, Syd. If you don't leave that hotel, I'm going to come get you."

"Don't worry, Dad. Nothing bad is going to happen."

One day, several years from now, I'd tell him about my adventure with the Smalls near Mount Ida. One day when we were by ourselves sitting on the beach, one day when my Mom actually did leave for the West Coast.

"Gotta go." I hung up before he could say more.

"How's Uncle George? Sounds like Aunt Mary Lou's still around," Ruth said.

"Not for long."

I hadn't yet told Ruth about the photo I found and she must have forgotten about me hiding it under my sweater, which was okay by me.

"What do we do now?" Ruth said.

"Let's try and locate Donna Jennings. She was Elsa's friend. Maybe she can tell us something."

While I called down to housekeeping services to see if Donna was working, Ruth gently folded the blue and yellow tent outfit and placed it back in its box. She looked sad, but she'd get over it.

"Donna's working on the 8th floor," I said. "Let's go."

We found Donna Jennings in room 809. She was emptying ashtrays into a trashcan. I knocked on the open door.

"Yes, ma'am. Do you need something?"

It looked like Donna had her work cut out for her. The place was a disaster and the smell was intolerable; stale beer, nauseating cologne, and cheap cigars. Then I saw a familiar item on the dresser, a St. Christopher medal, and I realized we were standing in the doorway of Muldoon's room.

"Miss Jennings? I'm Sydney Lockhart and this is my cousin, Ruth Echland. I can see you're busy, but can we talk to you for a moment about Elsa Dubois?"

Donna Jennings turned stark white and dropped the ashtray she was holding. "I don't know anything about Elsa. You have to leave. I have work to do."

Ruth and I stepped into the room and I closed the door.

Donna went to pick up the phone. I rushed over and placed my hand over hers and pushed the receiver down. "I was with Miss Fredricks Saturday morning when we found Elsa. I know that you and Elsa were friends. I'm just trying to find out what happened."

"You're not supposed to be in here." Her hand flew from the phone up to her throat. She backed away, and then pulled a chair in front of her as if to ward off any potential attack. "If Mr. Charles finds you in here, he'll . . . he'll . . . fire me," she stuttered and then pretended to cry.

"We'll leave as soon as we find out what we want to know," I said, "and not before."

"Sydney," Ruth said. I shot her a shut-up glance.

"Why were Elsa and Ellison going to Little Rock?"

Donna picked up the chair and held it close to her body.

I rolled my eyes, pried the chair from her fingers, and slammed it down. "Sit down," I said and handed her a tissue.

"Little Rock?" she said.

"You and Elsa were friends. She must have mentioned it."

"I don't remember her saying anything about going to Little Rock." She blew her nose, eyed me over the tissue, and quickly looked away. Donna would never make it as an actress. It was obvious she was lying. I decided to jar her memory.

"Elsa came to my room after Ellison's murder. She told me they were planning a trip to the state capital. But I got the impression that the trip was not necessarily a romantic weekend away. She sounded as if she still planned on going, even without her boyfriend."

Donna hugged her arms around her chest and shivered.

"Listen, I know this is hard for you," I said, sitting down on the edge of the bed and looking her in the eye the way I used to do to a contrary student. "The sooner they catch the person responsible, well . . . maybe—"

"—things will get back to normal?" Donna said. "Elsa was my friend and . . . things will never be back to normal." This time the tears were real.

I sighed, walked over, and opened the window to let out the noxious smells. In the few moments it took Donna to release her grief, her fear from earlier seemed to evolve into anger. She went to the bed and ripped the sheets from the mattress with such force I heard the static electricity crackle. "I can't believe anyone would kill her. She was such a sweet girl."

"Yes, I know. I can't believe anyone would do that to her, either."

Donna didn't comment. The bed sheets were in a pile on the floor. She was now attacking the furniture with a feather duster.

Ruth opened her purse and pulled out her cigarette case. She offered it to Donna just as the lamp she was dusting started to teeter. I grabbed the lamp and then took Donna by the arm and directed her to sit again.

"They're clove," Ruth said. "I special order them from Neiman's."

"My grandmother used to smoke these," Donna said. She lit up, inhaled, and seemed to savor the memory.

"Mine, too," Ruth said. "That's who got me started smoking them."

I didn't know who was the better liar, Ruth or Donna. Score a point for my cousin though. She was getting the hang of rooting out information from reluctant sources.

"I used to like working here, but now I don't even like being in these rooms alone. Looking over my shoulder all the time. Worried that I might be next."

"You poor thing," Ruth said. She reached over and patted Donna on the knee.

"Can you believe how some people live? Look at this mess. It's like this every morning." Using her thumb and forefinger, she picked up a dirty sock and threw it on a pile of clothes resting on an armchair. "I shouldn't talk about our guests, but this guy's a real pig. I hope he'll be leaving soon."

Discussing Muldoon's pigginess was not on my agenda, but Donna was starting to relax so I allowed her and Ruth a moment of smoking pleasure as I glanced around Muldoon's room. I'm not sure what I was looking for, but ever since last night when I saw him walking back and forth in front of the hotel at three in the morning, I wondered what he was really doing. I realized that I hadn't mentioned that fact to Dixon. It didn't seem important at the time. And maybe it wasn't, but Muldoon was the first person to bring Metzner to my attention.

I used the excuse that I had to go to the bathroom, just to have a look at the more personal habits of Mr. Muldoon. Ruth and Donna were now telling grandmother stories—well, at least Donna was. Ruth was making up more bullshit.

I closed the door and after a few seconds, flushed the toilet to cover up any noise I made opening the medicine cabinet. There was the usual man stuff: razor, comb, after shave, tube of Brylcreem—each and every item had at least one strand of hair adhered to it. I could understand how Donna hated cleaning this room, not that her duties involved removing body hair from Muldoon's personal items, but the sight was enough to spoil one's day. I picked up the razor, unscrewed it, and examined the blade. What the hell did I expect to find, dried blood? As if a razor would be used was a murder weapon? But I was desperate; I had no evidence that pointed to anyone else. The razor was clean. I put it away and closed the cabinet door. I pulled back the shower curtain and noticed a small kit on the shelf of the tub. It was open with more toiletries sticking out. I picked it up and pawed through it. I jerked my hand away when I noticed a small box of prophylactics. I was about to set the kit back on the shelf when I noticed something that shook my bones. The kit fell from my hands, its contents scattered across the floor. I quickly gathered everything up and put the kit back where I found it.

I walked back into the room, fearing I'd have to explain my prolonged absence and the noise I'd made, but Ruth and Donna were chitchatting away. It was clear both had been crying. Ruth gave me a look as if she'd forgotten I was there. "Both our grandmothers were named Evelyn. Can you believe that?" Ruth said. "Such a coincidence and both died in the same year."

Donna, tissue back in her pocket, was dotting her cheeks with Ruth's lace handkerchief, trying to compose herself when she suddenly burst into tears again. "I told her not to do it. I told her she'd regret it later."

Ruth and I exchanged glances. "Do what?" I mouthed to Ruth. She shrugged, then walked over and sat down beside Donna on the bed. "There. There. It's okay. Told who not to do what?"

"I promised her I'd never tell a soul. But now she's dead . . . murdered."

Well, that answers the who question. I sat down in the chair across from Donna and Ruth. "What did Elsa do, Donna?" I tried to sound as sympathetic as I could, but I was getting antsy.

"I told her God would punish her, and He did, even before it ever happened."

"If you know something that could help the police find Elsa's killer, you need to speak up," I said.

Donna just shook her head and continued to cry.

"Were Elsa and Ellison going to Little Rock to get married?"

She shook her head again. "They should have gotten married. Then none of this would have happened."

"Was Elsa expecting?" I said.

Donna nodded. "She wanted to . . . to get rid of the baby." She had twisted Ruth's handkerchief into a long narrow coil. "I told her it was wrong. But she wouldn't listen."

"She was going to Little Rock for an abortion?"

The word made Donna shudder. "I told her that she should get married. That once the baby was born, everything would be fine."

"Maybe Ellison wouldn't marry her," Ruth said. "Maybe he was the one who didn't want the baby."

Another wave of sobs gushed and Donna uncoiled the soggy hanky, using it to cover her face.

"I don't know if this had anything to do with why Elsa was killed, but you need to tell the police," I said. "Lieutenant Dixon's on the case."

Donna sniffled enough mucus back up her sinus cavity to drown an elephant. "Listen, I gotta finish up here before that hairy ape comes back." She stood up and grabbed the duster. It was clear the conversation was over.

Ruth and I rose to leave. "I'm staying in 1018 and Sydney's next door to me. Come by if you want to talk some more," Ruth said.

Suddenly there was a loud knock at the door. "Donna, are you in there?"

Donna gasped. "It's Mr. Charles. Hide. Quick, in the bathroom."

Ruth and I scrambled into the bathroom and gently closed the door. Putting our ears to the door at the same time, we bumped heads. Actually my chin grazed the top of Ruth's head.

"Why is this door closed, Donna? I want all maids visible for your own safety."

"Sorry, Mr. Charles. I opened the window to air the room out and a gust of wind slammed the door shut."

"Who's staying in here? This place is a disaster. What's that odor?"

"Mr. Muldoon. It's his cigars you smell."

"What's wrong with you, girl? Your eyes are all red and teary."

"It's the cigars. I . . . I think I'm allergic."

"I can't have my maids looking like they've been drinking. Let me get you a wet wash cloth."

The bathroom doorknob turned. My hand flew up to Ruth's mouth before she could let out one of her infamous squeaks.

"No sir! I'll be fine as soon as I leave this room, my eyes will clear up. Besides, you don't want to go in that bathroom, believe me. I'll have it cleaned up right away."

"I'll have a word with this Muldoon. Hopefully he'll be checking out soon. Disgusting! And leave this room door opened!"

"Yes, sir."

We waited a couple of minutes. Donna opened the bathroom door and poked her head in. "He's gone. That was close. You two need to get out of here."

"We're on our way," I said.

Ruth was out in the hall in a flash and in another flash was back in the room. "Oh, my God!"

"What?!"

"Muldoon just stepped off the elevator!"

"Shit! Did he see you?"

"I don't think so, but he's headed this way."

We ran back as Donna was closing the door.

"Muldoon's coming," I hissed.

"Back in the bathroom," Donna ordered.

We barely had time to close the bathroom door when Donna said in a shaky voice, "Oh, Mr. Muldoon. I'm not finished with your room. Just give me a few more minutes."

"Take your time, little lady. I just need to get something from the bathroom."

"No!" Donna shouted. "You can't go in there! I mean . . . the . . . the toilet's overflowed. Maintenance is on the way up right now."

Donna might not make a good actress, but she was a natural in the ad-lib department.

The doorknob turned again. "I won't go in. It's sitting on the back of the tub. I'll just reach in—"

"Let me do it, Mr. Muldoon. We . . . the hotel has a policy that guests not . . . well, we don't want you to see anything that'll leave you with a bad impression. And the smell in there is awful."

"Oh, alright. Just quit blabbering."

Donna pushed the door open a few inches and Ruth and I squeezed back behind it. Donna reached in. I grabbed the kit and put it in her hand.

"Thank you," she said.

"Thank you?" Muldoon said. "Who are you thanking?"

"Oh, I mean. Thank you for being so understanding. Here's your kit. You can get what you need out of it and I'll put it back."

"Never mind. I'll take it with me. I'm going down to the spa." We heard him walk out.

"Crazy broad," he muttered.

We waited until we heard the elevator ding and then left 809 to Donna.

"Man, that was close," Ruth said.

"Too close. Hurry. Down to the end of the hall. We'll take the stairs in case anyone else decides to visit room 809. Hey, Grandma Echland's first name isn't Evelyn and she never smoked clove cigarettes."

"I have two grandmothers," Ruth said.

I gave her my stern eye.

"Okay, so her name wasn't Evelyn, either. But give me credit. I did get Donna to open up."

"You did good," I said and draped my arm over Ruth's shoulder.

Just as we reached the stairs, we heard a racket coming from the end of the hall. The little boy who'd dug up the plant and later tried to eat a pine cone was running from his father. He ran straight for me and tried to hide behind my legs.

"Sorry. Sorry," his father said, grabbing at his dodging son.

I reached behind me, grabbed the little boy's hand, and pulled him around. He looked up at me and smiled, then opened his mouth and spit out his latest prize. I caught the item before it hit the floor. And for the second time in fifteen minutes, my knees went weak and my heart leapt to my throat. My first impulse was to call Dixon and report my discovery. But what would I say? I'd been in Muldoon's room snooping through his things?

The main picked up his son, nodding more apologies. I took the slimy item and slipped it into my pocket. Ruth and I made our way into the stairwell and up to the tenth floor.

"What is it?" she said. "You look like you've seen a ghost."

"It's nothing. I was surprised by what we'd found out from Donna Jennings. I need to let the information digest." I forced a smile. I wanted to tell Ruth that the little boy had spit out my stolen pearl earring. I also wanted to tell her that I'd discovered its twin tucked inside Muldoon's kit.

But I didn't.

Chapter 16

When Ruth and I returned to our rooms, I faked a headache just to get some time to myself. I expected her to whine and pout, but she surprised me.

"I've things to do," Ruth said. "I was so worried when you disappeared that I let everything go."

I imagined nails, hair, eyebrow plucking. But she caught me off guard again when she said, "I have to catch up on my reading." The thought that she may be developing an interest in the literary world was dispelled when I noticed that spread across her bed were the latest copies of *Harper's Bazaar*, *Glamour*, *Ladies' Home Journal*, and *Mademoiselle*.

I left Ruth to catch up on the latest fashions. I mean, who else would tell me what Doris Day was wearing lately, or whom Eva Gardner was divorcing. I had a quiet dinner in my room, then pulled out *The Catcher in the Rye*, but couldn't get through one paragraph of Holden Caufield's yammerings. I don't know if it was the teacher in me, or my recent brush with death, but I wanted to take the young man by the shoulders and shake some sense into his adolescent brain. His problems were teeny weeny compared to my recent adventures.

After the third time I dozed off and was awakened by the book hitting the floor, I gave up and got ready for bed. I'm not comfortable sleeping in the nude, but I didn't have much choice. I threw the robe on the foot of the bed and climbed in between the cold sheets. I suspected my night would be fitful, but as soon as my head hit the pillow I zonked out. The next thing I knew, my face was buried in a pillow dampened with drool. The smell of coffee shocked my brain. I opened one eye to see Ruth standing over me, hands on her hips.

"You've slept for more than twelve hours straight, Little Missy. I'm sure you needed it after your little adventure Saturday night so I won't give you a hard time."

"What time is it?"

"Eight o'clock." She jerked the cover away and screamed. "Syd!"

I jerked the covers back. "I don't have any damn pajamas!"

"I noticed. That's why we have to get an early start."

"Early start for what?"

"Shopping!" she sang.

"Shower," I moaned.

"I'll order us breakfast," Ruth said. "We can eat in our rooms and plan our day." She turned her back to me and faced the wall. "Now get up!" Then she clapped twice. "Chop. Chop."

"You've lost your mind, Ruth. Never mind. That's not possible. You need to have one before you can lose it."

"Sticks and stones. Sticks and stones."

I rushed to the bathroom before listening to anymore of Ruth's cheery philosophizing. That's one thing I can say for the girl, mayhem and misfortunes didn't get her down for long.

When I finished my ablutions, Ruth was sitting on my sofa with a perplexed look on her face. "What is it?" I said.

"I just called my maid, Sophia. She said that Maryanne Newton called me this morning."

"Maryanne Newton?"

"We graduated high school together."

"Oh, right. You two hated one another. She was the one who was chosen homecoming queen and—" I knew immediately I shouldn't have brought that up. "—you got runner up," I said, trying to sound Ruth-cheery.

"Runner up doesn't count. No one remembers runner up."

"What did she want?"

"She's chairing the planning committee for our ten-year reunion next spring. Sophia said Maryanne wanted a current picture of me for the brochure."

"So, why's that a problem?"

"I don't trust her. I'm not sure how to handle this."

"Well, I know you'll think of something."

"You're right. It's not important now. Shopping's what's important."

"We can shop, but later today. I've got an article to write. Let's see some of the sites. It'll be good for us to get out of the hotel. But first I need to call Dad and tell him to wire me some money." I paused. "I'll have to tell him how I lost my cash and clothes."

"I got money. Don't worry about it."

"I'll pay you back as soon as I can." That wouldn't be as easy as it sounded. As it is, I was barely getting by.

Our breakfast was delivered. Ruth poured fresh coffee for us as I finished getting ready. We ate in silence. Ruth was contemplating Maryanne Newton, I'm sure. I took the opportunity to look over my brochures on Hot Springs' attractions. I wanted to visit the main ones, but I planned to keep an eye out for places that tourists might miss. I had the day scheduled, putting shopping last on the list. But I wasn't optimistic about the day, knowing I'd spend most of my time worrying about staying alive. I shook off that thought. Ruth's problem was more manageable.

"You could send her that picture of you the *Dallas Morning News* used last year when you started the volunteer beautification program to paint Texas flags on all the city trashcans. Weren't you wearing a cute little red, white, and blue outfit with a single star on your chest?" I knew Ruth hated that picture. She looked like the Texas flag she'd wanted displayed. I don't know if that was intentional, but the picture was probably what spawned two letters to the editor during the next week, which suggested designing a new state flag.

"You're funny, Sydney Jean Lockhart. Real funny."

"Hey. Did you know that not far down Whittington Road is the Hot Springs Alligator Farm? Been there since around the turn of the century." I waved the brochure at her. "And across the street is the Hot Springs Crystal Shop. They're top tourists spots. Let's check them out. It's a beautiful day. We can drive around in my rented convertible. It'll be fun."

"Sounds good, but let's take my car instead," Ruth said. "I need to break it in."

Although my cousin and I have always been competitive in the food and men department, I'd never considered her as needing to one-up me when it comes to material possessions. But when the valet drove up in Ruth's new Styline, I was the one left speechless. She had failed to mention that her new car was a convertible, that it was bright red, that it was flashier than my rental.

"Would you like to drive it?" she asked.

"No, it's your car. You drive."

She shrugged and got behind the wheel. Ten minutes later we were standing behind a fence gazing at a pool of hungry alligators, watching a guy feed the creatures chunks of meat from the end of a giant toothpick. Every time one of the animals lunged from the pool and snatched the meat from the stick, the small crowd that had joined us at the fence clapped and hooted. I took a few photographs, but I couldn't get into enjoying the show. I was never much of a zoo person. I always wondered how the animals felt living in small confined enclosures. Visions of the root cellar flashed in my mind.

We walked on to view a family of white-tailed deer nibbling on vegetation. My melancholy intensified.

Ruth leaned against the rail and pulled out her cigarettes. "What gives? You've been brooding ever since we left the hotel. It's not like you, Syd." She opened her purse. "Clove or menthol?"

"Menthol."

She handed me a cigarette after stuffing it into an ebony holder. "You should be celebrating."

"Celebrating!"

"That you're still alive."

I appreciated Ruth's optimism, but popping a champagne cork after Saturday's ordeal was not going to do it. I knew I should tell her about what I'd discovered in Muldoon's bathroom, but my intuition told me to keep quiet for now. "I'm just trying to piece things together," I said. "I feel sad about what happened to Elsa. I didn't really know the girl, but she had her whole life ahead of her. Your theory might be right. At first maybe Ellison wouldn't marry her, then he had a change of heart. That's why he came back to the hotel to see her. But why risk talking to her at the Arlington? Why not go see her at her house?"

"Who did Elsa live with? If she still lived with her parents, maybe Ellison seeing her at her home was out of the question."

"Good point. But what does this have to do with their murders? Maybe Ellison didn't steal any money. Maybe he made himself scarce for another reason. That means that everything we've learned has been useless in discovering who killed them."

We stubbed out our cigarettes and strolled over to a tall cage containing a pack of raccoons. We watched as two fat fur balls washed their carrots in a small pool of water. We had to laugh. They were so cute. I took some more pictures and my mood lifted a bit. We left the Alligator Farm.

This place would add a nice touch to the article. At the Hot Springs Crystal Shop we learned a little about Arkansas' geology and how these colorful rocks were formed. I purchased an aquamarine crystal about the size of a baseball (it'd make a nice paperweight) and Ruth selected a rose colored one she planned to take to her jeweler so he could turn it into a pendant for a necklace. We stepped outside into the bright sunlight and immediately heard a loud roaring—our stomachs calling us for lunch. We looked at one another and burst out laughing. Two of a kind, we were.

"How does barbecue sound?" I said. "There's a place called McClard's on Albert Pike Road. Been there since the '20s. I heard it's the place for barbecue."

"I'll drive," she said. "You navigate."

I walked over to get inside the car and froze in my tracks. Muldoon was sitting on a bench in the park across the street. He looked away, but I'd already caught him watching us. Perhaps it was only my imagination. Why wouldn't he be sitting in the park? It's not a far stroll from the hotel. Why wouldn't he notice us? After all, we'd spoken to him in the mineral pool and later in the lounge. I looked again. He was lighting a cigar. A dripping golden retriever who'd just run through the creek that bisects the park was headed toward the bench chasing a ball. Muldoon moved from the bench as the dog shook, spraying water in his wake.

"What are you looking at?" Ruth said.

"Nothing," I said. I got in the car and glanced in the rearview mirror. As Ruth pulled away from the curb, I saw Muldoon get inside a white Studebaker. Wasn't Chester Salami driving a Studebaker? What the hell did that matter? A lot of people drove Studebakers. Whittington Avenue ends in a roundabout, and as we circled, I lost sight of Muldoon's car.

McClard's was crowded and we had to wait a few minutes for a table. The delicious smells wafting from the kitchen made our stomachs growl in unison again.

"Quit drooling, and give me two dimes, rich girl."

Ruth opened her clutch, dug around in the bottom, and handed me the coins. I walked over and pulled two root beers from the cooler. Ruth and I sipped and studied the blackboard menu.

"The mixed plate looks good," she said. "A slice of roast pork, a rib, a sausage link, and a slice of brisket. That's what I'm having."

"Too much meat for me. I'm having the chicken plate with cole slaw and beans."

"Look, they have banana pudding."

We toasted our good fortune by clinking root-beer bottles in celebration for finding the perfect barbecue joint. A table by the window had vacated and I took it. Ruth went to the counter to place our orders. I scanned the parking lot for a white Studebaker. I didn't see one, but there were several places along the road where he could be parked and waiting. I learned a long time ago to trust my intuition. Muldoon was outside my room moments before I was abducted and he had my earring in his possession. No, it was not my imagination. I took the seat that allowed the best view of the parking lot and the road.

"You know, Syd. We should do this more often." Ruth sat down and placed a numbered chip on the table. "We're number thirteen."

"Looks like something left over from a casino," I picked up the chip and tossed it into the air. "Do what more often—eat barbecue or become embroiled in a murder investigation?" I took a swallow of my root beer.

She giggled. "No. I mean just hang out together. Eat, drink, watch raccoons wash their carrots."

She caught me unaware and I snorted root beer up my nose. Ruth could be really funny at times. I sucked in some air and started laughing. "It sure beats the hell out of teaching school and comforting distraught divorcees," I said, once I caught by breath.

"Maybe I should forget about abandoned women and open a home for unwed mothers."

"You're thinking about Elsa."

"It was really sad what happened to her, although I've never met the girl. No matter how much money you have, making it alone can be hard."

"Yeah. I know. Since you brought the subject back around to murder, I guess I better tell you that it's possible that we're being followed."

"Metzner!" Ruth looked around as if expecting to find a thug lurking around with a blindfold in his hip pocket.

I told her about Muldoon.

"You need to tell your detective."

"He's not my detective, but I agree. I'll call him when we get back to the hotel. We have one more stop. I want to see the Oaklawn Race Track. That's another Hot Springs institution we can't pass up."

"Number thirteen," someone behind the counter called.

"I'll get it." I walked to the counter, set two plates on a tray, and carried them over to the table. Together they must have weighed ten pounds.

Unashamed over our gluttony, we dove in. Just as we were enjoying our banana pudding, Grady walked in. At first I didn't recognize him. He'd traded his rumpled suit for a casual pair of slacks and a black and white diamond-patterned shirt, and minus his fedora, he looked free of the perpetual burden he seemed to carry while at work.

"Hey, Miss Lockhart, Miss Echland, see you found Hot Springs' favorite barbecue place."

"Hi, Grady. Day off?"

"Day off is right; night off—no way. I'll be on duty this evening."

"Grady, know a guy named Muldoon?" I asked. "He's staying in 809. Seems this isn't his first time in Hot Springs. He knows a lot about the city."

"Ex-Marine. Yeah, I know the guy. Comes to the Arlington a couple of times a year. Think he lives somewhere around Longview, Texas. Why?"

"He's the one who told us about Metzner, and a few hours later we were sitting in Metzner's suite."

"The guy acts like a big shot. He used to come to town to gamble. He likes to talk big; likes to toss down a few too many at times. I've had to pay him a visit once or twice to tell him to pipe down. Harmless, though. He been bothering you?"

"No," I said. "I've just noticed him around, that's all."

"Well, don't let him rattle your cage. If he does, give me a call."

Grady's take-out order was ready. "Probably see you at the hotel later." He started to leave and turned around. "Ladies?"

We looked up.

"Why did the cop cross the road?"

"Haven't the foggiest, Grady," I said.

"To arrest the chicken for jaywalking."

Chapter 17

I'd called the racetrack before we left the hotel. Since racing season didn't begin until February, I had to make an appointment for a tour. A man named Leroy Peevey was to meet us in the lobby.

We pulled up into a massive parking lot, which must have covered four acres. A few cars were parked near the entrance, otherwise the lot was empty.

"Park by the front door," I told Ruth. "The track is closed so we shouldn't have any problem parking here. Mr. Peevey's waiting for us inside."

As I followed Ruth to the entrance, I glanced around for Muldoon and his car, but didn't see him. We stepped inside. A light shone in the lobby, but the rest of the building was dark, giving the place a cavernous feeling.

"Hey, look at this," Ruth said.

On the wall right in front was a giant framed photo of a horse and jockey. We were studying the picture when suddenly the place was flooded in light. A middle-aged man, wearing a brown suit walked up behind us.

"Gushing Oil, the horse that is. Little guy on top is named Popara—winner and jockey of last year's Arkansas Derby. Spectacular race. Won by seven lengths. A few lucky folks made a bundle on that race."

"Why's that?" Ruth asked.

"Odds were eleven to one. You must be Miss Lockhart," he said to Ruth.

"No. I'm Ruth Echland. This tall, skinny redhead is Sydney Lockhart. We're cousins."

"I can see the resemblance," he joked. "I'm Leroy Peevey. Sorry the ponies aren't running now. This place really hops during racing season."

"Nice to meet you, Mr. Peevey. We'll have to come back," I said. "At least I can get a feel for the place and take some photos."

"You can at that. Always happy to show folks around. I'll start at the top. There's a great view of the entire track and stables from the roof. Follow me."

I could have easily stayed off the roof considering the last time I climbed onto a roof for a view, I found a murder victim. But, I'm a professional, and duty called.

"We're celebrating our fiftieth anniversary in little more than a year. Been open since 1904," Leroy Peevey said, leading us past a long row of betting windows.

"How long have you worked for Oaklawn, Mr. Peevey?" I pulled out my notebook.

"Long time. Started out mucking stables in the twenties and worked my way up to PR. My official title is Assistant Director of Publicity. All that means is I get a smaller office and less money than the director. I also have to do the grunt work my boss doesn't want to mess with. Sometimes I get lucky, though, and have the opportunity to give a private tour to two nice looking ladies."

Ruth giggled. "Damn right," she whispered over her shoulder.

I'd have nudged her in the ribs, but that would've meant having to squat down, so I tweaked her hair instead.

We climbed several flights of stairs. Mr. Peevey pushed open a heavy door and we stepped out onto the roof. He was right; the view was spectacular. The grass around the track was emerald green and manicured to within an inch of its life. The stark white fence surrounding the track, along with the orange/brown turf made for a colorful photo. I snapped away and listened while Mr. Peevey talked. It was obvious he liked his job. He spoke with pride and pleasure as if the track belonged to him.

"It reminds me of the place in Kentucky," Ruth said. "The track with those two tower things."

I felt the blood rush up to my hairline. I should have told Ruth to keep her mouth shut as if it would have done any good.

Mr. Peevey laughed. "Churchill Downs and the twin spires."

"Right. That's where they had the Kentucky Derby one year." Ruth looked over at me and smiled. If my hands had been free of notepad, pencil, and camera, I would have had them around her throat.

"Had a Derby winner here a couple of years ago. Lenny-Go-Lightly won the Arkansas and went on to blow them away at Churchill a few weeks later. We thought surely he'd take the Triple Crown, but Hill Prince blew past and won the Preakness by three lengths."

"Too bad," Ruth said.

I could tell by her tone, she had no idea what he was talking about and didn't really care. She was holding her hair in place with her gloved hands.

I'd done a little research on recent winners. It's always a good policy to have background on the subject before an interview. Gives the writer some credibility.

"I read about that race. Wasn't there an investigation?"

"Yeah. Owner of Lenny-Go-Lightly felt that the jockey didn't ride him right. Bumped the horse next to him. But nothing ever came of it. Sometimes horses wake up and don't feel like running, or they're just as happy to follow another horse across the finish line. A lot of folks lost their shirts, and a few made a nice wad."

Only a few feet from the track and right next to the grandstand I noticed a quaint cottage tucked amidst a grove of maple trees.

"Who lives there?"

"Guy who owns the track. Uses the house to entertain the big-shots who come to the races."

"Like who?" Ruth asked.

"Like the Babe for one. The slugger loved to throw a few bucks on the horses when he was here during spring training."

"How about any of those gangsters we've heard so much about?"

"Ruth!"

"Oh, sure," Mr. Peevey laughed. "We had those, too. Come in to the box area. We just renovated it. Put in steam heating and there's talk of a new clubhouse dining room. Since the closing of the casinos people have started flocking to the track. It's been great for business."

"Speaking of gangsters, do you know a guy named Metzner?"

"Ruth!"

"You mean that flashy fat guy who used to live at the Majestic? He's dead. Isn't he? How do you know about him?"

"Just heard the name one night when we were in the mineral pool," I said. I was not about to let Ruth tell Mr. Peevey about our kidnapping. Mr. Peevey was now walking toward the south side of the roof with his back to us. I took the opportunity to pinch Ruth in the arm. She squealed.

"What was that?" Mr. Peevey looked over his shoulder.

"A bird," I said. "Sounded like a pigeon."

"Got too many of them here on this roof."

Ruth rubbed her arm and tried to kick me, but I was too fast for her short leg.

We followed Mr. Peevey to the other side. I kept looking over my shoulder, half expecting to find the ex-Marine lurking behind.

"Look at all those white barns," Ruth said, pointing to an area beyond the track.

"Our stables. In a few weeks time that place will be crawling with trainers, stable hands, jockeys, owners, not to mention some of the best thoroughbreds in the country."

I had a good shot of the parking lot from here. No Studebaker. No Muldoon. I began to relax a little.

"Let's go," Mr. Peevey said, heading toward the stairs. "I want to show you the Jockey's Club, pretty fancy place."

The Jockey's Club was indeed fancy. It looked like a gentlemen's club complete with deep lounge chairs and sofas upholstered in rich red leather. Dark mahogany paneling covered the walls. Sleek chrome and leather-topped barstools lined the bar. Hanging on the walls were oil paintings of jockeys atop their steeds. I sniffed the air and caught the lingering scent of expensive cigars and heavy furniture polish. The place had such a masculine feel, I wouldn't have been surprised if at one time the Oaklawn Jockey's Club was off limits to women.

"At one time this was a men's only bar," Mr. Peevey said, "but the rules have relaxed. I for one, like the ladies being here. They add a touch of class to this place."

"Very impressive," I said.

"There's even talk about putting a television in here so folks can watch the race without even going out to the grandstands. What'll they think of next?"

"I bought a television last year," Ruth said. "That invention will not last past this decade, mark my word. Just a flash in the pan. Here today, gone tomorrow. Like any fad, short lived."

I reached over to give her another pinch, but she jumped out of the way and stuck her tongue out at me.

"Why would anyone want to watch the race on a television screen when they can see it live?" I asked.

"Comfort. All about comfort," Mr. Peevey said. "We're getting to be a lazy people. But I agree with you, Miss Lockhart. There's nothing better than being out in the grandstands, watching those horses run. Do it long enough and it gets in your blood. I don't mean the betting part. I mean horses have an effect on people. You watch them run; you see their ears prick up when they pull ahead; the look in their eyes when they know they've won. Makes you want to be around them; makes you want to stroke their necks and feel their sweaty coat; makes you want to . . . to be a horse." Mr. Peevey blushed. "I'm sounding like an idiot. Sorry, lost myself for a moment."

I let Mr. Peevey have his moment and walked ahead pretending not to notice him pull a handkerchief from his pocket and dab at the corner of his eye. But I couldn't ignore the prickly feeling that had just assaulted my left shoulder, like a spider crawling across my skin. For some unknown reason, Mr. Peevey's passionate soliloquy sounded too familiar. "The look in their eyes when they know they've won." Maybe it was Dixon—his unnerving cockiness. Maybe it was Chester Salami glaring at me as the Smalls drove me away from his clutches. Maybe I was losing my mind. Maybe I should make this roof tour my last and jump. Instead I swatted at the imaginary spider and headed for the stairs.

Mr. Peevey escorted us out the building and to the parking lot. "Come back during racing season and I'll give you a tour of the stables; not many folks are allowed there. Hope you enjoy the rest of your time here. Hot Springs is a fine little city. Where are you staying?"

"We're at the Arlington," Ruth said.

Mr. Peevey whistled. "I heard about what's been happening there. That bookkeeper used to be a regular here at the track."

"Ellison James?" I asked. "You knew him?"

"Mr. James had a thing for the ponies. He was pretty good at picking winners, too. In fact, on Derby Day last year he laid down a picture of Benjamin Franklin on a long shot in the second race. His pony came in."

"What were the odds?"

"Thirty-eight to one."

"He won $3,800?!" I said. "That sounds a bit fishy. Who puts a hundred dollars down on a long shot, unless they had some inside information?"

"Ellison was often . . . lucky." Mr. Peevey raised his eyebrows. "Hey, that's none of my business, though I guess it doesn't matter now—me telling you that. I mean since the man's dead. Right?"

"Right. Since the man's dead, I hope you don't mind me asking. You think he may have gotten a hot tip?"

"Looks that way, but impossible to prove. Hey, gotta go. I'm expecting a call." He pushed his sleeve back and checked his watch. "Call if you have any more questions. It was a pleasure, ladies."

I looked at my watch too and was surprised at the time. My feet hurt and I wanted to park myself on something cushy. As if reading my mind, Ruth slipped off one of her spiked heels and massaged her instep.

"Let's go," I said. "Cocktail time. Let's try the Park Hotel today."

"Why? I like the lounge in the Arlington."

"Change of scenery."

The Park Hotel's lounge was not as elegant as the Arlington's, but the place had charm, like sitting in someone's living room. Prints depicting Hot Springs in her heyday hung on dark paneled walls. We made ourselves at home in two deep-stuffed leather lounge chairs and kicked off our shoes. It wasn't the Jockey Club, but it would do. Moments later, our martinis were on their way.

"I think you should call your detective and give him that information about Ellison and that long shot," Ruth said.

"He's not my detective! Would you stop with that?"

Ruth smiled at me like the she-devil herself.

"I'll call when I get back," I said.

I knew we were both tired. Ruth seemed lost in her thoughts and I was thinking that I should probably wrap up my story and get the hell out of town.

Finally Ruth let out a sigh and said, "Syd, I'm sorry."

"For what?"

"Buying you that outfit yesterday. I knew you wouldn't like it, but—"

"Got caught up in the moment?"

Ruth laughed. "I guess. I knew it wasn't your style, but you have to admit, it is boss."

"Maybe when we exchange it you should ask if they have it in your size. It'd look wonderful on you." It wouldn't improve the appearance of a goat, but then again I'm no fashion expert.

Ruth sipped her martini and smiled over the rim of her glass.

We sat quietly enjoying our drinks like two old ladies who'd known each other forever. It was comforting not having to say anything—a rare moment for both of us. Then, just as quickly as it came, my relaxed mood shifted back to the melancholy that had come over me too many times since we left the Arlington for our day of exploration. The murders, the kidnappings, Metzner, Muldoon—all still a mass of confusion, even more so since we'd spoken to Mr. Peevey. Al Capone, horseracing, Ellison James, bookies, now I began to wonder if the murders were linked to the racing business.

I watched Ruth as she spiked her olive, studied it, dipped it back into her gin, and swirled it around. I looked closer and saw my reflection in her martini glass. I couldn't believe that a little more than twenty-four hours ago I'd crawled out of a root cellar, spent an adventurous morning with the Smalls, used a jug of hooch to blow up a cabin and start a small forest fire, and ended back up in the hotel with a rip in my PJs and singed eyebrows only to discover that my room had been ransacked and most of my possessions stolen.

Ruth set the olive to swirling again and my reflection joined in. She repeated this gesture every couple of minutes. After the fourth time my head was beginning to spin. "What the hell are you doing to that olive? Just eat the damn thing!"

Ruth jumped out of her reverie, raised her eyebrows, and said, "Testy, testy. I'll be right back."

As soon as Ruth left, and oxygen started to diffuse back into the lobby, my mind started to drift again. I was wondering how my girls were doing. If only they could speak and answer the phone themselves. Using Scott as a go-between was annoying. Maybe I could call tomorrow when he was at work. If my luck held, Jeremiah would still be there. Ruth skipped back to the lounge, smiling like a she was up to no good.

"Where'd you go?"

"Pay phone. I called Maryanne Newton and volunteered to co-chair the reunion committee. Now Miss Homecoming Queen can't make a move without me."

"Smart, Ruth. Hey, sorry about snapping at you a minute ago. Seems as soon as I let my mind relax, I get all twisted up in the murders at the Arlington.

"Great title for a book—*Murder at the Arlington*—maybe you should write it."

"Maybe I will."

Chapter 18

I was about to suggest that we return to our hotel and call it a day. Despite the two murders, I liked the place. I liked my room. I'd have to come back sometimes, under better circumstances.

Suddenly I was exhausted. But before I could open my mouth, Ruth jumped up. "Shopping! It's ti . . . me," She sung her announcement in an annoying falsetto. "We only have a little more than two hours before the stores close. I firmly believe we could do some real damage."

I'd totally forgotten about shopping. At this point I'd rather return to see how the Smalls were doing at Mount Ida. In fact that quiet little root cellar sounded kind of nice. I looked at my watch. "Okay, Ruth. We shop. First I need coffee."

She gave me that pouty face, then found the waiter and ordered two coffees.

"Where's that shop of yours?" I asked. I added double sugar to give the caffeine a boost.

"Two blocks down Central. Maurice's. You'll love it."

"I need everything. A skirt, a sweater, couple of blouses, shoes, bathing suit, and pajamas, even a coat or jacket."

"We'll need a department store for that. Let's exchange the outfit first."

I tried on two outfits at Maurice's and claimed that neither fit. The clothes in this shop were atrocious, so much so that Ruth bought two dresses, a skirt and a sweater in addition to exchanging the blue and yellow eyesore for one in her size.

"Hey," I said. "Who needs clothes? You or me? Let's go."

We drove to Monnigs Department store and I had little less than an hour to outfit myself with a new wardrobe. While Ruth headed for the gloves, I found a sales clerk and told her exactly what I needed. She walked behind me and caught whatever I pulled off the shelves and racks. I wouldn't win a fashion contest, but I'd selected a few items I could live with. The only thing I really didn't like were the baby doll PJs. Not my style. I prefer the kind of nightwear I can walk around in and not have to worry if someone is looking through my window. These skimpy baby dolls made me blush.

I headed for the register when the sales clerk pointed out a white rayon blouse. She held it up, turning it around for the full effect. The neckline draped across the front and over the shoulders, then dipped deeply down the back forming a V. A string of covered Victorian-style buttons trailed down from the V to the waist, tapering the blouse along the ribs.

"We just got this little number in yesterday. You can wear it with your skirt as well as your slacks." She paused for effect. "It was made for you."

I looked down at the clothes on the counter and realized she was right. I'd gone for practical and I needed at least one sexy item—every girl does. Guilt and fear surfaced for a brief moment as I did a quick mental calculation of what was left in my bank account. I had just enough to cover the expense of this trip. I hadn't planned on buying a new wardrobe. What the hell? I'd live off peanut butter and jelly sandwiches for the next month. I grabbed the blouse and threw it on the pile.

"Black, white, navy, gray." Ruth walked up. "Are you joining the service, or maybe the Salvation Army?

I noticed she'd purchased a pair of gloves in every color. "I didn't have a lot of time," I said.

Then she picked up the baby dolls. "Yeah right. Here, I bought you a clutch. It's your favorite color, black. And a compact, and a wallet. I knew you wouldn't think about those things."

"How about gloves?" I joked.

She tossed a pair of red ones on the pile. "A little color never hurt."

I looked at my watch. Three minutes until closing. Still time. "There are a couple more things we both need. I know you close soon—"

"No problem, ma'am. What can I show you?"

"Dungarees, flannel shirts, bobby socks and two pair of saddle shoes, a size ten and a size . . ." I looked down at Ruth's feet. "A size two."

"What?!" Ruth shouted.

"Tomorrow we hike. And we can't do that in heels and skirts."

"I don't own a pair of dungarees and I've never worn flannel," Ruth said.

"Soon you will." It was my pay back for the red gloves.

"Saddle shoes are for Musketeers."

"Don't worry. You can wear your gloves while we hike."

"And I don't wear a size two! My feet aren't that small. I wear a size five, narrow."

The sales girl laughed.

We walked into the hotel lobby carrying enough boxes to form a notable shelter, or so I thought. As we passed the front desk, Mrs. Willis had no problem recognizing us behind our cover.

"Miss Lockhart. There . . . you . . . are. We've been calling your room all day." Her toned sounded like my mother's when I was sixteen and tried sneaking in the house after curfew.

"Lieutenant Dixon is looking for you." Now she sounded like a probation officer, speaking loud enough to grab the attention of everyone in the lobby. "Here." She ripped off a sheet of paper from a tablet with such force the tablet took flight across the front desk. "Here's his number."

Since my hands were full and setting the boxes down was no easy task, I said, "Thank you, Mrs. Willis. I know the number." It was a lie, but listening to her huff and squeal was worth the bit of untruth. I actually did have the number up in my room.

The elevator door slid open and the old man ambled from his stool and helped us with our boxes.

"That's what I like to see," he said. "Two ladies out enjoying themselves. Looks like you bought out the store."

"Almost. Miss anything at the hotel today?"

"I'll say. That detective's on the scent of something. He's been all over this hotel again. Here we are. Tenth Floor." He locked the elevator and helped us carry our boxes to the room.

Once inside, Ruth flopped down on the sofa and kicked off her shoes. "Wonder what that was all about?" she said. "Think the cops are ready to make an arrest?"

"I'm too tired to care. I just want to try out my new bathing suit."

"Shouldn't you call Dixon?"

"He knows where I am."

I opened a box, which I thought held my bathing suit. Instead I found my new black clutch. I clicked it open and expected it to be stuffed full of white tissue paper. It was stuffed with a big wad of cash. I was moved.

"Ruth, this is way too much." I took most of the money and handed it back to her. "It will be a while before I can repay you."

"Phooey. I was thinking of starting a new foundation anyway. You can be my first victim, I mean candidate, I mean beneficiary. It's a foundation for single, self-employed women, where I provide funds until they can get their business off the ground. There are plenty of those organizations for men. Mine will be just for women."

I gave her a hug. "Come on, let's go soak," I said.

I felt every pore in my weary body sigh with pleasure as the steamy water crept up to my chin. I located a hot-water jet and let the stream gush onto my lower back.

"Let's talk about Muldoon," Ruth said, easing down in the pool next to me.

"Let's not. We've talked enough."

"But he could be watching us now." She looked around. "He could be watching with binoculars from any of those windows. He could be behind one of those bushes along the trail. He could—"

"He could be lying on the bottom of this pool watching bubbles swirl around our toes while breathing through a hose. Let him watch. I really don't care."

"Sydney?"

"What?"

"Maybe we should leave?"

Ruth sounded as frightened as I felt. Visions of Ellison and sweet, little Elsa resting in pools of their own blood seemed to assault me whenever I closed my eyes. Then I thought of my parents, their wedding photo stolen from my room, my mother heading for California. She was annoying, aggravating, and nosy, but she was my mother. Whoever had stolen my clothes had the photo.

"I'm staying, Ruth. You can leave, but I'm staying."

"You're just too stubborn for your own good."

Before our little discussion could turn into an argument, we were interrupted.

"I don't think this is a good idea. Whoever heard of sitting in a pool outside in November," came an agitated voice.

Ruth and I stopped bickering and turned to watch an elderly couple shuffle up to the pool.

"You should have worn your robe," the woman said. She hung her robe on a hook by the shower and stepped in the pool one toe at a time.

"You always know what to do, don't you?" said her husband.

Great—just what we needed—company. I hoped they weren't the chatty type, but before I could close my eyes the wife said, "Isn't this just heavenly?" She smiled a smile that made her full round face look like a moon pie. "We come here every year at this time. Where are you young ladies from?" Since Ruth was in a conversational mood, I let her answer and went ahead with my plan to pretend sleep.

"Texas. I'm from Dallas and my cousin's from Austin," Ruth said. "How about you?"

"We're from Ardmore, Oklahoma. Lester and Jean Cooper. Lester's into oil. A lot of oil in Texas. Right Lester? Scoot over, honey. I need that jet. My shoulder blades are tighter than your purse strings." Jean hooted at her own joke.

I cracked open one eyelid and Lester looked as bored as me.

"What about your husbands? What do they do?" Jean said.

Yeah, Ruth, tell her about our husbands, I wanted to say, but sleeping women don't talk.

"Sydney's husband is president of Texas Bank and my husband, Andrew Rockefeller, well . . . to be honest, Jean, I'm not sure what Andy really does." Ruth giggled and her accent took a turn toward East Texas. "Something with stocks and bonds. It's all just too complicated for me."

"Not the East Coast Rockefellers?" Jean said.

I cracked another eyelid and saw Ruth answer with a smile.

"Jean, don't pry." Lester found his voice.

"Shut up, Lester. I'm just being neighborly."

"Ruth, speaking of husbands, we're supposed to meet Hugh and Andy in a few minutes."

"Oh, they can wait."

I pinched Ruth on the thigh, but the one who screamed was Jean Cooper. My eyes popped open to see the woman standing in the middle of a stream of scarlet water swirling around her buoyant butt.

Ruth was still in the shower when Dixon knocked.

"Where in the hell have you been all day? Not out starting more forest fires I hope."

"Funny. I've been working, conducting interviews for my article."

"Where's your cousin?"

"Trying to scrub the blood from her body. Who's was it by the way?"

"Your friend Metzner. I got a call from him this morning. He said he was ready to talk."

"Confess?"

"Who the hell knows? He was dead before I could get to him. Throat slit and stewing like a goose in a soup pot down in that hot-water holding tank in the basement. The mineral pool will be out of commission for a while."

The image of the flamboyant fat man cooking in the bowels of the hotel turned even my stomach. "Four people murdered in less than four days," I muttered.

"Glad you can count," he said. "I was afraid it would be six. Before Metzner hung up the phone, he said that you and your cousin wouldn't make it back to the hotel in one piece. I sent one of my deputy's here, but you two were nowhere to be found." His voice softened. "I didn't want two more bodies on my hands by the end of the day." He took his handkerchief out of his pocket and wiped his forehead.

"You need to tell him about Muldoon," Ruth said. She stood in the doorway wrapped in her bathrobe, wearing slippers and twisting a cigarette into its holder. What skin was showing (ankles, hands, and face) was scrubbed raw.

"Who the hell's Muldoon?"

"Ex-marine, staying in room 809." I paused. I was anxious to tell him everything, but that would mean having to reveal that I'd been snooping in Muldoon's room. Well, I've confessed to worse. I remembered my pearl earring, pulled it out of the dresser drawer, and gave it to him. I figured that was a good place to start.

"What's this?"

"My earring. It was taken from my room with the rest of my things on Saturday night."

"I'm missing something here. What does your earring have to do with this Muldoon?"

"Let me tell him," Ruth said, and she plowed into the story before I could object.

"It all started in the mineral pool when big hairy Muldoon told us about this gangster guy Metzner." Ruth paced. "A few hours later we were kidnapped by said gangster." She stopped, turned, and looked directly at us—her right elbow cupped in her left hand and a clove cigarette protruded from her fingers. "Then later Sydney looked out her window and saw Muldoon walking around at three o'clock in the morning. He kept looking up at her room. Moments later there was a brawl in the hall and Sydney rushed out." Ruth turned to me. "Not very smart, cousin." She flicked ash off her cigarette and continued. "Then Sydney was kidnapped . . . again by same said gangster. Her clothes, jewelry, purse were stolen, everything but her undies, but I guess . . . you already know that." Ruth tried to blow a smoke ring. "Later that day, after Sydney's miraculous escape and her return, she found one of her earrings in Muldoon's shaving kit while she was in his bathroom. And guess what?"

Dixon and I were too dumbstruck to respond so Ruth continued.

"Not two minutes later, the little foreign boy—I think the family's from somewhere in Asia—ran into Sydney in the hall right outside Muldoon's room and spit out the other earring—it was in his mouth. Then, today when Syd and I came out of the crystal shop—she bought a large bawdy blue-green one, but mine's a cute little rose-colored number—Muldoon was watching us from across the street. How do you like that?"

Dixon looked at me with such a strange expression; at first I couldn't read it. Then I realized that the man was about to cry.

I smiled at him.

"I need an aspirin," he said.

Ruth rushed off to her bathroom to fetch said medicine.

"Maybe you can clarify?"

"Sure. My crystal was actually aquamarine and is not bawdy."

Ruth came back with the bottle of aspirin and a glass of water. She'd changed from her bathrobe into a neat red suit, along with red pumps. "I ordered room service. Sydney and I are starved. You look hungry, too. I also ordered a bottle of wine. I know you're on duty, but one little bitty glass won't hurt."

"Miss Echland?"

"Yes?"

"Call room service back and tell them to bring a bucket of ice and a bottle of their best bourbon."

"Yes, sir."

"It's gonna be a long night," Dixon said, swallowing what looked like a handful of aspirin.

Then Dixon did something I hadn't seen him do before. He loosened his tie.

"All right. I have questions and I want answers." He picked up the phone. "This is Lieutenant Dixon. Find Grady Broussard and tell him I want to see him in room 1019. Now!"

It was the first time I'd heard Grady's last name. And it fit. He looked like a wiry little Cajun. I heard Ruth in her room ordering Dixon's bourbon and to that she added another bottle of wine and doubled the food order. I wished I could share Ruth's festive attitude. Instead I felt a bit overwhelmed.

Chapter 19

Grady arrived before the food and booze. He sauntered in, sat down in my desk chair, and tilted it back, balancing it on the back two legs. "How's it going, Ralph?"

"Make yourself at home, Grady. We got business to take care of," Dixon said.

I moved my boxes of clothes to the other side of the bed.

"I, for one, need a meal before I conduct any business," Ruth said.

"Hey, since we're waiting for grub and libations, I'll bet you guys haven't heard this one," Grady said. "There was a teacher, a doctor, and a cop waiting at St. Peter's gate. St. Peter comes out and says, 'We're filling up quick, so if you guys want in you have to answer one question correctly.' He turned to the teacher. 'Who killed President Lincoln?' Teacher said, 'John Wilkes Booth.' St. Peter let him in. Then to the doctor he asked, 'Where did President Lincoln take the bullet?' 'In the head,' the doc said and followed the teacher in. Then it was the cop's turn. St. Pete asked, 'Where the hell was a cop when they needed one?'"

Laughing at his own lame joke, Grady almost fell off his chair.

Dixon stared, expressionless.

Ruth said, "I don't get it."

Now I was the one who needed said aspirin.

There was a knock at my door. Dixon opened it and Mickey wheeled in the cart of sustenance. For some reason, it was a comfort to see Mickey. He was like the little brother I didn't have. No, I haven't forgotten about Scott. Like I said, Mickey was like the little brother I didn't have.

"Time for a powwow?" Mickey asked.

"Just mind your own business, son," Dixon barked.

Ruth rushed over and slipped a five in Mickey's shirt pocket. He thanked her, winked at me, and slid out the door. I wanted to follow, but despite the crowd in my room, I was sure my absence would be noticed. Ruth went about laying out the food. She used my writing desk as a makeshift buffet table. She was in her social element now, humming, refolding napkins into some sort of triangular shape, according to Amy Vanderbilt, I'm sure. She had ordered sandwiches, potato salad, baked beans and pecan pie . . . a la mode.

I opened my mouth when I saw the ice cream, then quickly shut it. She was the party coordinator, let her worry about it.

Dixon plunked ice cubes into two glasses, filled them with bourbon, handed Grady one (I guess it was understood that no self- respecting man would drink wine with his ham and cheese) then started ordering people around.

"I want to know everything." He looked from me to Ruth. "Where you've been; who you've talked to; what was said . . . everything."

"Maybe we should invite Donna, then?" Ruth chirped.

"Who the hell's Donna?"

"Donna Jennings, Elsa Dubois' friend, she's a housemaid here," Ruth said.

"And?" Dixon inclined his head forward.

"She's the one—"

"Ruth, honey, I'll have a glass of wine, since you're playing hostess," I said.

"Red or white."

"You choose." I continued for Ruth. "We spoke to Donna yesterday and found out why Elsa and Ellison were going to Little Rock."

Ruth handed me a glass of red wine and plate of pecan pie a la mode. I didn't question her choice of last course first. I wasn't ready to hear another Ruthism. I still had a slight headache.

"And . . ." Dixon said again, taking a bite of sandwich and washing it down with bourbon.

"And Elsa was . . . expecting. She was planning to see a doctor. She didn't want to have the baby."

Dixon chewed and swallowed. "We knew about the expecting part. Showed up in the autopsy. Except Ellison James wasn't the father. Wrong blood type."

"So, I was right," I said.

"About what?" Dixon asked.

"After talking with Elsa, I had a hunch that she and Ellison James weren't romantically involved."

"Well, she was involved with someone," Dixon said.

"Tell him about the bathroom," Ruth said.

Ruth always left the good parts for me. I explained to Dixon why I was in Muldoon's bathroom and how I found my earring in his travel kit.

Dixon sat his sandwich down on a plate (Ruth had passed them out with the napkins). "Grady, use the phone in Miss Echland's room and get Donna Jennings up here, then call the front desk and find out what you can about this Muldoon guy. Where he's from. When he checked in." Dixon picked up my phone and called for Officer O'Riley to join us.

I heard Ruth mumble concerns about not having enough food.

"Donna's gone home," Grady called from Ruth's room. He came in and handed Dixon a piece of paper. "Here's her address. She doesn't have a phone. I'll call about Muldoon now."

Dixon looked at me. "What else?" He took off his jacket and hung it on the back of a chair. His white shirt was pressed as flat as cardboard.

"After Donna told us what she knew, I advised her to call you. I guess she chickened out. She was pretty upset."

"Thanks for letting me in on this investigation," Dixon scoffed.

Grady came back in. "Muldoon's checked out."

"When?"

"This afternoon around 4:00."

"Damn!"

"I've seen the guy here a couple of times before," Grady said. "He never caused any real trouble—just loud mouthing in the bar—so I had no reason to get to know him."

"Muldoon told us that he comes here a couple of times a year," I said, confirming Grady's information. "You said he's from Longview, Texas, right Grady?"

"Best as I know."

"How long will it take you to find out exactly when Muldoon was here during the last year or so?" Dixon said.

"Just another phone call to front desk."

"Do it, then. And make sure no one checks into that room. I want it searched and fingerprinted."

There was another knock on the door. Dixon answered and Officer O'Riley walked in.

"What's up, boss?"

"Get a couple of boys to room 809 and go over it thread by thread. Here," he handed O'Riley the paper with Donna's address. "Go find this girl. Name's Donna Jennings. Works here at the hotel. Find out everything she knows about Elsa Dubois. Don't let her give you any lip. If she does, haul her down to the station for some real questioning. "

"Oh my," Ruth said. "She's such a sweet girl."

Yeah, Ruth, I thought. You're the one who brought this sweet girl's attention to the cops.

"And locate that foreign family," Dixon said. "Find out what they know."

"About what, exactly, boss?"

"About anything," Dixon barked.

O'Riley rushed out the door.

"Well, Muldoon's not from Longview, Texas," Grady said, hanging up the phone. "Every time he's registered—once on May 11, again on June 13 and this time November 16—he gave his address as Fort Smith, Arkansas."

"Ring up the operator in Fort Smith and see if she has a number for Muldoon. First name?"

"Stanley."

"November 16th; that was the day after I checked in," I said. "Speaking of checking in, any leads yet on why my room was ransacked and my clothes stolen?"

"Someone was looking for something," Dixon said, refreshing his cocktail.

"That's obvious," I said. "But what were they looking for? And why would it have been in my room? And why steal my clothes?"

"I can't answer the first two questions, but my guess is they stole your clothes to cover their tracks. Make it look like a robbery."

"It's got to be Muldoon," I said. "Since he had my earring. He must have dropped the other one in the hall and the little boy found it."

"Maybe Muldoon has a thing for women's clothes," Grady said.

"I don't think so," Ruth said. "Sydney's clothes would never fit the big guy. Besides, he left her undies."

We all turned and gawked at her. Ruth blushed all the way up to her blonde roots. "I mean . . . well . . . don't those sort of guys usually . . ."

"Weren't you going to call Fort Smith?" Dixon said to Grady.

"I'm dialing," Grady said, making a circular motion with his index finger. He disappeared back into Ruth's room.

"Since we're laying cards on the table," I said. "I found out something about Ellison James."

"Talk."

"Seems he was hot on the trail of some fast horses. I toured Oaklawn today and James either had a knack for picking winners, or had an inside line on the horses. He laid a hundred bucks on a long shot in the Arkansas Derby and walked away with a wad of cash. That might explain his flashy clothes."

"Hallelujah!" Dixon shouted and raised his arms in the air. "You're telling me something I already know. Imagine that."

"You don't have to get snippy." I sulked and finished off my pie and wine while Dixon read through his notes.

A few minutes later, Grady stood at the adjoining door again. "No Muldoon in Fort Smith, either; or if he's living there, he doesn't have a phone. Got his license plate number, though. Arkansas: T12-362."

My phone rang. Dixon answered. "Get the prints, then. And put out an APB on an Arkansas plate number T12-362." He slammed the phone down. "Eight zero nine's clean. Nothing there."

Dixon paced silently around the room. He glanced at the mess of boxes pushed aside on my bed, stopped for a moment, and continued pacing. I could almost hear his brain racking. Grady, having had no further orders, grabbed another sandwich and refreshed his highball.

My ice cream and pie appetizer did just that, enhanced my appetite and spiked my blood sugar. The sulking subsided. I refilled my wine glass and reached for a half of a sandwich. "What I can't understand is why Metzner and Chester Salami were killed? I figured they were behind what happened here at the hotel, but now that they're dead . . . well, what do you think . . . Ralph?"

Lieutenant Dixon twitched at hearing me call him by his first name, but recovered quickly. "Chester . . . Salami?"

"That's what we called the thug who abducted us and chased Sydney around the woods. He smelled like salami." Ruth had finished eating and was now part of the conversation again.

A minute smile spread across Dixon's lips. He quickly recovered, but not before I noticed a shadow of a dimple in his left cheek; and not before I dribbled red wine down my new white blouse. I ran into the bathroom to dab the stain and to keep anyone from seeing me blush. What the hell was wrong with me? As soon as Dixon started acting human, I started acting like a girl.

When I came back into the room, Dixon was putting on his jacket. The party was evidently over.

"I want you two to stay put in these rooms tonight. I don't care if the damn hotel catches fire. As soon as I can, I'm placing a guard outside. "You," he jabbed a finger in my direction, "will call me before you do anything tomorrow. Understand?"

I nodded.

"Come on, Grady. Let's go."

Grady was the first to walk out. Dixon followed. As he passed me, Dixon leaned close and whispered, "Nice new PJs . . . Syd. You shouldn't leave them in the box." The dimple made another momentary appearance.

Chapter 20

Dixon said we couldn't leave. He didn't say we couldn't have company. I called room service and ordered another bottle of wine just to have an excuse to talk to Mickey. He'd proved a valuable ally and topnotch snoop.

"That went well," Ruth said. "Except for maybe the ice cream."

"What were you thinking?"

"I got caught up in the moment. You know how I am."

I started taking my new clothes from their boxes and putting them in the drawers.

"I think you did okay in your selections," Ruth said, "considering the little time you had." I detected a slight disapproval in her voice, but appreciated her attempt at kindness.

"I do miss my jade sandals though. I never got to wear them with my new green cap that Rita gave me."

"You must be devastated."

I threw a wine cork at her.

Before she could find something to throw at me, Mickey arrived with our order. We got down to business for the second time that night.

"When do you get off work, Mickey?"

"I just punched the time clock before I came up. I'm at your service. Need me to do any more investigating?" He eyed the buffet table and raised his eyebrows. Ruth took the hint and filled a plate for him. Party number two had commenced.

"Who is that old lady who writes those murder mysteries where she gathers people together in the library in order to find out who done it?" Mickey asked.

"Dorothy Sayers," Ruth said.

"It was Agatha Christie," I said.

"That's her." Mickey bit into his ham and cheese (swallow). "Is that what happened here tonight?"

"Not exactly. It was more like a rehashing of information, which didn't get us very far. And yes, I need your help. Ruth and I are restricted to our rooms until a guard can be posted."

"And you want me to snoop?"

"You got it. I also want to know if you hear of anything weird going on."

"I could write a book of weird things. Normal people don't stay in hotels or if they do, they turn weird after they check in. You know . . . have to act right when they're at home, then they go on vacation and anything goes." He stuffed a spoonful of potato salad in his mouth and continued. "Last week (swallow) we had a mayor's convention. The mayor from Eureka Springs was found sleeping in the hall, wearing only his socks and shirt. Another guy, I forget where he was from, got his head stuck between the wooden slats under his mattress." He took another bite, chewed, and swallowed. "The maid found him just as he was beginning to turn blue. Claims he'd had a nightmare. I figure the nightmare didn't get what she'd been promised and there was a row."

"Oh, my," Ruth said.

"Where should I start?" Mickey said.

"The eighth floor," I said. "There was a guy named Muldoon staying in room 809. He checked out today."

"You mean that gorilla guy with the loud mouth?"

"That's the one. He was watching my room and then he began following us."

"Creepy."

"Also there's a foreign family on the same floor. They and Muldoon had something in common, earrings that belong to me. Dixon's boys will question them, but your eyes and ears, being unofficial, may prove more helpful."

"I'll see what I can find out. I've got the nose of a bloodhound."

"Mickey, just be careful. Don't do anything foolish. Two hotel employees have been murdered."

"I'll be fine. I know how to take care of myself."

I had no doubt that Mickey could do just that. The young man possessed a street savvy that would rival any young urchin in a Dickens novel. I also had no doubt that if I returned to this hotel in thirty years, Mickey would still be here doing a much better job of running the place than the Hamston Charles.

Ruth packed up the rest of the food and let Mickey take it home. My cousin would make a great mother. Maybe after this was over, I should concentrate on finding her a husband. With her money, that should be easy.

"Nice young man," Ruth said.

"He is. Maybe I shouldn't have gotten him involved. If anything happens to him, I won't be able to live with myself." Suddenly I felt the weight of what I'd just done. And the excitement of the evening began to wane.

Ruth promised to keep the sleeping pills in the bottle and I promised not to open the door no matter what. It was one in the morning and I was beat. I took a shower, slipped on my bathrobe and climbed into bed. My new PJs remained in their box.

The ringing of the phone jolted me awake. Sunlight brightened the room like a summer's day. I just managed to catch the receiver as the rest of the phone fell to the floor.

"Hello?"

"I thought you were an early riser."

I sat up in bed and pulled the sheet up to my chin. "Usually, but I had a couple of guys in my room last night, drinking and eating until the wee hours of the morning."

"I only had one sandwich and less than half a bottle of bourbon."

"You should have tried the pecan pie a la mode. It's not bad with booze. Find Donna Jennings?"

"At the grandmother's house, hiding like a frightened rabbit in a hole. Didn't tell us anymore than she told you."

"Have you found a bodyguard for us? I don't look forward to sitting in my room all morning. I'd planned to hike the trails and then let someone's magic fingers at the Buckstaff Bathhouse undo the damage."

"You're free to move about as you wish, hon." Dixon sounded happy— a new emotion for him. "We made an arrest early this morning."

"No! That was quick. Who?"

"Your friend Muldoon. We found him down the street at the Happy Hollow Courts. We also found his prints all over town—your first room, your current room, Metzner's apartment. My boys found the gun used to kill Chester Morani. It was in the trash bin behind the Majestic Hotel. Registered to one Stanley Muldoon."

"Wow! I'm impressed. You work fast."

"So I've been told."

"What was his motive? Something to do with gambling?"

"In this town? What isn't?"

"But what about Elsa? Was she involved?"

"Probably not. Saw or knew something she shouldn't have. We don't know much right now. Muldoon's not cooperating."

"He didn't happen to be wearing my clothes when you arrested him, did he?"

"No girlie clothes, hon. I'm afraid you'll have to take that loss. Enjoy your day."

He hung up without saying goodbye. I thought of my mother and all of a sudden the day seemed less bright.

I heard Ruth stirring. "Ready for coffee?" I called to her.

"Bring it on," she said. "Who was that calling so early?"

"Dixon. Once you're fully awake I'll tell you all about it."

"I look like a teenager," Ruth said, standing in front of the mirror, which hung on her closet door.

"You're cute." Actually she looked much younger than a teenager, more like a little girl wearing her big brother's clothes. We had to roll up the pant legs of her dungarees. The tail of her flannel shirt hung down to her knees.

"I'll need something for my head," she said.

I had my Chicago Cubs cap, but we didn't think about headgear for her while shopping. "Got a scarf?"

"I do. But the color's all wrong. It will clash with my outfit."

"Nothing clashes with gray flannel and denim. Besides we'll be in the woods. No one will see us. Let's see the scarf." She pulled out something that could have passed for a flag of some foreign country—Italy, maybe. It was red, green, and white striped and loud enough to incite a coup.

"Perfect," I said. "If we get lost, a rescue plane can easily spot us. Let's go have breakfast and then hit the trail. According to this map, the trail starts across the street behind the Medical Arts Building and continues to Blacksnake Road at the west side of Whittington Park. We can stop there for a snack. And if we're not too tired we can continue up over Sunset Mountain all the way to Gulpha Gorge Road. A good four hour hike . . . if we keep up a quick pace."

Ruth gasped. "Four . . . hour . . . hike."

"It'll be good for us. I've made appointments at the Buckstaff at three. You'll sleep like a princess tonight."

Ruth looked in the mirror once more. "Can't we just order room service and have breakfast here in the room?"

"Sure. No problem." Asking Ruth to wear her outdoor duds in the woods was one thing, but asking her to appear in the Arlington's dining room was another.

I called Mickey, the scent hound, and told him his snooping was no longer necessary. He was disappointed, but he's young. He'd recover. Then I called room service and ordered French toast, bacon and fried potatoes. I asked for two bananas, two bags of peanuts and an extra pot of coffee and a thermos. After we finished eating, I packed the thermos of coffee and food and a canteen of water into a backpack. "We can take turns carrying this. Ready?"

Ruth looked as if she were being led to the gallows.

"Come on. Cheer up. It's a beautiful day. The leaves are changing colors. You'll love it out there. Remember when we were in the Girl Scouts—"

"I hated the Girl Scouts. I lasted only one summer."

"That's because you tipped the canoe and fell into the lake. No big deal."

"No big deal for you. You can swim."

"There are no lakes out in these woods. We'll have a great day. Promise." I grabbed my camera and we left.

The trail finally leveled out once we reached the top of West Mountain. I took it slow for Ruth's sake. My long legs covered two strides compared to her one. To her credit, she trudged along without complaining. We reached a lookout point where a rock wall divided the point from a small parking lot.

"Let's rest here," I said. I took Ruth by the shoulders and turned her around. "Look."

"Oh, my. What a view!"

The town of Hot Springs spread out below us. The cupolas of the

Arlington Hotel rose above the treetops to our left; Hot Springs Rehabilitation Resort stood to our right, in between was Bathhouse Row and Central Avenue. The moment was interrupted by the whine of a car engine.

"What's that?" Ruth asked. She turned around and noticed the parking lot behind us. "A car!"

"Right. The map shows a road off Whittington Avenue which circles the mountain to the summit."

"You mean we could have driven up here!"

I filled the thermos lid with coffee and handed it to her. "You first," I said. She was mollified when she tasted what was left of last night's bourbon, which I'd used to spike the coffee.

While Ruth was finishing her caffeine cocktail, I stepped away and focused my camera.

"Ruth."

She turned and I snapped her picture. She threw the thermos lid at me. "If anyone sees me looking like this I'll kill myself, after rubbing you out first."

Now warm and refreshed we packed up and set out for Sunset Trail—if you could call it that—to Music Mountain. The foliage was so thick, we couldn't have seen a sunset unless the mountainside was cleared of trees. A wooden sign pointed us in the right direction. The narrow path almost disappeared in places. This was definitely not one of the most popular trails in the park.

"Listen," I said, stopping for a moment.

"I don't hear anything."

"Exactly. When was the last time you've heard such silence?"

"Last summer when I was in Neiman's for their end-of-the-year clearance sale. Some lady dropped her cigarette on a table of negligées and started a small fire. There was an announcement that we had to evacuate the store. Fifty women were speechless. You could have heard a pin drop. Do you think we might run into a bear?"

"No bears here. A cougar maybe, or a skunk."

"Funny."

I wasn't joking though, not this time. I stopped again a few yards down. There was a fluttering in the trees. I scanned the area.

"What is it?"

"Shhhh. Look. Over there—pileated woodpecker!"

"Where?"

"Up higher. That oak tree."

"Wow! It's huge. Beautiful!"

"You'd never see that in downtown Dallas. Admit it. You're enjoying yourself. You should have stuck with the Scouts a while longer. I would have taught you how to swim."

"Yeah . . . well," Ruth shrugged. "It is beautiful here."

It was dark enough under the trees to need a flash. I snapped in a bulb, took a picture, snapped in a second bulb, but the bird flitted to another tree, stayed a moment, and then flew off.

"If that picture turns out, it will be a great addition to the story. We're fortunate to have seen it. They're rare, you know."

"Really? Why?"

"Usual reason. More people, less room for nature."

"Sad."

I hung the camera around my neck and I looked at my watch. We were lollygagging. At this rate we'd be late for our spa appointment. I looked at the map. "The top of Music Mountain should be just ahead. We'll stop for a quick snack and then we've got to step it up. We're less than halfway."

There was no marker indicating the summit, but we continued to climb. Soon the trail started to descend. I declared that we had reached the top. To celebrate, we sat down on a huge rock and enjoyed our peanuts and bananas.

"Why do you think Muldoon killed those people?" Ruth said.

"I was wondering about that. Things don't add up. Ellison James was killed the afternoon before Muldoon checked in."

"If he had connections with Metzner perhaps he was staying with him at the Majestic."

"Then why come to the Arlington?"

"To find what was in your room?"

"Possibly. I don't think he planned to kill those other people. I think things started to go wrong and one thing led to another. There's something else that doesn't fit."

"What's that?"

"Why did Muldoon check out of the Arlington and check into the Happy Hollow Courts a couple of blocks away? If he thought the police were on to him, why not leave town?"

Ruth finished her banana and tossed the peel. I picked it up and put it in our sack.

Ruth rolled her eyes. "Well, that's obvious."

"It is?"

"He wasn't finished with his business; whatever that was. And things were getting too hot for him at the Arlington. At least Dixon caught him. And everybody that works at the hotel is safe, including us."

Don't ask me why, but for some reason I didn't feel all that safe.

We packed our trash and headed out. A slight breeze started to blow from the north and the temperature dropped a few degrees. I kept a steady pace and heard Ruth huffing behind me, but she kept up. I knew we were both thinking the same thing, steam bath, whirlpool, masseuse. Suddenly it got quiet and I looked behind me. Ruth was standing still, her head cocked.

"Hear a bird?"

"I think we're being followed."

"This is a public trail. It's another hiker, or maybe a deer. Come on. We have to make some time."

We moved on. After a couple of minutes, she stopped again. I was getting aggravated. At this rate we'd be here after dark.

"Step it up, Ruth. Don't be so paran—"

The shot rang out. Ruth screamed. I turned around in time to see my dear cousin pitch forward, her eyes wide open, a look of shock frozen on her face. She hit the ground and tumbled down the slope.

"Ruth!" I turned and ran after her. I tripped just as I saw the flash from the second shot. The bullet cut through the air and zipped past my ear. Before I could make sense of what was happening I was rolling down the hill, too. Finally all movement stopped. I looked around and saw Ruth lying in the brush. She wasn't moving. I crawled over to her and dragged her behind a boulder. I looked down at my hands and then at Ruth's shoulder and started to cry.

Chapter 21

I'm not sure how long I sat there, holding Ruth in my arms. Right after we'd taken cover, I heard excited voices in the distance. Maybe a scream, I couldn't be sure. Now all was silent. Ruth's breathing was steady, but the blood was beginning to soak through her shirt. I pulled the scarf from her head and lifted up her shirt collar. It was a small wound—shot through the shoulder right above her clavicle—the bullet appeared to have made a clean exit. I grabbed the napkins from the backpack, pressed them over the wound, and tied the scarf over her shoulder to stop the bleeding. I listened for footsteps, movement through the brush. All I heard was the wind creaking the branches above. Whoever shot at us was either waiting for us to make a move or had left. I needed to go for help, but I couldn't leave Ruth. I could do nothing but stay put and wait. We had seen no other hikers on the trail. In fact we were probably the only two that had taken this isolated path in weeks—the shooter and us.

Ruth started to come to. I had to do something. I had to keep her from going into shock.

"What . . . Syd?"

"It's okay. I'm here. You had an accident."

She tried to sit up.

"Don't move."

"What happened?" she whispered.

"Listen, sweetheart. Your shoulder's hurt, but you'll be fine. Just listen to me, okay?"

She shook her head.

I took her jacket from around her waist and draped it over her shoulders.

"I'm bleeding."

"Just a little. Can you sit up now?"

She tried to raise herself and I helped her lean against the rock. Her eyes were glassy. "What happened?" she asked again.

I held the canteen up to her. "Take a drink."

She shook her head and looked around. "I fell, but . . ."

"We need to get out of here and find the road. Do you think you can stand up? I can't leave you here."

Her eyes grew wide and she grabbed my arm.

"We're only about a mile from Blacksnake Road. I'll help you. We're going to have to walk. Once we get to the road, we'll flag someone down."

Then, as if assaulted with the memory of what had happened, she said, "Someone shot me! Syd, someone shot me!"

"Looks that way, but it's not a bad wound." I looked around. "It'll be rough going at first. I don't want to make our way back up to the trail in case the shooter is still up there." She let out a cry. "We need to climb down into the ravine. Follow it, and then try to find the trail again. Once we do, walking will be easier. Okay?"

"Okay," she said.

I helped her up. My little cousin—I think I could have carried her if I had to. I pulled her arm around my neck, grabbed her around the waist and we started off.

"Have you lost weight?" I asked, trying to sound casual.

"No."

"I think you have. You look really slim in these dungarees.

"Well, maybe a couple of pounds."

"I don't know why you don't wear jeans more often. They're really cute on you."

"I'm not too short?"

"No way."

"Maybe I will then. I'll have to hem these up. The cuffs look stupid."

We started walking and I could feel Ruth tense with pain.

"Hey, this is the latest style. Haven't you seen Rosemary Clooney's newest record cover? She's wearing rolled-up dungarees just like yours," I lied.

"I love Rosemary Clooney."

"You kind of look like her."

I glanced at Ruth's face and saw a slight smile, and then I noticed the tears dripping from her chin.

The ravine was rocky and we were moving slowly. I stopped a few times and listened. If someone was following us, they were doing a good job at not showing themselves. After several yards, the ravine meandered to the left, leading deeper into the woods.

"We need to start up now," I said, "Otherwise we'll lose the trail. It's not too steep in this spot. Ready?"

Ruth nodded. I knew she was trying her best not to cry out. Once we reached the trail, I eased Ruth to the ground. Her skin was as pale as the white gloves she usually wore.

"Rest a minute." I took the canteen out of the backpack and poured her a lid full of water. "Not far now. Just beyond the next bend." I didn't know what the hell I was talking about. The map was not that detailed, but I had to sound convincing for Ruth's sake . . . and for my own.

"Who would shoot me, Syd?"

"We'll figure that out as soon as we get back. Try to think of something else. A sale at Neiman's; a nice, big martini with extra olives—"

"Maybe a pleated woodpecker?"

"Hey, a pleated woodpecker sounds good to me. I need to check your shoulder. Okay?"

I loosened the scarf and, although the napkins were soaked with blood, the flow seemed to have lessened. "Looks good. You'll be in shopping shape in no time."

I helped her to her feet and she let out a stifled cry. "You're being too brave. Scream if you want to."

We continued on. I didn't hear another peep out of Ruth and I knew I had to hurry. I was afraid she was growing weaker. I started to silently pray. Halfway through the twentieth Hail Mary, I saw the road up ahead.

"Look! We're here!"

"Thank God," she said.

Thank God indeed, I said to myself.

When we reached the road, I sat Ruth down again. My heart sank. Blacksnake Road was no bigger than a gravel trail. It looked almost as deserted as the path we were on. I looked at the map again. About three miles to the northwest, the road linked up with Highway 227. Unless someone was looking for a shortcut into town or planning to visit the far reaches of Whittington Park, no one would be driving our way. I gave Ruth some more water and noticed her shivering. I pulled off my jacket and put it around her shoulders.

"Won't be long now," I said. I didn't get a response. "Ruth?"

Her eyes swam in her head. I needed to get her to a hospital and quick. I fought as hard as I could to keep my tears from coming. Then I heard it—the strain of a car engine coming up the road. A rusted green pickup crested the ridge. I started waving my arms. An old man was driving and next to him sat a huge white dog. The driver slowed to a stop.

"Need some help?" he said.

"Please. My cousin's hurt. I need to get her to the hospital."

For an old guy, he jumped out quickly and ordered his dog in the back. Then he helped me lift Ruth into the cab and within a few seconds we were off.

"What happened?" he asked.

"Someone shot at us and hit Ruth." I couldn't hold it back any longer and burst into tears.

"Damn hunters. They know better than to hunt on parkland. Happens every year. Some innocent person looks too much like a deer. We'll be at the hospital lickety-split."

I didn't bother to tell him I feared that the hunter had not mistaken his target.

Sitting and waiting for word from the doctor, I poured the remainder of the spiked coffee into the thermos lid. I was staring into the lukewarm liquid when I heard a familiar voice.

"How is she?" Dixon sat down in the chair across from me.

"Don't know yet. It didn't seem too serious. But she passed out just as we drove up." I sat the lid down and buried my face in my hands. This morning I would have died rather than let Dixon see me cry, right now, I didn't care. He moved to the chair next to me and put his arm around my shoulder. Thankfully he didn't say anything. That would have made it worse. After I managed to swallow back the tears, he finally spoke. "This was all my fault," he said.

I jerked my head up. "Your fault?"

"I was too quick to make an arrest."

"What do you mean?"

"Muldoon's not our man."

"What?"

Before he could explain, a heavyset man in a white coat walked up.

"Miss Lockhart?" he said.

I stood up. "Yes, how is she?"

"Lucky. Clean shot. If a bullet could fly through a shoulder and miss everything important, it did with Miss Echland. She'll be fine. She should be able to go home after a good night's rest here."

Relief washed over me in such a wave I felt my knees go weak and I swayed. Dixon grabbed me and sat me back in the chair. I looked up at the doctor and drew in a deep breath, "Can I go in to see her, Dr. . . . ."

"Dr. Jansky. She's asleep right now. Maybe I should take a look at you."

"I'm fine. Just exhausted."

"You can go in, but don't stay too long. The anesthesia hasn't completely worn off."

Dixon started to follow. Dr. Jansky stopped him. "Not you. I want Miss Echland to rest."

"I'm Lieutenant Dixon," he pulled out his ID. "I wouldn't disturb her, but it's important I ask her a few questions as soon as she wakes up."

"Five minutes, then," Dr. Jansky said, and then led us to the room.

I don't think I've ever seen Ruth look so small. Her shoulder was swathed in gauze and bandages. I stepped over and picked up her hand. Dixon walked over to the other side of the bed. "She thought she heard someone following us," I said. "I should have listened to her. It all happened so quickly. One moment we were trekking down the trail and a second later Ruth was shot."

Ruth's eyes fluttered. "Francie?" She said.

"No sweetheart, it's Sydney. We're in Hot Springs, remember? How are you feeling?"

She turned her head and opened her eyes. It took her a few moments to focus. "Water."

I raised her head and placed the cup and straw to her lips.

"The doctor says you'll be as good as new in a couple of days."

She moved as if to sit up, so I propped up her pillows. Then she noticed Dixon and smiled. "My hair," she whispered.

"You look wonderful," I said.

"Like a millions bucks," Dixon added. "Feel like talking a little?"

"Sure."

"Remember what happened?" he asked.

She glanced around the room for a few moments and then said, "Syd and I were in the woods. Then I fell. It felt like a horse had kicked me."

"Did you see anyone?" he asked. "Take your time. Just relax and try to remember."

"I thought I'd heard someone behind us . . . footsteps. I stopped a few times to listen, but the sound disappeared. I looked around and didn't see anything."

"And you?" he said to me.

"Nothing until I heard the shot . . . and Ruth's scream. I turned around and saw her fall down the slope. I scrambled after her, just as a second shot buzzed by my head. It was really dark. All I saw was the flash when the gun fired the second time. The guy who gave us a ride to the hospital said it was probably a hunter who had mistaken us for a deer."

"This was no accident. Hunters use shotguns or rifles. Ruth was shot with a small caliber gun, probably a .22."

"Someone tried to kill me?" Ruth said.

"Maybe both of you, or they meant to frighten you and came a bit too close. But we'll find out. Until then I'm posting a guard outside your door."

"But I thought . . . Oh, my," Ruth said and reached for my hand.

"Don't worry, you're safe," Dixon said. "I promise."

Dixon didn't sound convincing enough for me.

"Five minutes are up," Dr. Jansky said as he pushed open the door. "Miss Lockhart, you can stay for a while, but the Lieutenant has to leave. No more questions today."

Dixon stepped out and motioned for me to follow.

"I'll be right back," I said to Ruth. "I want to make sure Dixon knows what the hell he's talking about. You know how cops are." I smiled at Ruth and winked.

As soon as the door closed behind me, I came unglued. "Don't tell me that you let Muldoon out of jail! It's only been a few hours!"

Dixon pulled out his cigarettes. The nurse behind the counter at the nurse's station cleared her throat and frowned so he returned them to his pocket. "We're still talking to Muldoon, but he's not our man."

"Hell, who could it be? Chester Salami's dead, Metzner's dead, and you've still got Muldoon." I didn't realize I was shouting, until I was shushed by the same nurse.

"I can't say. Not now."

"I want some answers!" I hissed. "My cousin's lying in there with a gunshot wound. We both might have been killed."

"Calm down, Miss Lockhart. We're doing what we can."

Dixon's tough-guy facade had returned and I was back to Miss Lockhart. Well, we'll see who's got guts. "Make . . . sure . . . you . . . do." I punctuated every word with a poke of my index finger on his chest. I turned on my heel and went back into Ruth's room. She'd fallen back to sleep for which I was grateful. I knew she'd have more questions and I wasn't up to lying to her.

Chapter 22

Once Officer O'Riley arrived to stand guard outside Ruth's door, I went back to the Arlington to gather a few things so I could spend the night at the hospital. Ruth was physically fine, but I knew she'd be frightened.

I came through the employees' entrance so I wouldn't run into anyone. The story of our adventure had to be all over the hotel, if not the entire city. I grabbed a change of clothes and left. I made one stop before the hospital and was back just as Ruth was waking up. Her color was much improved and the best sign was that she was hungry. I waved a paper bag under her nose and a slow smile spread across her face.

"McClard's?"

"McClard's. Barbecue, beans, potato salad and—"

"Banana pudding?"

"You got it."

I started removing all the hospital things from her tray and sat out the food. "We eat first and then we talk. Two smart Texas women should be able to figure out what's going on, don't you think?"

"Two smart Texas women wouldn't be stupid enough to get shot in the woods."

"Pessimism is not your thing. You must really be hungry."

Ruth ate, but not with her usual aplomb. Neither did I for that matter.

"I should probably call Francie," I said.

"No! If you do, she'll come home. I mean, I don't want to ruin her vacation."

"Ruth, she's your mother."

"That's exactly what I mean."

While Ruth's father was alive, Francie's sole purpose in life was to hover and protect her family. I figured it was her way of keeping things together. Uncle Martin tended to stray and when he did Ruth and Francie huddled like two chickens without their rooster. After his death, things changed quickly as mother and daughter discovered that life after Martin Echland was pretty damned good.

"Mother's finally realized that I can take care of myself and I don't want her to think I can't."

"But Ruth, getting shot wasn't your fault. You can't keep this from her."

"Oh, I don't plan to. I'll give her a call in a couple of days, after I'm out of here. Can't you imagine how she'll react getting an overseas call from a hospital? She doesn't even know I'm in Hot Springs."

"I guess you're right."

"Now, tell me what you and Dixon were shouting and hissing about out in the hall."

"I thought you were asleep."

"I know you did." She smiled.

"Okay. I don't know much. He wouldn't tell me, just that Muldoon's still in custody, but there's reason to believe he's not the one responsible for the killings. You know, the more I think about it, the scarier it gets. I think we're dealing with someone bigger than Metzner."

"Think Muldoon was working for Metzner or whoever is behind this?"

"That's a possibility. He's probably spilling his guts at the police station. They may be keeping him locked up for his own protect—"

We heard voices and then a knock at the door. "Sorry, ma'am," O'Riley said, "but we can't be too careful."

"No harm done, officer."

The door opened as a bunch of yellow and white gladiolas walked in on spiked heels. "Can I come in?" Rita peeked from behind the flowers. "First time I've ever been frisked."

"Rita. How nice of you to come," I said.

"I heard what happened," she said, looking around. Not finding a large enough surface, she sat the flowers on the floor. "How are you Miss Echland?"

"Call me Ruth. I'm fine. Those flowers are beautiful. Thank you. That was sweet."

"They're from the hotel, and speaking of sweet, these are from me." She opened her purse and pulled out a box of assorted Belgian chocolates. "There's a candy store in town that imports these. I knew you'd enjoy them."

Ruth tore open the box with such finesse, I knew she was on the mend. The aroma of sweet confection darted out and headed straight for our noses. Only after scrutinizing each one with a critical eye, and selecting a nugget from the middle of the box, did Ruth offer Rita and me a chocolate. We sat in silence, surrendering the next few moments to our taste buds.

Finally Rita said, "Who needs sex when you have these?" She licked her fingers and came back to earth. "Hey, what's with the guard? I guess the rumor about a nearsighted deer hunter isn't true."

"Evidently not, but we don't know much more than that," I said. "Dixon's sealed his lips."

Rita seemed to contemplate her next words. "If this is connected to the murders, it might take the authorities a long time to get to the bottom of this."

"You're probably right. But I have no intention of hanging around Hot Springs any longer than necessary. Actually, my work here is finished," I said. "I've gotten what I came for." And lost a lot more. My clothes were no big deal, but my parents' marriage license was another story.

"Dixon won't let you go if he thinks someone's trying to kill you."

"Well, he'd better find out and quick. He can't keep us here under guard forever."

"Before you leave the three of us should go out to dinner. Hate to rush off, but I have to be back at work. Mr. Charles sends me out on errands and then gets cranky if I'm not back in what he decides is a reasonable amount of time. Call if you need anything. I'm so glad you're okay, Ruth."

Ruth and I indulged in a few more chocolates after Rita left.

"She's a nice lady," Ruth said.

"She is. She could do better than public relations at the Arlington. I don't think Mr. Charles realizes what a jewel he has."

"Probably does, but he's envious, so he gives her a hard time. Are you serious about going home?"

"Yes, as soon as we can."

"How long had you planned to be here?" Ruth studied a dark chocolate nugget, sniffed it, and put it back.

"A few days."

"I say we stick it out." She picked up the same piece and bit into it. "For no other reason than to satisfy our own curiosity."

"Curiosity killed the cat, you know."

"Don't you think that's an overused cliché?"

Ruth was becoming too smart for her britches. She was also assuming she was my partner in this endeavor. I guess by now, she was.

We'd decided to keep Ruth's "accident" from the family for now. Aunt Francie would be in Europe for at least three more weeks and by the time she returned Ruth's stitches would be out. In fact the story would make a nice telling at Christmas when we gathered in Galveston. A little spiked eggnog after everyone stuffed themselves with turkey, dressing and pecan pie, and the incident might even sound funny. Well, in a slapstick sort of way.

"What's my doctor's name?"

"Jansky."

"When he comes by tonight to check on me, I'm going to insist he release me in the morning."

"Ruth, another day and night in the hospital is a good idea. You don't want to get up and about too soon."

"Nonsense. We have work to do. Lying here won't get us anywhere."

Why was I letting Ruth call the shots? Was it because I felt responsible for her getting shot? After all, she tried to tell me that someone had been following us. I decided to tolerate her bossiness, but I wouldn't allow it to get out of hand.

"Okay," I said. "I'll abide by whatever your doctor says. Right now, I'll let you rest while I go and get my pictures developed. The photographer at the newspaper office will develop them for me. I want to see if my film turned out before I leave Hot Springs. Can I bring you anything?"

"How about a couple of magazines? Vanity Fair and Harper's."

"Right. I'll be back as soon as I can. If you see a nurse, tell her to bring in a cot so I can stay here tonight."

"Right O."

Damn. Either Ruth was still happy from the drugs or escaping death had given her a boost.

I was in the waiting room of the Hot Springs' *Sentinel-Record*, reading the latest edition while waiting for a man by the name of Yancy Summers to fetch my film—fellow newspaper people are more than willing to assist. I was deep into an article about Eisenhower's plan for his first six months in office when the front door of the Sentinel flew open.

"Hurry! Get it upstairs for the morning edition, Larry!"

"We still need to talk to those two broads. I couldn't get past the nurse at the hospital and the other one isn't at the hotel."

"We'll do a follow up later. I want this story in the morning paper, interview or not. Just use what we got from the police record. We haven't had a shooting in a long time. And, Larry, make sure those yoyos get this on the front page."

I slumped down in my chair and hid behind the newspaper. Sounded like Ruth and I would make the headlines. Great, as if we really needed the publicity.

"Miss Lockhart?"

I peeked one eye out from behind my cover to make sure it wasn't Larry or his partner. It wasn't.

I put the paper down and stood up.

"I'm Yancy Summers. Let's go into my lab before the reporters find out you're here." He held a handkerchief over his nose and sneezed.

"Thanks. I'm not in the mood to answer more questions."

Yancy was at least six feet tall and couldn't have weighed more than 140 pounds. He was wearing a photographer's apron and visor and his hands were stained dark.

"How's your cousin, by the way?"

"Off the record?"

"Off the record. I just print the pictures, not the stories."

"She's doing fine. Very lucky."

"Nice to hear it." He sneezed again into his handkerchief and blew his nose. "Damn cold. Happens every year about this time. Must be the sudden drop in temperature.

The chemical fumes in Yancy's darkroom took my breath away. No wonder he was so thin. After having breathed this noxious odor for any length of time, one's insides would surely shrivel up and refuse to function properly. I suspect it didn't do much for Yancy's cold, either.

"I can have these slides for you in the morning. Except for you getting shot, not much has happened, at least not anything worthy of photos. Last week we put out our annual debutante edition. Talk about pictures. If I had to develop one more smiling face dressed in ruffles and lace, I'd puke." Then he colored slightly. "You weren't one of those Texas debutantes, were you?"

"Not me, Yancy. I was paddling a canoe down Lake Austin while those belles were shopping for their gowns. I have a shot of a pileated wood-pecker. If it turns out, could you make an enlargement?"

"No problem." He threw his head back and time froze while the sneeze made up its mind whether or not to materialize. "Ah . . . choo. Sorry. My shift ends at six in the morning. Just come back here to the lab and I'll have your slides in an envelope with your name on it here on my desk. Let me show you out the back way so you don't have to risk running into our reporters."

I thanked Yancy and headed back to the hospital. It was almost dusk and I couldn't believe all that had happened in this one day. This morning Ruth and I faced the day with bodyguards, only to be delighted that they were not necessary, only to meet a bad guy in the woods and then end up with Ruth in the hospital. I naturally thought of my family and realized that a call home was overdue. I decided to call Scott instead of my parents. With any luck, Jeremiah would answer. I found a pay phone in the hospital's waiting room.

"Hello."

I guess I'd used up all my luck for today.

"Scott, how's it going?"

"How's . . . it . . . going? Is that what you asked?"

"Uhhhhh—"

"I was beginning to think that your cat was from some other planet. Food went in but nothing came out. Her litter box was untouched. Then, yesterday morning, I noticed a bad odor in the kitchen. I looked in the pot of my favorite ivy and saw that the soil was lumpy and dirt was scattered all over my just-waxed floor."

"Scott—"

"Then I noticed the plant's leaves were turning yellow. And do you know what I discovered? Mealworm's been using it as a litter box."

"Scott—"

"I'm not finished. This morning I panicked and thought I'd lost my wal-let. Then I noticed another pile of lumpy soil, this one in the backyard. Seems your poodle decided to bury what was left. My twenty-dollar bill must have upset the little girl's tummy, because she threw up all after-noon. But don't worry, Syd, dear. Jeremiah took her to the vet and she is doing just fine. In fact, she and Jeremiah are taking a nap right now. So, how's your vacation? Coming home soon?"

"I'm working. I'll replace your ivy and buy you a new wallet, Scott. I'm so sorry. They must miss me."

"I don't think that's it, Syd. Your pets hate me."

Scott was almost right. Not just my pets, but all pets. Once when we were little, Scott's goldfish, which he kept in the bathroom, jumped from his bowl and escaped down the toilet. Then his guinea pig chewed its way through its box and moved into the backyard pecan tree with the squirrels. Muffy resided there for at least two years. During the fall when the pecans were ripe, Scott couldn't go into the backyard without being pelted with the nuts. Little Muffy would be sitting on a branch with his rodent pals, smirking.

"Tell Jeremiah I'll pay him for the vet bill. I'll take you two out to dinner at the Night Hawk."

"I've got more serious things to worry about than setting a date for dinner."

"Mom."

"Oh, you remembered."

"Dad's keeping me updated."

"I'm sure he is."

"Listen, Scott, what am I suppose to do?"

"Instead of vacationing all over the country you could be here with your family."

"I'm not vaca—"

Click.

Chapter 23

Sleeping on a cot was worse than sleeping on the ground. At least on the ground my pillow wouldn't keep falling down. About two o'clock I gave up and stared at the ceiling and listened to Ruth snore. I thought about my simple life back in Austin—my pets, my little apartment, tapping away at my typewriter, working on my current assignment. Would life ever be normal again? I thought about my crazy family in Texas; my wounded cousin here in the hospital. I closed my eyes and prayed. Why me, Lord, why me? Okay, so it wasn't a real prayer, but I didn't expect an answer anyway.

At three I went to the cafeteria with Ruth's magazines. The nice thing about a hospital is that it never closes, the coffee is always hot, and the younger doctors pull night duty. When I got bored with the magazines, I watched the interns file in and out. Around five the newspapers were delivered. I refreshed my coffee and slid a dime into the newspaper rack.

The next thing I knew, a young doctor was holding my hand asking me if I was okay.

"I'll be right back with something for that burn."

"What?" I said.

"Your hand. You spilled your coffee and burned your hand." He wet a napkin and wrapped it around my fingers. "I'll be right back."

I looked down at the newspaper, now soggy from coffee. Staring back at me was Ruth's smirking face right there on the front page of the *Hot Springs Sentinel Record*. It was the photo I'd taken of her in the park before she was shot. The scarf on her head looked unbelievably ridiculous. Damn Yancy. Wait until I get ahold of him. I hoped to God the wire hadn't picked up the story, otherwise the same photo would end up on the front page of every newspaper in Texas, including the state's oldest newspaper, the *Galveston Daily News*.

I don't know what felt better—the salve or the application thereof.

"Are you accident prone, Miss Lockhart?" the young doctor chuckled.

"I suppose you think it's funny that you know who I am."

"Sorry, but after the day you and your cousin had yesterday, any tall, good-looking redhead will grab attention in Hot Springs." He smiled and nodded at my forehead. "Those stitches look ready to come out. Let's walk over to my office and I'll take care of it right away."

I touched the stitches at my hairline. That frightening incident at the Crooked J seemed eons ago. Considering what's happened here in Arkansas, I think I'd rather tangle with Gerald any day.

On the way to Ruth's room I ran into Dr. Jansky. "Get any rest last night?" he asked.

"Not much. Ruth wants to go home today. You think it's too soon?"

"Let's go find out."

Ruth was sitting up when we walked in.

"How's my patient?" He started removing the bandage.

"Other parts of my body hurt worse than my shoulder," she said.

"Not unusual—bruises from your fall. I'll give you some aspirin. Take two every four hours and don't go on anymore hikes for a couple more days."

"Does that mean I can leave?"

He stuck a thermometer in her mouth. "As soon as I complete the release forms, I'll call Lieutenant Dixon. He told me to inform him when I release you." He turned to me. "Are you two going back to the Arlington?"

"Looks that way," I said. "At least for a few days."

"If she starts feeling worse, for any reason, I want you to call me right away. I'm serious about her doing nothing more than resting in her room." He plucked the thermometer from Ruth's mouth and smiled. "I'll send the nurse in to put on a new dressing."

As Dr. Jansky left the room, a nurse's aide brought in a tray she claimed was Ruth's breakfast. She sat it on the tray stand and removed the metal lid. Ruth sniffed and turned up her nose. "Take that away. I'll just have coffee."

"I have to leave it here. Hospital rules." She huffed and left.

"Set that on the floor before I get sick from the smell."

"You're looking good this morning." And she was too, better than I looked and felt. "Well, you got your wish. I guess lounging in bed in the hotel is better than lounging in bed here. I'm going to the hotel to take a shower. I'll bring you a decent breakfast. By the time I get back, hopefully you'll be ready to leave."

"Sounds good. Is the morning paper here? I want to see if we made the news."

"Uhhh . . ." What exactly did Ruth mean by here? Here, as on this floor? Here, as in this room? "I haven't noticed. It's still early. I'm stopping by the newspaper office to get my slides; I'll pick one up then. Here." I gave her the magazines. "There's an article in *Harper's* on how to marry the man of your dreams and still keep your sanity."

"Hey, what happened to your hand?"

"Cute young doctor, hot coffee, you know the story."

"Does he have a brother?"

"Didn't get that far. Be back later. Don't go anywhere."

"Funny."

I stopped by the nurses' station and asked for the nurse who was to apply Ruth's new dressing.

"Would you do me a big favor?" I asked. "Could you keep my cousin from seeing the morning paper?"

"Sure, Miss Lockhart. Don't worry."

Yancy was true to his word. The envelope was on his desk. There was a note attached. "Slides turned out good. Come back later for the enlargement. I wasn't able to get to it. Damn cold threw me for a loop and I went home early. I should have it ready this evening anytime after seven."

If he hadn't been sneezing yesterday, I could have sworn that he was avoiding me after giving Ruth's picture to the reporters. Before I left, I laid the slides on the light table. He was right. I was turning into quite a photographer. The shots were postcard quality. The racetrack's grandstand glittered under the deep blue sky and the bright colors of Arlington's lobby shone through the smoky haze. Even the raccoons at the Alligator Farm had given me their best profile.

On the way to the hotel, I drove past Bathhouse Row. Ruth and I had missed our three o'clock appointments yesterday at the Buckstaff. I still wanted to include information on the bathhouse for the article, so I parked across the street on Central Avenue and decided to take my chances this

morning without an appointment. Like Ruth, I felt the aftershock of yesterday's tumble. I walked up to the front desk and had barely gotten into
my apology for missing my appointment when the attendant said she
heard about the shooting and if I didn't mind waiting a short while, I
could have my belated massage. She showed me to the dressing room. I
changed out of my clothes and slipped on a bathrobe, then was escorted
to the ladies' waiting room. There were three other women swathed in
white robes. They looked up as I walked in and without any pretense
started whispering. I sat down on a sofa on the other side of the room,
opened a magazine, hid behind its pages, and tried to look small.

After a few minutes, a voice called, "Mrs. Martin?"

"That's me," said a woman who was as tall as she was wide.

Then a few minutes later, "Mrs. Jackson?"

The other woman raised her hand. "Here."

With twenty minutes left before it was my turn, there was only me and
one other woman waiting. I slumped further down into my chair and held
the magazine so close to my face it was impossible to read. Just as I got
the idea to pretend I was dozing, I felt a presence next to me.

"Excuse me."

I looked to my left. The woman had joined me on the sofa.

"I couldn't help but wonder."

"Yes, I'm Sydney Lockhart and my cousin's doing just fine."

"Oh, I'm so glad to hear it. Bless her heart." She put her hand over her
heart to express her relief. "The newspaper said that it was a hunting accident, but no one believes that."

"Why?"

"Well, with all that's been going on at the Arlington the last few days,
we're beginning to wonder."

"Are you from here?"

"I am. I'm Margaret Rochester." She held out her hand.

"Glad to meet you, Mrs. Rochester. It must be nice to be able to visit
the bathhouses whenever you want." I wanted to move the conversation
away from yesterday's incident and the hotel murders.

"Absolutely. I have an appointment here every Wednesday morning
while my husband, Frank, plays golf at the Hot Springs Country Club. He
likes to get in nine holes before work."

"What does your husband do?"

"He's a lawyer involved in public service. You know how that is."

"Sure." I actually didn't.

"We stayed in the Arlington for a couple of weeks while our house was being remodeled. That hotel's one wild place; let me tell you."

"Mrs. Rochester?" the attendant called. She left for her appointment before I could ask about her wild time at the hotel.

Rochester. The name sounded familiar. Frank Rochester. Could that be F. J. Rochester, the attorney general Grady told me about? But the Rochesters wouldn't be living in Hot Springs. They'd be in the capital.

The spa treatment at the Buckstaff lacked the fluff of the Arlington. The massage oil had an antiseptic smell as opposed to the fragrant oils Myra used, but the experience was wonderful nonetheless. I truly envied Margaret Rochester having a standing appointment. I could really get into this lifestyle if it weren't for the murders. Feeling halfway human, I went to pay at the front desk and the clerk handed me a slip of paper. I unfolded it and read, "Miss Lockhart, please call me at TR-3856. Margaret Rochester."

I returned to the hotel, washed my hair, and got dressed. I thought about throwing the paper with Margaret Rochester's number away, but my curiosity got the best of me. She answered on the first ring.

"Mrs. Rochester? This is Miss Lockhart. I got your message."

"Great. How about coming over for coffee . . . make it breakfast? I live in the Trivista neighborhood right before you get to the racetrack."

"That's very nice of you, but I'm sort of tied up here—"

"You might find the visit . . . useful. Hot Springs hasn't treated you too well, and I . . . let's just say that I want to extend some true Arkansas hospitality." She laughed and added. "My lady friends at the garden club would never forgive me if I didn't take the opportunity to leave you with a good impression."

"I'll have to check on my cousin at the hospital first. She's going to be released this morning. If everything goes well, I could meet you around ten."

"Wonderful. My address is 322 Trivista Drive. Take a left off Central. The road curves to the right. My house is the second one on the left, red brick with white columns.

As much as I hate garden club and socialites, Margaret Rochester was right, my perspective on Hot Springs was somewhat skewed. However, I had a feeling that the invitation was more than an innocent social call.

•

Ruth was sitting on the edge of the bed dressed in yesterday's hiking clothes. "Where the hell have you been? I'm ready to blow this place."

"Glad you're feeling perky."

"It's not that. I want to get back to the hotel and change into some decent clothes."

"You'll change into your PJs. Bed rest, remember."

"Phooey. Where's my breakfast?"

"Forgot. We'll order room service when we get back. Has Dr. Jansky finished the paper work?"

"I'm cleared to leave. I can't believe you forgot about feeding me."

"Feeding you? What am I? You're handler?"

She stuck out her pouting lip.

"Sorry. How about Dixon?"

"He wants the policeman outside to stick to us. We're under orders to stay put in the hotel again."

"Good idea." I'd have to get my brain working and figure out a plan to get Ruth back to the hotel and keep my appointment with Margaret Rochester. I looked at my watch. It was nine o'clock. Surely, I'd think of something. Having a cop accompany me to the Rochester house wouldn't be very sociable, even if she were the AG's wife.

"What?"

"What what?" I asked.

"You've got something up your sleeve. I can tell. Your eyes are darting around and you're looking everywhere but at me."

Ruth and I had definitely spent too much time together these last few days.

"Let's go."

Officer Bud O'Riley followed us out of the hospital and back to the hotel. He walked us to our rooms and planted himself outside.

I ordered breakfast for one. "Ruth, I didn't sleep much last night and I'm not hungry. I'm going to go to my room and try and catch some Zzzzs."

She squinted at me. It was her way of telling me she suspected I was up to something. I didn't give her a chance to ask any questions. I walked into my room and closed the door. I picked up the phone and luckily the cord was long enough for me to drag it into the closet so I could make my call without being heard just in case Ruth was listening. I called the Venetian Room and asked if Mickey Saunders was working. He was, but today, I was told, he was wearing his bellboy hat. I then called down to the front desk and was relieved when Mrs. Willis did not answer. I asked for Mickey and after a couple of minutes he answered. I told him my plan and it worked like a charm.

Chapter 24

The Trivista neighborhood was ancient and wealthy. The maple trees that lined the streets must have sprouted before the Civil War and the colonial mansions were sprawling and opulent, definitely old money.

Margaret Rochester's house was gorgeous. The entrance was bigger than my apartment. Artwork covered the walls and a grandfather clock older than our country chimed ten. The maid allowed me to gawk for a few minutes and then brought me to the conservatory where I waited for my hostess. The giant sunroom was filled with so many varieties of plants, I felt like I was in a botanical garden. A tree-size schefflera filled one corner. Pots of leafy philodendrons lined the opposite wall. A series of glass shelves contained dozens of blooming orchids.

The maid brought in a tray with a silver coffee service and a plate of butter cookies. I hoped this wasn't the breakfast Margaret had promised. My stomach let out a rumble that sounded like an airplane on takeoff.

"Help yourself, ma'am. Mrs. Rochester will be down in a moment. Breakfast will be served shortly." She raised her eyebrows as if hearing my body noises was just too offensive. She left and I shoved two cookies in my mouth. I fixed myself a cup of coffee and wandered around the conservatory. I was gazing at a white orchid that looked so delicate I was afraid it would disintegrate if I breathed on it when I heard a voice behind me.

"It took me years to develop a white one," Mrs. Rochester said. "Isn't it lovely?"

I washed my cookies down with a gulp of coffee and wiped the crumbs from my mouth. I turned around and at first didn't recognize Margaret Rochester. Last time I saw her, her hair was pinned up and she was wearing a bathrobe. Now she was decked out in a red Chanel suit, red pumps, a string of pearls and matching earrings. I was glad I had chosen to wear my new navy skirt and white Victorian blouse instead of slacks and a sweater. I still felt underdressed.

"It's beautiful. So, you're the one with a green thumb?" I couldn't imagine the woman ever getting her well-manicured nails in a pot of dirt.

"Just the orchids. Growing them is my hobby."

Had this room been on the roof, I would have felt like I was in Nero Wolf's nursery. Suddenly I wanted a beer.

"You must be hungry." She looked down at the plate of cookies. "Good. I thought we'd have breakfast in here. It's such a beautiful day."

Near the schefflera was a small table covered with a white cloth and set with Wedgwood china. Mrs. Rochester brought over the coffee service and we sat down. She refilled my coffee cup and poured one for herself.

"Is your cousin back at the hotel? I wish she could have joined us, but I'm sure she's still recovering."

Just then the maid walked in and whispered something in her employer's ear. "Excuse me, Miss Lockhart. I have a phone call that can't wait. I'll be right back." She picked up the plate. "Have another cookie. Alma, bring a fresh pot of coffee." She left the room.

I opened the French doors and stepped out into the garden, which sloped down to a small pond at the end of the property. An old black man, stooped and slow moving, clipped at some already manicured Burford hollies. He looked over and I waved. He nodded and went back to his work. Living in an apartment seemed too stifling all of a sudden. Mealworm and Monroe would love a backyard like this—hummingbirds swarming the crepe myrtles, shade from large Spanish Oaks; soft, thick grass that felt like a deep, lush carpet—instead they had a small patio bricked over except for a swath of grass that was almost the size of Monroe when she stretched out for her nap. No matter how many articles I wrote, I'd never be able to afford a place like this. My thoughts turned to my single status. A status I enjoyed, most of the time.

I heard Mrs. Rochester laughing as she joined me. "I hope you don't mind. Someone will be joining us for breakfast."

"A friend of yours?"

"Not yet. Although I did have a delightful conversation over the phone with her just now."

"Oh?" Suddenly I felt the cookies drop to the bottom of my stomach like a lead ball.

"Your cousin Ruth. Her police escort is delivering her as we speak."

"Damn," I said.

Mrs. Rochester chortled. "You left my phone number and address on the desk in your room."

"Damn," I said again.

"Don't worry, I'm glad she's coming. Come on. I'll show you Franklin and Eleanor."

"Who?"

"Two turtles that live in the pond."

I was getting tired of small talk. I wanted to know why this woman invited me here. It was probably nothing more than curiosity about the two women who blew into town right before four people were murdered. Curiosity—that cat-killing fiend. I don't care what Ruth says about the expression being a cliché, cats have nine lives; I don't.

"Mrs. Rochester, it was very nice of you to invite me here. But—"

"But why?" she said. "My husband, Frank, is the attorney general."

"I recognized the name, but I thought the attorney general would live in Little Rock."

"Frank has an apartment there. When he had the opportunity to take over as attorney general—the man who was in office was convicted of fraud—there was no question as to where we'd live. This place is my family home." The pride showed in her straightened posture.

"Your garden is lovely," I said, hoping my sincerity overshadowed my envy.

"It was a mess when we moved in. After my mother died, my dad let the place go. Frank and I moved in to take care of Dad and to spiff things up. It took me forever to find a decent gardener. You know how that is."

"Decent gardeners are a thing of the past." What the hell was I saying? I wouldn't know a decent gardener if he walked up and bit me on my ass.

"The boy I have now does an acceptable job, when he's not napping."

"Boy? You mean that old man I saw clipping the hedges. He's hardly a boy."

"He's colored. What do you expect me to call him? Mr. Jones?"

"Only if that's his name."

Mrs. Rochester pinched off a dead rose blossom. She either didn't hear my comment or simply ignored any further discussion of her insignificant gardener. Prejudice is still rampant in the South, but its ugliness never fails to astonish me. I was about to thank her for inviting me, use the excuse that I felt a migraine coming on, and get the hell out of here.

"Helloooooo!"

Mrs. Rochester and I looked up and standing in the doorway of the conservatory was my cousin—dressed in her blue and yellow circus-tent outfit, wearing a matching hat made of straw flowers, waving her yellow gloved hand like Miss America on some charity mission.

"Ruth?" Mrs. Rochester asked me.

"Ruth. We'd better go before she comes outside and one of the hummingbirds tries to nest in her hat."

I made the introduction and we sat down at the table. Alma added another place setting and moments later we were dining on Eggs Florentine, crustless toast, and strawberries and cream. The sun was shining into the room, warming it up. Mrs. Rochester picked up a small silver bell and tinkled it. Alma appeared instantly and was told to turn on the ceiling fan. The switch was just an arm's reach away and had I known what my hostess was ringing for I would have saved Alma the trouble. I felt bile rising in my throat.

"You look a bit flushed, Miss Echland," Mrs. Rochester said. "This room get rather warm in the late morning sun."

I looked over and sure enough Ruth was red in the face and the cheeriness of a few moments ago had vanished.

"Are you okay?" I asked. "Maybe you should have stayed in bed."

"Nonsense," she said. Her voice sounded weak and unconvincing. I knew she was fading and I needed to get her back to bed. Enough of this tea-party facade.

"Mrs. Rochester—"

"Right. It's time we got down to business. We may be able to help one another."

"How?" I said.

"My husband took this job by promising to rid Arkansas of gangsters, which he did, and quickly. Frank's a brilliant man. Anyway, it was understood that if he failed . . . was unsuccessful, he . . . wouldn't run in the next election." She looked at Ruth, then back to me as if to make sure we understood the direction in which the conversation was going. Then added, "This situation is very important to my husband's career."

I looked at Ruth and noticed her jaw was clenched. It was obvious she was in pain.

"And now with these recent . . . unfortunate events—"

"His neck's on the chopping block," I said.

"Well, something like that."

"Where do we come in?"

"Oh, for heaven's sakes!" She threw her napkin down on her plate and stood up. She walked over to a credenza, pulled open a drawer, and dug around in the back until she found a gold cigarette case. "Miss Lockhart, may I call you Sydney?" She stuck a cigarette in her mouth and continued to root around in the drawer. "Frank hides my cigarettes. He doesn't like me smoking."

"Syd, sure. Here, use my lighter."

"Thank you. Call me Margaret. Look around this place."

"Very impressive," I said. I glanced at Ruth and her flushed face was now turning white.

"No shit!" Margaret's profanity caused Ruth and me to jump. "Coming back here to live in my family home was a dream come true. I don't want to move, or leave my father. The longevity of an AG is short. Do a good job and you're a hero. One little, bitty thing goes wrong and your head's on the chopping block." She took a long draw on her cigarette.

"I don't consider four murders in less than a week a little bitty thing."

"I like you, Syd." She blew a smoke ring. "You speak your mind. More women should do that."

"I still don't see how I can help you," I said.

"I've kept up with everything that's been happening since you've arrived. This case is all Frank talks about. You're smart. You notice things. You're right there in the thick of things in that hotel. I want your help solving these murders now. I lived in that hotel for two weeks. There's something fishy going on there. You can find out what it is."

Ruth picked up her napkin and started fanning herself.

"Lieutenant Dixon—"

"The Hot Springs Police Department is incompetent when it comes to dealing with the big guys."

"Big guys as in organized crime?"

"That's right. Frank's doing all he can, but . . ." She took another drag and slowly blew out a stream of smoke. "But his term is up and if he doesn't wrap up this case before the next election, he'll be out of office."

A loud crash sounded. Margaret and I looked around to find Ruth on the floor.

Chapter 25

On the way back to the hotel, Ruth and I rode in O'Riley's squad car (another officer followed in my rental car) and listened to him plead with me to never sneak out of my room again. His concern for Ruth's welfare worked to my advantage; otherwise, I'd have been in much worse trouble. Mickey had expertly delivered the officer a message—my message—that Dixon wanted to speak to him pronto. O'Riley followed Mickey down to the third floor offices to take the Lieutenant's call. But when he picked up the phone, the line was dead and Mickey was gone.

"I knew something was fishy," O'Riley said. "So I rushed back to your room and Miss Echland was standing in the hall shouting for me to hurry up. If Dixon finds out that you got away from me, he'll make sure I'm demoted back down to beat cop, Miss Lockhart."

"Sorry," I said. "We just won't tell him." I liked Officer O'Riley. He was a nice man. I promised him I'd be good. Then I reminded myself that I shouldn't make promises unless I knew I could keep them.

"I don't understand. I felt great this morning."

"Drink your orange juice. You were still feeling the effects of those drugs. I told you to stay in bed. You were shot less than twenty-four hours ago. I should take you back to the hospital."

"You shouldn't have lied to me, Syd!" Tears started sliding down her face. "You shouldn't have. We're a team. And look at this!" She plucked up the newspaper and slapped it down on the bed. "How did they get this picture?"

"Sorry, Ruth. I didn't give it to them, honest."

"Honest! I'll never trust you again."

"Please don't cry. Listen, things just happened fast this morning. I wanted to find out what Margaret Rochester had to say. I knew you'd want to come along. I was only thinking of your wellbeing. If you stop crying, I promise I won't lie to you again. And if you promise to stay in bed, I'll let you wear my monkey socks."

"Oh, please! I'd rather be shot in the shoulder and left in the woods for dead."

"Or kidnapped by a man who smells like salami," I added.

"Or have my hair done in that blue-haired salon on the mezzanine."

We burst out laughing.

"Or have to wear dungarees and flannel."

"My . . . shoulder," Ruth said and leaned over in bed. "It hurts when I . . . laugh. Stop . . . it!"

That made the situation worse. I rushed to the bathroom to keep from peeing in my pants. I was straightening out my garter belt when someone knocked. This primping procedure couldn't be hurried. Before I could finish, a second knock sounded even louder. "Hold your horses!" Still in a laughing mood, I added, "I'm straightening my seams!"

I threw open the door and Dixon stood there smirking. I turned and walked over to the sofa and sat down. I waited for another lecture. Dixon removed his hat and addressed Ruth first.

"I hope you've learned your lesson, young lady."

"I sure have. I know not to wait until 10:30 for breakfast."

Ruth and I started giggling again.

Dixon stood there with his hands on his hips. "Pull yourselves together, I have a lot to say."

"Okay," I said. I drew in a deep breath. "We're listening. Shoot."

I looked over at Ruth and we tried hard to keep it down, but the snickers turned back into hoots and we lost it.

"You two women are insane. Get serious." Then he turned his attention to me. "If you pull another stunt like that, I'm throwing you in jail."

Suddenly my humorous mood turned to concern—concern for Officer O'Riley. "Please don't blame O'Riley. How did you find out?"

"He told me. He's a good cop. Honesty is the best policy, in case you haven't heard."

"That's what I told her," Ruth said.

"Whose side are you on?" I said. "Besides, didn't I tell you to stay in Dallas? Didn't I?!"

"Don't shout at me!"

I guess it's true what they say about emotions swinging like a pendulum during a crisis. Ruth and I went from feeling anxious to amused to angry. Dixon pitched his hat on the bed and called for room service to bring up coffee. "Why didn't I become a Methodist preacher like my mother wanted?" he said.

He made us rehash everything since I arrived last Saturday. He read through his notes, asked some of the same questions, a few new ones, and beat the information to death.

"We've been over this before," Ruth said.

"There may have been something you forgot." He paused, scrutinizing his notes, then said. "Why were you at the Rochester's house this morning?"

"I don't have to tell you everything, hon," I said.

He raised his eyebrows and the warning look he gave me was enough to intimidate a rock.

"Okay, I met her at the Buckstaff and she invited us . . . me over for coffee."

"Just like that? Two ladies having coffee?"

"Well, there was an ulterior motive."

"I'll bet! That woman can't keep her nose out of her husband's business anymore than you can keep yours out of mine."

Ruth squeaked.

I bit my lips.

Color rose past Dixon's collar and up to his hairline.

Visions of my children, I mean pets, Mealworm and Monroe, romping in a gardenlike backyard flashed before my eyes. Dixon and I were sitting in the sunroom having breakfast. I was scribbling notes for my future bestseller, Dixon was hidden behind his newspaper. Of course our pond turtles would be named something less haute than Franklin and Eleanor, maybe Fred and Ethel. He put the paper down and asked what my plans were for the day. I told him that I'd made arrangements for the turtle pond to be cleaned out and the crepe myrtles to be pruned. I complain about the incompetence of our gardener. He said that if he wasn't too busy, we'd meet for lunch at the country club, otherwise, I'd see him after work. We'd have cocktails by the fireplace while the cook prepared prime rib for dinner. Finally, he got ready to leave, kissed my cheek, and told me to enjoy my day. I shook these lunatic daydreams from my head, and refrained from slapping my own face.

"What exactly did she want?" Dixon finally spoke.

"To show off her turtles. Never mind." I gave a dismissive wave. "She's afraid Frankie will lose the election if you and your boys don't drop the net on this case."

"And she has more confidence in your ability to solve these murders?"

"Woman's intuition," Ruth said.

"Look where your intuition has gotten you two. I hope you told Mrs. Rochester to take a hike."

"I didn't have time to tell her anything. Ruth fainted."

"It was way too hot in that sunroom," Ruth said in her own defense.

"I've put two officers outside these doors, O'Riley and his partner, Stockton. The only way you'll be able to sneak out is through the window, ten floors down."

"Actually, it's only two floors down," I said. "The eighth floor wing extends out below us."

Dixon looked out the window. "Even you wouldn't be that foolish. I gotta get going."

"Hey, wait. You said you would give us the latest. Did you find out anything from Donna Jennings?"

"Not a single word; the girl's clammed up tighter than an oyster."

He grabbed his hat.

"You haven't told us anything new."

"Here's something for you," Dixon smiled. I looked for the dimple; it wasn't there. "A man named Henry Irving is coming this afternoon to interview you. Don't be difficult. Tell him whatever he wants to know."

"Who's he?"

"He's with the FBI." He turned and walked to the door.

"That's it. That's all you're telling us." I followed after him.

"It's the Fed's investigation now. Can't say more. Just stay put."

"For how long?"

"After Irving gets his information, then we'll talk. If it were up to me, I'd send you two hightailing it back to Texas. Hey, your left one's crooked."

"Uh?"

"Your left seam, it's crooked. Shame on you."

"Aren't you staying for coffee?"

"No longer in the mood for coffee. It's rather warm in here." He grabbed his hat and left.

"I think he likes you," Ruth said.

"He just gets a kick out of annoying me."

"Same thing. Do you like him?"

"No."

"Yeah, I can tell."

It's a good thing Ruth didn't indulge in sarcasm too often; when she did, she was good at it.

"While we're sequestered in these rooms, waiting for the FBI guy, I might as well type my article."

"I'm going to sleep."

"One of your better ideas."

"Wake me in time for dinner."

I called Rita and asked if I could borrow a typewriter, then laid out my notes on the desk. I'd covered everything: the hotel, the bathhouses, Oaklawn Racetrack, the National Park hiking trails, sites around the city, a bit of history. Putting it all together would be easy.

One of the officers knocked on my door. "Miss Lockhart, Miss Fredrick is here."

"Come in."

Rita walked in pushing a small table on wheels on which sat a Smith Corona. Behind her was a waiter with the coffee. "You must hate being stuck here in your room," Rita said.

"I do, but considering what happens whenever I leave, I think being here may be a good thing."

"I'm on my lunch hour. Want some company?"

"Sure. I'll order something from room service?"

"Just coffee. I'm trying to lose a few pounds."

"You? You look great."

"Thanks, but it gets harder every year. I had to decide to give up lunch or afternoon cocktails. Easy decision. How's Ruth?"

"After this morning, I think she's finally realized that bed rest is the order of the day."

"This morning?"

"We were having breakfast with Margaret Rochester when Ruth fainted."

"Margaret Rochester? The attorney general's wife?"

"That's the one. I met her at the Buckstaff early this morning. She invited me over. You wouldn't believe what she wanted."

"Oh, I can guess. She thinks everything that happens in Hot Springs is her business. Just because her family has roots that go back to when Arkansas belonged to the Indians, she thinks she owns this town, hell, this entire state."

"She's worried about her husband's upcoming election."

"Not surprised."

There was another knock on my door. "That must be Henry Irving."

"Who?"

"An investigator with the FBI. Dixon said he was coming around to ask questions. Seems this case has crossed state boundaries."

Rita stood up. "Good luck. Keep the typewriter as long as you need it." She brushed past my visitor as he walked in. I turned around to push my typewriter out of the way and give us some room.

"Miss Lockhart."

The blood froze in my veins. That voice was hard to forget. I turned around and there he was, smiling with the stogy stuck in the corner of his mouth.

"Officer O'Riley! Officer O'Riley! I picked up a vase and held it over my head. "How did you get in here?!" "Don't come any closer."

Muldoon sauntered in, sat down on my sofa, and flicked an ash in my ashtray.

Officer O'Riley rushed in. "What is it, Miss Lockhart?"

"What is it?!" I pointed to Muldoon.

"Mr. Irving? I thought Lieutenant Dixon told you he was coming.

Chapter 26

I waited for Muldoon to stop laughing. I thought he was going to choke on his cigar, which would have been fine with me. While he pulled himself together, I started pulling my thoughts together. Of course, now it made sense. How could I have missed seeing it? He showed up the day after the first murder and had been nosy around ever since.

"I hope you don't mind if I ask to see your identification. Not that I don't trust you, but I don't trust you, or anybody in Hot Springs for that matter."

"You're one tough gal." He reached in his jacket pocket and produced his ID. "We've been on this case for months. My job is to keep tabs on this hotel. You made that hard to do."

I studied his identification and gave it back, along with the ashtray. "That thing smells horrible. Do you mind?"

"No, ma'am." He stubbed out his cigar. "Anyway, things were going well until you sneaked into my room and started snooping around. Next thing I know, that crazy guy Dixon slaps the cuffs on me and hauls me down to the station. It took awhile to prove I worked for the Feds."

"Sitting in jail wasn't as nice as sitting in the mineral pool, was it? Hey . . . you were the one who mentioned Metzner in the first place. You're the reason Ruth and I were abducted."

"That was unfortunate, but I needed to find out for sure."

"Find out what?"

"That you weren't the one."

"You thought I was behind the mess?"

"Two people were murdered within hours of your arrival."

"You could've gotten Ruth and me killed."

"I didn't think you'd do something as stupid as drop Metzner's name all over the Arlington. Besides, Metzner was small potatoes. That's why I wasn't worried about you two being led away from the hotel in blindfolds." Muldoon, I mean Irving, had the nerve to laugh.

"Small potatoes? Chester Salami dumped my ass in a root cellar and then came back and tried to kill me!"

"His name was Chester Morani. And you're still alive, aren't you?"

"And what about my room then? And my clothes and my earring?"

"What about 'em?"

I knew Irving wasn't as thick as he sounded. "When I was abducted the second time, I figured it was because they were looking for something in my room. Since you had my earring, you were in here, too."

"Whatever they were looking for they most likely found. After they left, I checked your room out. Nothing, except your earring in the hall. They must have dropped it. I took it for a little souvenir. The little kid must have found the other one. There was a trail of your things strewn down the stairs and out the seventh floor exit."

"I should hang a sign outside on the door: Public Welcome."

"Listen, Red." He pointed his fat finger in my face. "If I hadn't been arrested, your cousin probably wouldn't have gotten shot. So cut the tough-girl talk and hear me out. There's an organized-crime ring that's come to Hot Springs from the big city."

"Big city?"

"New York City. They've been spreading across the country like a slow growing fungus. Set up here a few months back. I'm trying to find out who's running the operation here in town."

"Why Hot Springs?"

"Why not? You can lop the head off of a weed, but if you don't pull up the roots, the weed starts growing again. Rochester didn't go deep enough and now we're having to do his job for him."

"So what do you want from me?"

"Just answers. From you and your cousin." He looked around.

"She's asleep."

"I can come back. But you'll do for now."

Irving grilled me, asking more of the same questions as Dixon had. What did I see? What did I hear? What did I know? My only question was "Why me?" All I did was check into this hotel. Not fifteen minutes later I found a dead body, only to find another the next morning. Things went downhill from there.

"Syd?" Ruth called from her room.

"My cousin. Excuse me." I went into Ruth's room and she looked almost as bad as yesterday morning after she was shot. I placed my hand on her forehead and was relieved to feel her cool skin.

"I feel like shit," she said.

"No wonder." I gave her two aspirin. "That's what happens when you don't listen to your doctor."

"Who were you talking to?"

"Nobody."

"You promised you wouldn't lie—"

"Okay, sorry. I just wanted a few minutes to prepare you—"

Ruth gasped, pointed to the adjoining door, then pulled the bedspread over her head.

"—for a new development. Meet Mr. Irving with the FBI."

"But that's Muldoon," Ruth cried from under the covers.

"His real name's Irving. He's undercover."

"Can you answer a few questions, Miss Echland?"

"She's not feeling well. Can't you come back?"

"I'm okay," Ruth said, peeking out with one eye.

Irving's questions centered on what Ruth heard and saw the night I was taken from my room. Her answers: "Nothing." Then he focused on what Ruth heard and saw when we were in the woods hiking. Her answer: "Except for footsteps, nothing."

He sat and stared at her for several minutes. She stared back. Before coming to Hot Springs the intimidation tactic would have worked, but Ruth had become pretty tough in the past few days. She won the staring contest and Irving left after telling us to contact him by way of Dixon.

"I'm going back to sleep," she said. "I don't want to think about any of this."

"Good idea. Call me if you need anything."

"Forget dinner. Wake me up in time for cocktail hour."

"Will do."

It was hard to believe it was only two o'clock. I finished my article and was getting antsy. I looked out the window at another beautiful day. People were on the great lawn pitching baseballs to their kids and throwing sticks to their dogs. I thought seriously about tying my bed sheets together and lowering myself down to the roof of the eighth floor like I'd told Dixon earlier. Then what would I do? The doors to the inside were probably locked and I'd be stuck on the roof forced to spend the afternoon with the pigeons. Actually that sounded better than wasting away my time up here, waiting for Ruth to wake up, waiting for cocktail hour to begin, waiting for—

Whack! Whack! Whack!

—another knock on my door. How could I complain about being bored? This room saw more traffic than the lobby bar when the Intones played. At least with a guard outside all I had to do was yell, "Come in!"

Dixon did, and made himself at home again. He fluffed up a throw pillow and sat down on the sofa.

I stayed put by the window, arms folded across my chest, daggers shooting from my eyes.

"You're cute when you pout."

"I'd offer you a bourbon, but Ruth and I finished it off."

"That's not very sociable."

"What do you want?"

For a moment he just stared. "To see how you held up with Irving."

"Well, what do you think?" I held out my arms and did a half-twirl. "How do I look? No whelps, bruises, or abrasions."

He smiled.

"Why didn't you tell me about Muldoon?"

Dixon stood and sauntered up to me. I thought he was going to cuff my chin. Instead, he cupped my face in his hands, leaned close, and gave me a kiss. Butterflies, which had been hibernating in my stomach for so long I'd thought they'd turned to stone, awoke. "I don't have to tell you everything . . . hon." He turned and walked out.

Chapter 27

Natural disaster. That's the only way to describe what happened. At first I felt like I'd been caught in a volcanic eruption, my blood seemed to boil and heat spewed up to my head like an Alka Seltzer fizz. I rushed to the mirror, certain that my hair had turned a deeper shade of red and that my ears were smoking. Then as quickly as the volcanic sensation had started, it disappeared, only to be replaced by the swirl of a Gulf Coast-style hurricane. My head wouldn't stop spinning. My insides were cold and my skin was hot and clammy. Even though the temperature outside was in the forties, I threw open the window. When that didn't help, I called room service. To hell with waiting for cocktail hour. This was not an ordinary afternoon. I needed a drink. Now.

I was stirring a pitcher of martinis when I heard Ruth. She must have smelled the gin.

"What time is it?" She called from her room.

"Almost four." I stood in the doorway, sipping my liquid tranquilizer decorated with a double olive condiment.

"What's up? You look . . . red. Not just your hair, your face, and . . . your eyes."

Although I'd promised I wouldn't lie to Ruth again, these were special circumstances. So I just twisted the truth.

"It must have been Muldoon, I mean Irving. Sorry, I couldn't wait. Want one?" I held up my glass.

"Sure. Just a light one, though."

How do you make a light martini? Add extra vermouth? Splash in some olive juice? I handed her mine and went back in the room for another glass.

"I thought I heard Dixon a while ago."

"He came in to gloat. Thought it was real funny that he didn't tell me about Irving's double life."

"That was pissy of him."

"Feeling better, now?" I said.

"Much. You know, Syd, I know we're booked here until Saturday. But do we really need to stay that long? You've gotten everything you need for your article. The case is pretty much solved."

Except for the "we" this and the "we" that, Ruth was right, again. But it wasn't the murder and who committed it that was keeping me around. As absurd as it sounded I wanted my parents' wedding picture. And come hell or high water I was going to get it. But I knew if I disagreed with her, she'd needle me until she got her way. So, I decided to try a little child psychology.

"You're right. You should get home as soon as possible. You'd recover much faster in your own bed. I have a few more things to do and Rita wants to go to dinner one night before we leave. I could arrange for a ambulance to take you back to Dallas."

"But I can't leave you, Syd."

"With you laid up, you wouldn't be able to help much."

"Moral support. Besides, I think the best thing to do is for me to lay right here. A ten-hour road trip might be too stressful. I'll be good as new in a couple of days. Read me your article."

We managed to kill another two hours, discussing the article, talking, drinking, and just being girls.

Having exhausted all benign topics, Ruth finally said, "Imagine Margaret Rochester wanting us to solve this case so her husband would win his election. That was pretty brazen."

I didn't want to talk about the case, not about Margaret, or Muldoon/Irving, or Metzner, or shootings, or kidnappings, or romps in the woods with the Smalls. I just wanted to be back in my apartment curled up on my sofa with my cat and poodle. I wanted my simple uncomplicated life. I was beginning to wonder if I'd ever have that again.

"You okay?" Ruth asked.

"I'm fine." One lie usually leads to another. I figured what the hell. I needed to keep my mind busy so I wouldn't start daydreaming about turtle ponds and country clubs. "Margaret said a lot of strange things went on here. I think she knows something, but for some reason isn't saying."

"Why would she keep quiet with so much at stake?"

"Good question. But here's a good answer. She doesn't want it to get out that she blew the whistle on someone, doesn't want to get involved. Bad press."

"Makes sense." Ruth held out her empty glass. I refilled both hers and mine.

"But she didn't tell us much."

"That was because you fainted just as she was getting warmed up."

"We could always invite her over."

If I wasn't so bored out of my mind, I would have ix-nayed that idea.

At six fifteen Margaret was sitting with us in our hotel room turned-cell, and the second pitcher of martinis was getting low.

"I'm so glad you called. I really felt bad about this morning, Ruth. You were seated in the sun. I should have known better. I'm really sorry."

"It's my fault, Margaret" Ruth said. "I should have stayed in bed. I'm the one who's sorry."

"Well, I'm glad you came. Having you both at my house was delightful."

Holy shit! I felt like pulling out my hair. I didn't want this visit to be a social call.

"Listen!"

They jerked around and stared at me as if I'd just created the biggest faux pas of the year.

"Let's get down to business," I said. "In three days Ruth and I are checking out and when we leave here, I want to leave this murder mess behind. I don't want the FBI or Hot Springs Police Department pestering me when I get home."

"That's easy to say, Syd," Margaret said.

"What do you mean?"

"If it's the mafia, do you honestly think going back to Texas will end this for you?"

"Oh, Lord." My stomach did back flips for the second time today. The first situation was much more pleasurable.

"You think we could really get to the bottom of this in three days?" I said.

"You can try," Margaret said.

"What've we got to lose?" Ruth chirped.

"How about our heads? Margaret, you said something about the people in the hotel being strange."

"If Frank finds out I'm talking to you about this case he'll skin me alive."

"I protect my sources. You don't have to worry about that."

"I'm sure you can understand my hesitation. I have to be careful. When Frank and I were staying here, I overheard talk. You wouldn't believe what went on. We were staying on the eleventh floor and every day after lunch I heard that maid, the one who dressed like she worked in a brothel and had the morals of a rabbit, giggling in the linen closet. And believe me that bimbo wasn't reading the funny papers."

"Elsa Dubois, the girl who was murdered?" I said.

"She's the one," Margaret said. "I hate to speak bad about the dead, but she spent more time on the linens than she did changing them."

"Who was she fooling around with?" Ruth asked.

"Who cares? Miss Dubois' affairs aren't what's important here," Margaret said. "I also heard talk about a new boss in town who is come to resurrect the gambling scene. And that new boss is supposed to be working out of this hotel. You find out who that boss is and you can go back to Texas a free woman and Frank gets reelected."

"That's a pretty tall order," I said.

"You're up to it."

"What makes you so sure?"

"You've been here less than a week and—"

"I understand. But who exactly did you overhear?"

Margaret waved a hand at my question as if it were inconsequential. "Oh, you know, maids, waiters, masseuses, those people who scurry around here acting like they're busy. I didn't pay any attention to who was saying what, I just heard what was being said. You know, when you're married to a high-profile law- enforcement agent, you pay attention."

Pay attention, but not to those people who are unimportant, like the bimbo Elsa Dubois who'd had her throat slit because she's taken up with the wrong guy. Margaret Rochester, social niceties aside, was a bit too highbrow for my taste. I thought of Grady, Donna, Myra, Mrs. Lindstrom, Mickey and even sourpuss Mrs. Willis at the front desk. How many people did they encounter everyday, who took their services for granted, giving them a tip without so much as a 'thank you?' I looked at Ruth. The expression on her face seemed to convey my sentiments. Ruth could be as shallow as a puddle, but her heart was always in the right place. Right now, her lip was beginning to curl with indignation as Margaret contin-

ued with her banal assessment of the goings on here at the hotel. I wondered if she ever considered the fact that those people voted.

My thoughts wandered back to this morning. What the hell was I thinking; naming pond turtles Fred and Ethel and worrying about an incompetent gardener pruning the crepe myrtles? Hell, if I had crepe myrtles, I'd
prune them myself, or make my husband do it. Big, beautiful house or
not, living Margaret Rochester's life would choke the life out of me.

"Sydney, are you okay?" Ruth asked. "You look a bit odd."

I brought myself back to reality. Margaret and Ruth were staring at me
as if I'd lost my mind. "I'm fine. I was giving serious thought as to what
Margaret was saying." I was really giving serious thought about telling
Mrs. AG's wife to take a hike like Dixon suggested. But her story about
a boss coming to town confirmed Muldoon's, I mean Irving's, information.

"Margaret, you haven't told me anything I don't already know. If
there's something specific you found out, spit it out."

If Margaret was offended by my abruptness, she covered it well. She
stood up and walked around the room, her face twisted in contemplation.
She swirled the gin in her martini glass. "Okay, here it is. When I was
planning Frank's celebration ball, that PR woman and I—"

"Rita Fredricks?"

"That's her. We were walking through the ballroom discussing decora-
tions and menu items, those sorts of things. That manager was with us."

"Mr. Charles?"

"Right. Greasy-looking guy. Anyway, he was more annoying than helpful. We finalized everything and the PR woman—"

"Rita."

"Right, Rita told me I could come to her office the next day. She'd have
the plans typed up for me and have a price for the entire event. Not that
money was a concern, mind you. Anyway, I went to her office the next
day. The office secretary was there." Margaret paused, looked at me to
indicate I was to feed her the woman's name.

"Miss Roberts."

"Right. Miss Roberts. Rita had been called out of town at the last
minute. So, this Miss Roberts person gives me the file. Rita was nice
enough to get it ready before she left. I sat down and read through it. You
have to watch these people, you know. Pad the bill if they think they can
get away with it."

I wanted to remind Margaret about money not being an issue, but I let it drop.

"Anyway, Miss Roberts left for lunch. While I was adding up the figures, I heard a door slam and then people yelling. Since I was the only one in the outer office, I tiptoed into the next room. The argument was coming from the manager's office. I think he was on the phone because I heard only his voice."

"What was he saying?" Ruth said.

"Something about the new person in town needing to move very slowly, needing to take time to check things out before any decisions were made. Then he shouted to the person on the phone not to be so damn pushy unless he wanted things to fall apart and to get off his back. He said he could handle the cops."

"They could have been talking about almost anything, Margaret," I said.

"True, except this Charles guy said that the 'boss' knew what was best. At first I thought it was just hotel talk. Then as the weeks went by, and I started hearing from Frank about a crime boss, I began to wonder."

"And you never told your husband?"

"Oh, of course I did. But I'm not quick to meddle in his business. I ask every once in a while, and Frank tells me his boys are working of the case. You know now husbands are, tightlipped about their work?"

There was no doubt in my mind that Margaret hadn't forgotten that Ruth and I were single. My cousin and I looked at one another and shrugged—two husbandless women out in the world alone. Then Ruth said something that made me want to rush up and kiss her.

"I almost got married once, but I decided that sharing my money wouldn't be much fun." She stuck a cigarette in its ebony holder, lit up, and blew a smoke ring over her head. If she were twenty years older with longer, wavy hair she'd look like Marlene Dietrich in that Alfred Hitchcock movie *Stage Fright*. The one where Marlene talks her boyfriend into killing her husband and then double-crosses him.

Margaret was untouched by Ruth's display of cattiness. "Anyway," she said, "this boss, whoever he is, is working out of this hotel. You know it, I know it, and my husband knows it."

And so does Muldoon/Irving, I thought to myself.

"With all that's been going on, I figure that the boss is finally speeding things up. Two hotel employees are murdered, two gangsters are murdered, and you and Ruth were almost murdered. You find out who the Boss is and my husband will nip this potential crime spree in the bud."

"Four murders aren't a potential crime spree, Margaret, and your husband's late in nipping any buds around here."

"Well, you're right as far as hotel people and gangsters are concerned. But it's only a matter of time before real citizens fall victim, like policemen and business owners, and—"

"Sydney and me," Ruth said.

"Well . . . yes. I've got to go and see about dinner. We're having pork roast and that absentminded cook of mine always forgets to put in enough carrots. Frank likes his carrots."

"Good cooks, like good gardeners, are hard to come by these days," I said.

"Don't I know it," Margaret said. She grabbed her purse. "Keep in touch and let me know what you find out." She left.

"I must have been delirious this morning," Ruth said. "Before I fainted, I imagined I was having a fun time having brunch with Mrs. Frank Rochester."

"You were delirious, but you're looking better now," I said and smiled. "You now have that slightly inebriated glow about you."

Ruth giggled.

"What's so funny?"

"I was thinking about those raccoons in the zoo washing their carrots." She reached over for the martini pitcher. "I wonder if Margaret washes her husband's carrot."

"Ruth Echland!"

I grabbed the pitcher out of her hand before she could do any more damage.

Chapter 28

Ruth fell asleep, or passed out is a better way of putting it, before room service could deliver the pot of coffee and meal I'd ordered. Poor girl. She needed her rest. And I needed a little time to myself. Being stuck here in my room was comforting—sort of cozy. With two cops outside my door keeping bad guys out, I could relax and contemplate the day.

I couldn't believe everything that had happened since I woke up on the cot in Ruth's hospital room: my early morning massage and meeting Margaret Rochester, picking my cousin up off Margaret's sun-room floor, discovering Muldoon's true identity, and, I almost forgot, the incident with Dixon.

I went to the phone and picked up the receiver. I should tell him what I'd learned from Margaret. I put the receiver down. What had I learned? Obviously nothing that Dixon and Muldoon didn't already know.

I picked it up again. I should tell him about the conversation Margaret overheard when Mr. Charles was on the phone. What had she heard? Not a blasted thing. I put the receiver down. I had nothing to report. Besides I didn't want to appear forward. I didn't want to seem eager. I didn't want to be the first one to pick up the damn phone. After all, one little kiss does not a girlfriend make.

Just as I was about to fling the stupid phone out the window, it rang.

"Hello."

"Sydney, your mother's in El Paso at some fancy hotel downtown. You know where El Paso is? Halfway to LA."

"Dad—"

"She's not alone."

"What do you mean?"

"Your brother's with her. They got on the bus yesterday."

"What?!"

"Good riddance, I say. They're the loony ones in the family. They should be together. No skin off my teeth. Maybe I should move to Austin. Be closer to you. We'd have a great time."

"Dad, have you been drinking?"

"Lattie LaVelle stopped by to help me through this terrible situation."

"Dad, now you listen to me—"

Click.

I was about to pick up the phone to call him back, when it rang again.

"Scott's left me."

"Jeremiah, he'll be back."

"Oh, I don't really care. In fact, I'm celebrating. Did you know that Monroe looks cute in a party hat? Mealworm scratched the hell out of me when I tried to put one on her head."

"Just don't feed them any sweets."

"Whoops."

I hung up promising I'd keep Jeremiah informed of any further family crackups. I was no longer in the mood to call Dixon. In fact, I thought about pulling the phone wires from the wall. Suddenly I felt lightheaded, the cause of which could have been myriad things. The only thing to do was order room service.

Mickey brought in my shrimp scampi and Caesar salad. He looked at the coffee pot. "What, no wine tonight?"

"Overdid the martinis today. I need coffee."

He nodded toward my bodyguards. "Got two of them outside now?"

"One for Ruth and one for me. Dixon didn't want to take any chances. Sit down, or do you have to be back at work?"

"No time soon. Things are slow this time of day." He looked at my meal with yearning eyes.

I picked up the phone. "What would you like?"

"You mean it?"

"Sure. A snoop has to eat, doesn't he?"

"How about a hamburger and fries and maybe a beer?"

I placed the order, all except for the beer. I ordered a Royal Crown Cola instead. I didn't want to be accused of corrupting the young man.

"Find out anything?"

"I've been hanging around on the eighth floor. Those maids usually gossip like chickens, but everyone is so freaked, no one's saying a word. But I did find out that Donna hasn't been at work since Sunday. She called in sick."

"Since Sunday? Dixon said she was away visiting her grandmother."

"I don't know where she is, but she's not at work."

I couldn't blame Donna for not wanting to be here. But I couldn't help but be concerned. People around this hotel disappeared almost as often as they had their throats cut. I prayed the grandmother story was true.

"Ever hear of a crime boss moving back to town and homesteading in this hotel?" I said.

"Sure. That's an old story."

"It may be, but old stories have a way of coming true. You think it could be Mr. Charles?"

"Naw. He's not smart enough."

"How about Ellison James?"

"Hey, you might have something there. He was sort of shifty."

"I don't buy that story about him stealing money and disappearing. I mean, how much could he have taken from petty cash that would cause someone to kill him. Besides, from what I've heard he made a bundle at the racetrack."

"Could it have been that old gangster that kidnapped you?"

"Dixon assured me that Metzner was someone's henchman. And remember he ended up dead."

"If there's a boss at this hotel, I don't think he'd show himself. Just kind of run the operation from behind the scenes. I hear you're checking out soon."

"As much as I love the hospitality bestowed upon me, I can't stay here forever. I have what I need for the article. There's not much more to do, or see."

"Shows how much you know. You missed all the best places."

"I did?"

"Bet you never heard of Buddy Mack's in Malvern, the colored side of town? Best music you ever heard, a real jumping joint. Or the Stingy House out on South Central, or Hot Momma's somewhere in the woods on Lake Hamilton, or Dirty Reds on Blacksnake Road, or Smilin' Joe's in the basement of the Riverside Baptist Church, or the Capone Pad in the Ohio Club—"

"Hold on. Talk about shifty, Mickey. Those places sound like something from the rough and tumble times."

"You bet! But that's the real Hot Springs. Everybody thinks those types of places disappeared, and most did, but some just laid low until the coast was clear, then it was business as usual, only more secret-like. Why write about where mom and pop can take the kiddies?"

"Are you sure these places are still in operation?"

"All but the—"

Officer O'Riley opened the door.

Mickey said, "Shhh."

"Got another plate of food out here for you, Miss Lockhart. And a . . . soda pop?"

I'd become used to Officer Bud O'Riley. He looked like anybody's uncle. His black hair was absent of gray, although he must have been pushing fifty. With that benevolent face, he looked like a push over. I could see him in a candy store, doling out treats to a dozen neighborhood kids as they danced with delight. He was inspecting Mickey's burger and fries more for their culinary aspect than for any hidden weapons or hazards.

I took the food, thanked him, and closed the door. "Okay, continue."

"Anyway, they're suppose to be closed down of course, but they're not, except for Capone's pad. He's dead you know."

"I heard that. His pad's still there?"

"Yeah, sort of like a museum no one knows about."

"How do you know this, Mickey? You're not even old enough to drink, much less get into these places. Some of them sound like houses of ill repute."

Mickey huffed. He reached into his shirt pocket and pulled out a matchbook. He flipped it over to me.

I saw Buddy Mack's printed on the front. "So. This could have been around for a while."

"Open it."

I did. On the inside was printed: *New Year's Eve 1951*

"That was just last year."

"Told ya. These places play by their own rules, and the only one that matters is how you get in."

"And how do you get in?"

"Gotta know someone."

"And that's you?"

Mickey smiled, folding his arms across his chest.

"Eat. Your food is getting cold." Suddenly I wasn't hungry. I lit a ciga-rette and poured a cup of coffee. While Mickey noisily chewed and slurped, I paced, giving serious thought to this new, less than family-like story. My initial story would appeal to whom? The American Family? My mother? Mom and Pa Kettle? Margaret Rochester? I'm a reporter . . . a journalist. If there's a racy story out there somewhere, it's my duty to find it. Anyway, these places sound like just the sort of venue where one might pick up a clue about the mob. I wasn't doing very well here at the hotel.

"Okay. I want to see these places. All of them. Tonight." I slammed my palm on my forehead. "That's impossible."

"Why?"

I pointed to my door.

"Oh, your bodyguards."

"I don't think I can get rid of them again."

"We need Grady."

"Call him. Now."

While Mickey licked the catsup from his fingers and picked up the phone, I went to my closet and pulled out my black slacks, white blouse and saddle shoes. Since Hot Momma's was somewhere in the woods, spiked heels would not do.

"It's still early. These places don't start jumping until right before mid-night," Grady said. He looked at the list I made after I had Mickey repeat the names of all the joints. "We start here with Smilin' Joe's at the Baptist Church, then go out to Dirty Red's, swing into Hot Momma's on Lake Hamilton, Stingy House on Central, then back to Buddy Mack's in Malvern."

"What about Al's place? And what about Officer O'Riley?"

"He might be able to help us there."

"Officer O'Riley?"

"Yeah. Every cop in town knows how to get into Capone's pad. It's like on their private tour list. You know, Cousin Bob comes to visit his cop rel-ative, say O'Riley here, and Cousin Cop takes Bob over to see this place."

"Would Officer O'Riley do this, you think?"

"He doesn't look like he's having too much fun standing out there in the hall. Besides, Dixon didn't say you had to stay here, as long as you went out with your escort."

"No, actually Dixon did say that I couldn't leave the room and the last time I tricked O'Riley he told Dixon even though he risked getting in trouble."

"Ummmmm." Grady rubbed his chin. "O'Riley's a good cop, but he can't resist showing off Capone's pad. Just wait and see."

"But surely O'Riley wouldn't go with us to the juke joints."

"Who said he was invited." Grady said. "Once we get out, we find a way to lose him, a diversion."

Mickey had been listening to this without saying a word. Finally he piped up. "I have a plan!"

"Let's hear it," I said.

"Better you don't." Mickey arched his eyebrows.

"Why?"

"Just trust me," he said. "You, Grady, and Officer O'Riley be out on the roof of Al Capone's place at exactly eleven. My uncle's newsstand and pawnshop is down the street. You can see it from the roof."

"Danny Mueller's place?" Grady asked.

"That's it," Mickey said.

"What about the newsstand?" I asked.

"Just watch," Mickey smiled. "You'll be free of O'Riley in no time. We'll meet at Smilin' Joe's once you get away."

I looked at Grady. "He's a sneaky little thing."

"Yeah," Grady said. "He plans to run this hotel one day. I need to call in Jimmy Howser to take over for me. Tell O'Riley you want him to take you to Capone's pad. But don't do it until right before it's time to leave. Don't give him any time to wiggle out of it."

"I got work to do," Mickey said.

My cohorts left and I had a couple of hours to kill. I didn't know if I could stand the wait. So I did what I always do when I'm too anxious to do anything else. I rolled a sheet of paper in the Smith Corona and started clacking the keys. The title, "The Real Hot Springs."

Chapter 29

Officer O'Riley pushed opened the door and the smell of stale air escaped. He flicked on his flashlight and we followed him inside. "We're gonna make this quick," he said. "Stay with me. Don't turn on any light. Don't wander around. Don't move anything. Don't even touch anything."

"Got it," I said.

"Okay, we start in this room. It's the living room." He shone the light around. A glint of gold flashed from some object on the floor across the room. "Gold plated spittoon," O'Riley said. The light rose over recessed shelving in the wall behind the sofa. Liquor bottles containing various levels of alcohol stood still and undisturbed, as if waiting for the parties to begin again. "Bar." O'Riley's light washed over a painting on the wall above a roll-top desk. "Safe. Behind the picture." The light illuminated the fireplace. "Fire—"

"We get the picture, O'Riley," Grady said. "Let's move on."

We stepped lightly across a thick Persian rug toward a room on the right. Officer O'Riley stood at the doorway. "We don't go in here. Just look." In the middle of Al Capone's bedroom was something I'd never seen before—a round bed.

"Look at that," I said. "It doesn't look very practical."

"Unless you're round and fat like Capone." Grady laughed.

The bed was covered with a satin spread of gold and black stripes. On the other side of the room, away from the window, was a small sitting area. A gold brocade settee with a matching chair and an oak coffee table with matching end tables, were all neatly arranged on another expensive rug. I wondered how many shady deals had been made here in this room.

"Kitchen's nothing special, but you got to see this." O'Riley led us to the other side of the apartment. "I'll turn on the light here. There're no windows."

I checked my watch. In five minutes we needed to be on the roof looking toward the newsstand.

"Wow!" I heard Grady say. "This bathroom's bigger than my pad."

A gold tub large enough to bathe an elephant rested in the middle of the room. Al had a thing for gold. The faucets were gold, the light fixtures were gold, the ornate mirror was surrounded with a gold gilt frame. A black rug covered the black tile floor next to the tub. Evidently Al didn't like to place his precious tootsies on a cold, hard floor after his bath. A phone sat on a table next to the tub. Also on the table, an ashtray the size of a dinner plate was filled to the brim with half-smoked cigars. Hanging from a hook on the wall near the tub was a dressing gown of—you guessed it—black and gold silk.

"Seen enough?" O'Riley asked.

"Almost," Grady said. "Let's go out on the roof."

"I don't know about that," O'Riley said.

"Oh, come on, O'Riley. What harm will it do?" Grady draped his arm around O'Riley's shoulder.

"We need to get back to the hotel." O'Riley said.

"Just a quick look. I promise," Grady said. "Then we'll leave."

"Hurry then." O'Riley led us through the living room, pulled back the drapes, and slid open a glass door. Grady and I stepped out. I glanced at my watch again.

One minute.

I had no idea what Mickey had planned. I didn't want him to get in trouble. I didn't want anyone to get in trouble, Grady, Officer O'Riley, or me, but it was too late now. Whatever was going to happen would happen.

The neon lights of Danny Mueller's newsstand/pawn shop blinked on and off. Through the storefront window, I saw someone moving around. The person was small. It had to be Mickey. Suddenly the door flew open and the small guy, wearing a stocking cap, ran out and down the street. An old man rushed out the door. "Stop! Thief! Police! Police!"

Office O'Riley instantly put his hand to his gun. "Stay here! Don't go anywhere!" He ran back inside the apartment and seconds later we heard the front door slam. We waited until we saw Office O'Riley in pursuit. There was no way he'd ever catch Mickey. I was surprised he even tried.

"Come on," Grady said. "We gotta get out of here before he comes back." As I turned to follow Grady, I noticed a tall dark figure slip from the alley next to Mueller's and head quickly down the street after O'Riley. I stopped to watch, but before I could determine if anything fishy was going on, Grady grabbed my arm. "No time to hang around. Mickey will be fine."

"There's a weird guy hurrying down the street," I said.

"In Hot Springs? There are a lot of weird guys hurrying down the street. Let's go."

We ran back into the apartment and in our haste to leave, we slammed into the closed door.

"Damn! That louse locked us in!" Grady said.

"Shit! What do we do now?"

"Come on! Back on the roof!"

We were outside and down the fire escape in no time. I glanced down the street. All was quiet. No weird guys lurking. I felt better.

Grady had his Hudson parked in the alley. Before I could give a second thought to our deception, we were speeding down Central to our second destination of the night—Riverside Baptist Church where Smilin' Joe awaited us.

I felt bad for O'Riley, but my trepidation disappeared when I saw the church lit up like the North Star—a heavenly beam in an otherwise dark area of town. Gospel music floated out the windows and down the street. It took us awhile to find a place to park. When we walked up to the church, Mickey was standing on the porch smoking a cigarette. "What took you guys so long?"

"Any problem with O'Riley?" Grady asked.

"Last I saw of him, he was doubled over sucking air."

"See anyone else?" I asked.

"A couple of rats scurried into the gutter, but that's all."

"It looks like a service is going on tonight," I said. "Maybe we should-n't go in."

Grady and Mickey laughed. "There's a service every night," Grady said.

The church was packed. With arms rised, reaching for heaven, blacks and whites, young and old, were swaying to the sound of "May the Circle Be Unbroken." A mixture of sweat and strong perfume filled the air. We slipped into a back pew. At the pulpit stood a huge black man clapping his hands and singing at the top of his lungs, accompanied by a choir to his left. At least twenty black women, whose melodious voices were sure to bring Jesus back for his second coming, clapped and swayed as they sang. Then I noticed a familiar figure at the organ. Last time I saw him he was tickling the ivories in the Venetian room. As the notes of the last verse reverberated, the Reverend stomped his foot three times, making the floor vibrate all the way back to where we were standing. The hymn ended with the last stomp. The preacher lowered his arms and the entire congregation sat down in one smooth motion.

"Thank you for coming. Thank you for offering your souls to the Lord. Reverend Joseph Smiley welcomes everyone to Riverside Baptist Church. Jesus loves all sinners, colored people, white people, it don't matter. Jesus is colorblind. He don't see no difference."

"Amen!" a shout rose from the crowd.

I leaned over to Grady. "Reverend Joseph Smiley as in Smilin' Joe?"

"That's the one," Grady said.

"You!" Reverend Smiley pointed to a man in the front pew. "Are you a sinner?"

The man stood up. A hush fell over the crowd.

"Yes, sir!"

"Come up and repent! Repent in the name of Jesus!"

Grady and Mickey were bobbing their heads around to see. For me that was no problem. The sinner stood in front of the Reverend and received a blessing that consisted of being struck on the forehead with the palm of the Reverend's hand. The sinner yelled 'Amen!' He stuck his hand in his pocket and flung some change into a gallon-size tin can. The reverend jerked his thumb toward a door in the back of the pulpit and the repented sinner ran out and disappeared. The next time sinners were called, five men ran up for their forehead-smacking blessing, threw money in the can, and made a beeline for the door. The church never seemed to empty. New sinners came in as fast as repenters fled. I was beginning to wonder if the same people leaving through the back door were coming back around through the front for another dose of grace.

Every ten minutes or so, the Reverend nodded for the choir to commence singing. On the last notes of the hymn, he'd stomp again and shout for more people seeking redemption to come forward. After the third cycle of songs, stomps, and sinners, Grady leaned over and smiled at Mickey. "Our turn," he said.

I looked from Grady to Mickey and back to Grady. I couldn't believe what I'd heard, so I said, "I can't believe what I heard." My two companions grabbed my hands and before I could lodge a protest, we were heading down the aisle like Dorothy, the Scarecrow, and the Tin Man, skipping down the yellow brick road.

"Jesus loves redheaded white ladies!" the Reverend shouted.

"I thought Jesus was colorblind," I said to Grady.

"Shut up," he said.

In unison, we proclaimed our desire to cleanse our filthy souls, and smack, smack, smack, we were pure once again. Grady threw three dollar bills in the can. It was more than anyone had given, but without the loud clanking of coins against tin, the donation was almost a disappointment. We ran through the back door, which led to a staircase down to the basement. The lights were dim and cigarette smoke hung thick. The room was filled with those who'd just found salvation. With a pocket full of good luck from Jesus himself, they were all seated around several gambling tables—poker, blackjack, craps, roulette. The surprising thing was everyone was so quiet. Then as quickly as that perplexing thought entered my mind, the choir above cranked up and so did a jazz band playing at the end of the room. Voices rose in merriment. Quietness gone.

We walked around the room, soaking up the lively atmosphere. A waitress came by and took our drink order. We watched a poker game where the stakes were high. I counted at least two hundred dollars in the pot. While we enjoyed our drinks, we heard the three stomps from above and the room went quiet again.

"Reverend Smiley's signal to us that he's collecting entrances fees," Mickey said.

"So this is just a front for a gambling house."

"No way," Grady said. "Reverend Smiley's the real thing. He just has a unique way of fundraising. He alone has built a small children's clinic for coloreds in Malvern."

"He does this every night?"

"Every night," Mickey said. "Unless he gets word of a raid, then he closes the church until it's safe."

"That means until the right people receive their . . . shall we say charitable donations," Grady said.

We ordered another round, watched a small black woman, who looked like anybody's grandmother, slide the poker pot toward her. A couple of guys left the table only to be replaced by two more.

"Time to go," Grady said.

Next on the list was Dirty Red's on Blacksnake Road. On our way there, we drove past the hotel, turned left on Whittington, past the tourists attractions Ruth and I had visited a couple of days ago. My stomach knotted as we climbed toward Music Mountain. A short distance away was where Ruth had met with someone's bullet. Suddenly Dirty Red's didn't seem like a place I wanted to visit. Too late now. We were bumping down a rutted dirt road. Grady pulled up along side a long row of cars parked on the shoulder. I climbed out of the Hudson and took a deep breath. Overhead the stars glimmered and the man in the almost-full moon seemed to smile, and I took it as a sign that everything would be fine.

We heard the music long before we got there—jaunty, happy, carefree sounds that lifted my spirits.

"Gambling?" I asked.

"No, just your plain ol' juke joint," Grady said. "Plays the best swing this side of New Orleans."

The place, like the church, was packed with an amalgam of people, dark-skinned, light-skinned, and all shades in between. The band was making good work of a Les Paul number and the couples on the dance floor were swinging to the beat. In my whole life I'd never seen the jitterbug performed with such flair. Not even at the Crooked J. Luckily a couple was leaving and we grabbed their table.

Grady went up to the bar to order our drinks. Mickey could hardly sit still, and neither could I. It was my turn to initiate the trip to salvation, so I grabbed his hand and we bound for the dance floor. As with Vivian a few nights ago, I was destined to lead. Mickey didn't seem to mind when I twirled him under my arm. No one else seemed to notice or care. We ended the dance with a dip. As we meandered our way back, the music started again and a man cut between Mickey and me. He bowed gracefully and offered me his hand. This time I got to be the one twirled. My new dance partner had me by several inches. We danced three more when the band broke for intermission. He escorted me back to my table, both of us breathless and me thirsty.

"I see you've met Tooths Filsome," Grady said.

"You're a great dancer. I'm Sydney—"

"Lockhart. I know. Pleased to finally make your acquaintance, ma'am."

I didn't bother asking how my name preceded me. Like Mickey and I switching roles on the dance floor, it just didn't seem important.

"Join us." Grady pulled up a chair and the tall lanky man sat down.

I looked closely for a reason for Tooths' name. There were no missing teeth, nor were there too many. In fact, his smile was dazzling.

"Ain't seen you in here in a while," he said to Grady. "Must be working too hard."

"Always."

"Well, at least you still alive. Ain't had your throat slit none." He turned to me. "Where you from, gal?"

I was surprised Tooths didn't know this. "Austin, Texas."

"Ever been to the Crooked J? Never mind, no white woman with good sense would go there."

"You're right. I've been known to do some stupid things. I was there a few nights ago." I proudly pointed to my scar.

Tooths slapped his leg and hooted.

"You my kinda gal."

Our drinks arrived and Tooths left to dance with a woman who came by and grabbed him by the collar.

"Popular guy," I said.

"He's a dentist," Mickey said.

"I'm finally getting to meet the true pillars of the community."

"Don't speak too soon," Grady warned me. "The other places we're going to are a bit seedy."

The alcohol was beginning to make my head spin and seedy or not, I was ready to see more. The band started up and we left after Mickey and I danced a couple more times.

Chapter 30

Grady drove up and down several dirt roads on the way to Hot Momma's. "Lost?" I asked.

"Not lost. Need to find a safe place to park the car. This isn't exactly the best part of town. We'll have to walk a ways, but it'll be worth it."

Finally, Grady found a spot that was satisfactory. As soon as we stepped from the car I knew Lake Hamilton was nearby. The smell of river water, fresh and raw, filled the air. It was the smell of mud and catfish, digging worms and baiting trot lines. I instantly thought of my Uncle Jerome's farm near Austin where my parents would take us for the weekends. I'd run wild for the entire visit. I would imagine I was the daughter of some Indian chief trying to prove my worth to the tribe I'd planned on ruling one day. My mother had to threaten me to within an inch of my life in order to get me to come into the house after dark, otherwise I probably would have slept in the barn with the cows. I'd come home with bruises, cuts, scrapes, and torn clothes. Scott would come home immaculate.

"You gonna stand here all night daydreaming?" Grady said.

We walked down the road until Grady found a well-used trail leading into the woods. Before we got too far from the road, a flash of light caught my eye—moonlight reflecting off a fender. The car, driving down the route we'd just taken, had its headlights off. This time I didn't let Grady hurry me on. I stood, hidden by the trees, and watched. The driver slowed next to Grady's car and then drove on. I heard Grady and Mickey laughing and talking as they moved deeper into the woods. After a few moments, I turned to follow.

About two hundred yards dwon, I noticed a red light shinning through the trees.

"Hey, this place isn't a . . . brothel, is it?"

"Hot Momma serves the best steaks in town," Grady said. "What some guys choose for dessert is none of anybody's business."

"Damn," I said. "Well, I have to admit I'm getting hungry."

"Order the T-bone," Mickey said. "Melts in your mouth."

Hot Momma's was built on the shore of Lake Hamilton. The restaurant wasn't much more than a huge porch covered by a plywood roof. All the seating was outdoors. Several wood-burning stoves gave the rustic place a cozy atmosphere. Over to the side sat a giant brick pit covered with a grill where dozens of different cuts of beef lay sizzling. A man who looked like he'd spent his life riding bulls slathered the meat with a barbecue mop. He wore a white apron spotted with steak juice. I wouldn't have been surprised if this guy had butchered his own cows right here on the property. A small shed with a service window stood near the grill. The only other structure was an old house a few yards away—the dessert kitchen no doubt.

My stomach grumbled at the smell of steaks charring over an open flame. I was beginning to get lightheaded. This time we had to wait for a table. While we stood nursing bottles of Falstaff (a Royal Crown for Mickey), a woman who could be none other than Hot Momma stepped onto the porch. I expected her to be black, but Hot Momma was as white as white could be—skin, hair, clothes—everything white. Weighing in around three hundred pounds, she looked like a walking marshmallow. As the restaurant's proprietor made her way around the tables, greeting her guests, she spotted us and yelled across the porch.

"Well, I'll be a monkey's uncle. If it ain't Broussard. Where the hell have you been, Grady?" She came over and slapped him on the back. Grady tumbled into me and me into Mickey; three fallen dominoes waiting for a table. "Here to eat?" She picked Mickey up from the floor and stood him back on his feet while Grady and I righted ourselves.

"What do you think, Hot Momma? Of course we're here to eat."

"Don't get smart with me or I'll slap you."

I stepped out of the way. Being in her line of fire once was enough.

She turned around and glared at a couple sitting at a table by the rail. They'd obviously finished eating; their empty plates were pushed aside.

"Hey! You!" Hot Momma shouted. "Throw some cash on the table and move it! I got people who want to eat."

The startled couple did just that.

Hot Momma went over and gathered up the dirty plates, pocketed the money, and pointed for us to sit. We did.

"Minnie'll be right over to take your order. Relax."

I looked around and noticed two men standing by the serving window of the shed. Hot Momma walked over, stuck out her palm, and they handed over some cash. Then they stepped off the porch and walked toward the house. These guys must be ordering their dessert first.

Minnie took our order for three T-bones, medium rare. We sipped our drinks and listened to the sounds of plates clattering and people laughing. A cool breeze blew in from the lake. A murmur of thunder whispered from far off. I yawned.

"Too early for that," Grady said. "We got two other places to go. Unless you want to call it a night."

"Not on your life," I said. "I wouldn't miss Stingy House and Buddy Mack's for the world."

"Hey, Grady, maybe we shouldn't go to Stingy House," Mickey said. "That's a pretty rough place. Unless Gully Stine's there."

"If Gully's not at the door, we couldn't get in anyway."

I didn't have a chance to ask why Stingy House was so rough. Minnie walked up with three oval plates, which were too small for the steaks hanging over the sides. Juice dripped from of each one. She sat them down, left, and returned with a bowl of buttery corn on the cob and another with mashed potatoes smothered with white gravy. Suddenly I thought of Ruth and hoped she was still sleeping off her early inebriation.

For the next several minutes, we ate in silence, words being a sacrilege to this dining experience. The meat fell off the bone and didn't need chewing. I was determined to clean my plate. The food was too good not to.

I looked around and the other customers were lost in the dining experience as well. Compared to Smilin' Joe's and Dirty Red's this place was almost serene. Folks came for some serious steak, paid their money, and left without much lingering.

"Nice, quiet place," I said.

I'd spoken too soon.

"Miss! Oh, Miss!" A man raised his hand and shouted for Minnie to come to his table. He sat across from another man who was picking at his steak as if he'd been served something putrid.

Minnie walked over. It was the first time all night that she hadn't rushed across the porch.

"What?" she said.

"We ordered these steaks well-done."

"So?"

"So . . . they ain't well done. They're all bloody."

"Butch don't like to cook 'em dry. They don't taste good without a bit of blood."

The man picked up both his and his friend's plates. "Tell Butch that he ain't the one eatin' and that we don't like blood in our meat." He shoved the plates at Minnie.

"It ain't civilized, girlie," the other man said. He'd placed his hand on Millie's backside and patted as if she were a dog.

From the side of the shed I caught sight of a soft, white cloud beginning to materialize. It seemed to float across the porch and stop next to Minnie.

All conversation in the restaurant ceased. All plate- and utensil-noise ceased. The breeze coming off the lake ceased. No one breathed. No one swallowed. No one moved.

"Problem here?" Hot Momma said.

"They don't like blood in their meat," Minnie said. "It ain't civilized." She slapped the man's hand away and left the table.

"I'm truly sorry," Hot Momma said. "We all want to be civilized here. I run a civilized place. I like civilized." She turned to her other customers. "We all like civilized. Don't we?"

Everyone nodded.

Hot Momma leaned over the man to her left. She placed a hand on his shoulder. "Tell you what I'm gonna do." Then she grabbed his coat collar and lifted him from his seat. She grabbed the back of his pants, and in one fluid motion she tossed the guy over the rail and into the lake. "I'm just gonna send you on your way." The other guy was sneaking away from the table. Without looking behind her, Hot Momma swung her arm around, grasped the man's wrist, and pulled him up to her face.

"That woman's name is Minnie," she hissed. "And she ain't something to paw." She squeezed his hand. Through the silence, everyone in the place heard the crunch of bones and then his scream as he flew through the air and joined his partner in the lake. Hot Momma walked away to attend to whatever business she'd been taken from, and the crowd turned back to the civilized business of eating without complaint.

Just as I was stuffing the last morsel in my mouth (thankful I liked my steaks medium-rare) I noticed a familiar figure standing by the pit. He was leaning on the shed, legs crossed, arms folded across his chest. His head was cocked and he was giving us one mean look.

"Uh oh," I said.

Grady and Mickey turned around and saw him immediately. "Better invite him over before he shoots us." Grady waved his hand in a gesture for Officer O'Riley to join us.

The big cop sat down next to me creaking the bench. "I should arrest the three of you right now."

"On what charges?" Grady said.

"I can think of three for starters. One," he held up one finger, "lying to an officer of the law."

"It don't count if you're not under oath," Grady said.

"Two," he held up a second finger and turned to stare directly at Mickey, "shoplifting at Danny Mueller's place."

"My Uncle Danny gave me those cigarettes. I was just running home with them."

"Then why did he yell, 'Thief?'"

"He was probably drunk," Mickey said. "He gets confused after a few beers."

"What's the third reason?" I asked.

Minnie walked by with another armload of dripping plates and Officer O'Riley lost his train of thought. "It don't matter. You three are gonna be in a hell of a lot of trouble when Dixon finds out."

"Don't get so sore, O'Riley. So who's going to tell Dixon? You?" Grady said between nibbles on his corncob. "Then you'd be in trouble too, letting Sydney escape twice in one day. Hey, Minnie, bring Officer O'Riley one of those steaks, will ya."

Officer O'Riley took off his cap and rubbed his scalp in frustration.

"Hey, how many cops does it take to arrest a guy for shoplifting?" Grady said.

None of us said a word, so Grady answered his own question.

"A thousand. One to cuff the guy and nine hundred and ninety nine to set the shop back on its foundation." He doubled over with laughter while the three of us sat looking at him.

"I need a beer," Officer O'Riley said.

"Now you're talking," Grady cackled.

"How did you know where to find us?" I said.

"Been on your trail all night, just missed you at every stop. You dropped this in Capone's pad," he reached into his pocket and pulled out my list.

"At least we're all together again," Grady said.

And I felt safer for it.

As Officer O'Riley finished his steak his anger dissipated. He pushed his empty plate aside and looked at his watch. "Almost two. We best be getting back. No way you guys are visiting Stingy House, especially not him." He pointed to Mickey. "Hey, don't you have school tomorrow?"

I forgot Mickey was still in high school. He seemed to fit in no matter who he was with or where he was. Although imagining him sitting in a biology class studying the formula for photosynthesis was a stretch.

"Miss Lockhart wants to see the real Hot Springs," Grady protested.

"I'd say she's seen enough. Now here's what we're gonna do. We're gonna all get into my squad car. I'm gonna drop Mickey off at his house." Mickey started to object, but Office O'Riley stifled his whines by raising one hand like an officer stopping traffic or, better yet, like Reverend Smiley silencing his choir. Then I'm giving you," he looked at Grady, "a ride home and then taking Miss Slippery here back to the hotel."

"I got my car parked back in the woods," Grady huffed.

"Ha!" Office O'Riley blurted out. "That car of yours ain't going nowhere."

"What do you mean?"

"Need four tires to drive a car. Yours only got two, by now, proba'ly none."

Grady slammed his beer bottle down on the table. "It's your job to see that things like that don't happen to good people like me."

"We're on the edge of the city limits. Ain't got no jurisdiction here," Officer O'Riley said. "We stay outta places like this unless something really bad happens. It works best for everybody."

Hot Momma sidled up to the table and threw a beefy arm around Officer O'Riley's shoulder. "Nice to see ya, Bud. Want your usual dessert tonight, sweetie?" She kissed him on his head, then floated to another table.

"That woman's crazy." O'Riley flushed. "Let's get out of here."

Chapter 31

The three of us watched from the squad car as Mickey crawled into a window on the side of his house. Once inside he stuck out a hand and waved us goodnight. I sincerely hoped he'd wake up in time to catch the school bus.

"Come on, Sweetie, be a good sport and drive us to Stingy House," Grady said. "It's not too far from here."

"I know where the hell it is," O'Riley said. "There's no way you're getting in there."

"We can if Gully Stine's working."

"Gully Stine? Is he still around? I thought he was dead."

"He was, but he's back."

"Son-of-a-bitch . . . sorry, Miss Lockhart. He owes me some money."

"Let's go collect, Sweetie."

"Cut that Sweetie stuff out or you ain't going nowhere."

After a stop at Officer O'Riley's house so he could change into street clothes, we arrived on South Central Avenue. He slowly cruised down a street lined with beer joints. People were standing around cars, laughing, smoking, carousing. There wasn't a white person to be seen anywhere. As soon as they spotted the squad car, everyone stopped what they were doing and stared as we drove by. I wondered what kind of reception we'd get walking down this street to Stingy House. Just as I was beginning to hear Mickey's voice saying that maybe we shouldn't go, Officer O'Riley turned off the main street and down a dark alley. "Are you sure you want to do this?" he said.

I was about to tell him to drive me back to the Arlington when Grady answered, "Yeah, we're sure."

Two alleys later we drove up a steep hill and stopped in front of a tall steel fence surrounding at least a dozen warehouses and a huge parking lot. The railroad track ran along the south side of the fence. The place looked deserted except for a dim yellow light over the doorway of one building.

"This is Stingy House?" I asked. "Where's everybody? The place looks closed."

"It's open all right," Grady said.

"How do you know?"

"Light's on."

"There are no cars," I said.

"Folks park at the depot a block away and enter through the gate on the other side. Stingy House isn't always open. But if the yellow light is shining, it's open," Grady said.

I looked across the parking lot to where Grady was pointing and sure enough I could just barely make out two men and a woman coming through the gate.

"We're parking here," O'Riley said. "If I drive this squad car to the depot, everyone will scatter. We'll walk around to the other side."

We stepped out of the car. The quiet tremor of thunder I'd heard earlier had turned into a roar. I searched for the stars I'd seen while traipsing out on Blacksnake Road, but they all had more sense than any of us and had taken cover.

O'Riley snapped on his flashlight. Grady and I followed the cop to the railroad track. He stopped, looked both ways, listened, then placed his hand on the rail. "Just wanted to make sure. We gotta walk down the track for about fifty yards."

We started our trek down the rails when I looked to the right and realized that we were actually crossing a railroad bridge. I kept my eyes on O'Riley's back and kept walking.

"Damn, O'Riley," Grady said. "Why bring us this way?"

I was glad to hear the fear in Grady's voice. I was beginning to think he wasn't human.

"I told you I had to hide the car."

We approached the gate behind two identical black women, who were dressed in matching skintight red dresses, which they did justice to. Complimenting their outfits were silver shawls, silver spiked heels, silver gloves, and silver hats with brims wide enough to keep the sun, or in a more immediate situation, the rain, from ever finding them. At night the hats looked like shimmering flying saucers coming in for a landing. The gate opened automatically, they walked in, and the gate shut. I looked around for some sort of triggering device, when I saw it, right under my nose. The device was about four and a half feet tall, smoking a cigar. He was dressed in a black suit and a fedora. O'Riley handed the flashlight to Grady as we stepped off the tracks.

"Here," O'Riley said. "You gotta cover me."

Grady shined it in the guy's face. I almost fell over. Stingy House's maitre d' must have been a hundred years old.

"Gully Stine! You old son-of-a-gun!" Grady said. "When did you get back from New Orleans?

"Broussard!" Gully shouted. He looped his gnarly fingers through the fence wire. The gate remained shut. "Been here awhile. You still at the Arlington? Must not be doing your job with all the throat-slashing going on there."

"They don't pay me enough to keep people from being murdered. I throw the drunks out of the bar and keep them from drowning in the pool."

"Suppose you want to come in?"

"No, Gully, I came out here with my friends, a couple from Texas. We're out for a stroll along the tracks.

"Texas, huh? I been there once. A lot of tall people." He looked at me as if I were responsible for his shortness. I opened my mouth to apologize when O'Riley took my hand and squeezed it. I got the hint. O'Riley kept his head down and so did I.

"It's starting to drizzle, Gully." Grady opened his wallet and pulled out a five. Gully swiped the bill like a hawk grabbing a sparrow. The gate swung open and we slipped in. Halfway to the warehouse Grady said, "I thought you wanted to collect from Gully."

"I do, but on the way out. I don't want anyone knowing a cop's here. Listen, we go in, look around so Miss Lockhart can get a feel for the place, and get the hell out. Understand. In and out—should take no more than ten minutes."

The drizzle turned into rain and we hurried toward the warehouse. Grady opened the door and noise and light escaped like a charging bull. This place was not just a gambling hall, it was a full-scale casino with rows and rows of one-armed bandits. There must have been four hundred people inside. I wondered what Frank Rochester would think about his clean-up job if he saw this place.

O'Riley and I followed Grady to a blackjack table where he elbowed a guy out of his chair. The dealer dealt Grady his first hand. "Get us some drinks, will you dear?"

It was a couple of seconds before I realized Grady was talking to me. "If you call me dear again and ask me to get you a drink, I can't be responsible for what I might do."

"Sorry," Grady said. "Something happens to me when I start playing cards."

"Jeez," O'Riley said. "You two are loony."

"You get your own drink if you want it," I said. "I'm going to take in the scene."

"No!" O'Riley said, loud enough to make several heads turn. "You're staying right here."

"Let the girl—"

I poked Grady in the back.

"—I mean lady walk around. She can't go anywhere, O'Riley. There's only the front door and the escape door and it's closed."

"Escape door?" I asked.

"Big garage door over on that wall," O'Riley said. "Flies open in case the crowd needs to leave in a hurry."

O'Riley was still clutching my hand. I pried his finger loose. "I won't go far. Just keep an eye on my red hair. I should be easy to follow."

There must have been a hundred slot machines and each one was occupied. Bells rang, wheels clattered, people cheered and cursed. I walked by a table and heard someone say, "Hey, white girl. Why you wearing those men's stupid trousers and those stupid shoes?"

I turned and saw the red and silver twins perched on stools, sipping drinks as colorful as they were. I looked down at my attire. "For a fast get-a-way if necessary." I looked at their identical silver shoes. The heels were four inches at least, and as thin as toothpicks. A narrow ankle strap and a small slither of rhinestone-studded leather across the toes were all that held the shoes on their feet.

My answer must have satisfied them. The woman on the right changed the subject. "Ain't never seen hair that red unless it come from a stupid bottle."

"It's real all right."

"What's you name, party girl?"

"Sydney."

They looked at one another.

"Yeah, stupid, I know."

"It's a man's name. Man's trouser, man's shoes. You ain't one of them queer types are you?"

"No, just like my comfort at times. But I also like those shoes you are wearing."

"These?" The one on the left stuck her leg in the air. Her red dress slid down over her thigh. Three men walked by and fell over themselves.

"Really wild," I said.

"Sit down, Syd. Where you from?"

I was afraid they, like the entire town, had heard of the murders at the hotel and the woman from Texas and her short cousin who'd gotten shot, so I avoided the truth once again. "New Orleans. Here visiting . . . my cousins. They're showing me around." I pulled up a stool and sat down.

"What are your names?"

The one on the left answered, "I'm Nadine. She's Charlene."

They looked so much alike, I couldn't help but stare. As hard as I tried, I couldn't find one dissimilarity—not a slant of an eye, not the shape of the mouth, not even a facial mole.

"You mean you ain't here with you husband?"

"Not married."

"Not married? Everybody's married, sugar."

"Not me. Where're your husbands? I saw you two walk in unescorted."

This threw the sisters into a fit of laughter. "Our husband ain't here," Charlene said. "We leave him at home."

"Husband?"

"That's what I said, didn't I, Syd?" Nadine sipped her drink. "We just got one."

"Isn't that illegal?"

"Yeah, but Elroy don't know he got two wives," Charlene said. "Nadine's the one who actually signed the papers at the courthouse. But we switch off on occasion."

"You mean, he doesn't know?"

"He's sort of—"

"Stupid. I get the picture."

A waitress stopped by our table. "See'n as we friends, you can buy us a drink," Charlene said.

"What's the red concoction anyway?"

"Singapore Sling. Made with gin, brandy, and something red."

"We'll have three of those," I said. The waitress disappeared into the crowd.

"Hey, those really women's shoes?" Nadine said.

"Of course."

"Sometimes a girl needs easy-walking shoes." Nadine stared longingly at my saddle shoes. Probably thinking about her aching arches. "Here," I said, unlacing my right shoe. Try it on."

"Get out!" Nadine said.

"No, I'm serious. There're comfortable. Here."

It took Nadine a while to untie the knot on her shoe strap. When she did, she handed it to me. We switched.

I tied the silver spike onto my foot, stood up, and stumbled.

"Look here," Nadine said. "You gotta tie a double knot or they slide off. Gimme your foot."

I laid my foot in her lap and she tied a knot that would have earned her a girl-scout badge. Talk about tart shoes. These would have driven my mother crazy. Nadine had my saddle shoe on and she and Charlene were giggling so hard, they held on to one another to keep from toppling over.

I hobbled around with one leg shorter than the other. "How you managed to walk all the way from the parking lot in these, I never kn—"

"Raid!"

People started running toward the back wall in one huge mass, like a herd of thirsty water buffalo who smelled the river up ahead. In their wake, tables tumbled, chips flew, glassware shattered. Women screamed and men shouted curses. I turned toward the blackjack tables and O'Riley and Grady were nowhere in sight. I felt a rush of cold air as the escape hatch opened. I grabbed onto the table to keep from being shoved to the floor in the massive stampede when I realized the bigamy twins were gone, and along with them, my saddle shoe. I shoved my way through the crowd, looking for Grady and O'Riley. Coming through the yellow-lighted door were at least a dozen cops. My heart stopped when I saw that some carried clubs and the others rifles. One officer had a bullhorn. He shouted for everyone to freeze. I ducked behind a roulette table for a moment to think. That was all I had—one short moment. I decided to save myself. If I wasted time looking for my two escorts, I'd surely end up in the slammer.

Running toward the escape door with one leg four inches shorter than the other was not an easy endeavor. I was halfway across the room when I stumbled. I grabbed onto the guy in front. If I hit the floor, I'd be trampled. The guy was not happy about being slowed from his escape and he slammed his elbow into my chest and shook me off. Someone from behind rammed into my back and I was on my way to the floor again. I could hear my mother now. After the church service, after the burial, after the funeral meal, after all the mourners had gone home—my mother, slouched on the sofa, a handkerchief to her eyes, asking my father, "Why was Sydney Jean wearing that one silver shoe?"

Just as I began to wonder what dress my mother would choose for me to wear in my casket, someone grabbed my jacket collar at the nape of my neck and jerked me up. My gratitude was short-lived. As soon as I was on my feet, the person had me in a headlock. I saw the knife a split second before I felt blood trickle down my chin. Then before I could ask God's forgiveness for those sins I held back in confession, the knife flew from my attacker's hand and disappeared under stampeding feet. In his foiled attempt to slash another throat, the guy disappeared in the crowd, but not before I recognized him as the person who had followed Officer O'Riley outside of Danny Mueller's place. For some odd reason I wasn't afraid. Instead, I was madder than a poodle with a botched clip. I shoved my way through the melee in his direction. What I'd do if I caught up with him I wasn't sure. Knock him to the floor maybe? Demand he give me my parent's wedding picture back?

Jesus must truly love redheaded white women, because Officer O'Riley stepped in front of me and saved me from my madness. He whisked me around and spun me toward the bar. Grady was crouched beside a beer cooler waiting. As soon as he saw us, he pushed open a panel next to the cooler and a small door swung open. We crawled through, down some stairs, and into a cellar. I noticed a stream of people, mainly employees, filing into a back hallway. We followed.

"How do you know about this route?" I said running after Grady.

"Use to tend bar here."

The hallway was pitch black, but I kept my hand on Grady's jacket. O'Riley was behind me with his hand on my coattail. "Almost there!" Grady cried. I looked ahead and saw a dimly lit staircase. We emerged into another warehouse. Most of the people were headed toward a back door, but Grady led us in the opposite direction. "In here." We entered what appeared to be a small office. In the darkness I could barely make out several people sitting on the floor. "We wait," Grady whispered. "The cops know about that exit, we just wait them out." O'Riley and sat down next to Grady. No one spoke. After a few minutes someone lit a cigarette. "Put it out!"

Someone else ordered. "Moron."

"Watch who you call a moron, jackass."

"Shut up you fools before we're all arrested," Officer O'Riley said.

It was silent again. The room was stuffy and I imagined all of us suffocating once we used up all the oxygen. I took a deep breath to make sure I got my share. Then my lungs froze. The scent of lime was enough to make me move a little closer to O'Riley.

Chapter 32

After about fifteen minutes people started to move. We followed the crowd from the office and climbed a set of stairs to emerge into yet another warehouse and out the backdoor into the parking lot. I scanned the crowd as it scrambled toward the fence, but I didn't see him. Several cops now guarded the entrance gate that was earlier guarded by Gully Stine. The only way out was up and over. We scaled the fence like the others. I was careful not to get my spiked heel caught and thankful I'd spent most of my childhood climbing anything that didn't move. Most people headed for the woods, but we ran toward the tracks.

"What in the name of God is on your foot?" O'Riley called between gulps of air.

"It's a long story," I shouted over my shoulder.

We almost made it to the tracks when someone yelled, "Hey! You! Stop!"

"Keep going!" O'Riley yelled. "If I get caught I'm dead meat."

Running across the gravel parking lot and then the muddy field on the other side of the fence, I could handle—the railroad track was another story. With the cops chasing us, I couldn't take the time to stop and remove the shoe. I looked down and forced my eyes to focus on the railroad ties. It had stopped raining, but the clouds still lingered, making the night uncomfortably dark. I didn't bother to shout to O'Riley to pull out his flashlight. He was too far ahead, running like a rhino after a mate. I turned to glance behind me and was relieved to see that the cops were not coming after us. Evidently we weren't important enough for them to risk tackling the train trestle in the dark. They stood at the tracks and watched as we scrambled across the bridge. Just as I was beginning to feel the elation of freedom, I stumbled. I grabbed the rail to catch myself, and all bodily functions, involuntary and voluntary, stopped. I felt the vibration and knew why the cops were no longer in hot pursuit.

The whistle of the train split the night air and drove a spike through my heart. Grady came up behind me and yanked at my arm to help me up. His gesture was futile. I was anchored to the track—the silver tart shoe wedged between a tie and the rail.

O'Riley turned and shouted, "The train! Get up! Get up!"

"My foot's caught!" I screamed.

Grady tugged at my ankle. It didn't budge. I grappled at the strap, but Nadine's knot held tight. I understood now why trapped animals gnawed themselves free. I would have tried that, but when I saw the bright light of the engine illuminating the tracks, I knew I didn't have enough time to start chewing. The train had rounded the corner and another earsplitting blast from the whistle told me we were goners. I wanted to pray, but for some stupid reason, I concentrated on not wetting my pants, as if it mattered. O'Riley ran over, knelt down, and snapped out his pocketknife. What is it about impending death that turns people into idiots? I started screaming as I envisioned this Irish cop slicing off my foot. I felt the cold blade next to my skin and before I could push his hand away, I heard a snap. He'd sliced the strap instead. It didn't matter. For all his heroic efforts, we wouldn't make it to the end of the trestle before the train ground us into hamburger.

O'Riley threw a beefy arm around my waist. His other arm looped around Grady's neck. It's true what Newton postulated about gravity. Objects, no matter what their weight, if dropped from the same height will hit bottom at the same time. As soon as we flew from the trestle, O'Riley let go of Grady and me. From a height of at least thirty feet, the three of us hit the Ouachita River in one gigantic splash.

The impact paralyzed my lungs, which was a good thing because I was now several feet under water. I kicked for the surface, and just as I began to wonder what questions St. Peter had in store for me, my head popped above the surface and I sucked air into my burning lungs. The river was rushing due to the runoff from the night's rain. I went under again from the force of the water, but kept swimming toward the shore like we were taught at camp. "If ever caught in a rip tide, swim diagonally to the shore," our swimming teacher had said. This wasn't the ocean, but the same principle applied. The water slowed as I swam toward the riverbank. Then my knees hit mud, and I crawled the rest of the way. O'Riley was lying on the bank, heaving. I scanned the river and made out what looked like a bundle of rags caught on a downed tree branch. Grady was hanging on, but just barely.

"O'Riley!" I cried. "Help me with Grady, he's going under."

The big man sprang from the bank with a loud 'thuck' as the mud reluctantly let go of his body. I pointed to Grady and O'Riley eased out into the river, holding on to the tree limb. He plucked the little Cajun from the river and dragged him to safety.

The three of us sank back into the mud, cold and filthy, but alive and unharmed.

"Wife's in Pine Bluff visiting her mother. Come into the kitchen, but don't get anything dirty," O'Riley said. "I'll turn myself back into a cop, and have us at the hotel before . . .four."

Grady and I stood there by the sink. The mud was beginning to dry so we weren't in danger of mucking up Mrs. O'Riley's spotless kitchen.

"I didn't think you could look worse than that day you got back from your second kidnapping," Grady laughed. "But I was wrong. Hey, your chin's bleeding."

"Must have happened in the fall." I wasn't sure why I lied. The rate I was going, I shouldn't rack up any more sins. But after what I'd been through, I felt . . . dangerous in an invincible sort of way. I took the dishtowel from the sink and cleaned a spot on Grady's cheek. Then I kissed it. "Thanks for a swell evening," I said. "You're some fun date."

"We never made it to Buddy Mack's."

"Well, I'll have to come back one day."

"Warn me before you do."

I put my arm around Grady's shoulder. "This was your idea, dear, remember?"

"How could I forget?"

O'Riley, freshly scrubbed and spiffy in his uniform, walked in. "Let's go. I hope to Jesus I still have a job when the sun comes up."

Sneaking up the stairwell covered with dirt, wearing tattered clothes, was getting old. The only thing that made it better this time was a uniformed escort. O'Riley pushed open the door to the tenth floor.

"Holy Mackerel! Where have you been?" Stockton rushed up to us. "I've worn a path pacing this hall—"

"Just open Miss Lockhart's door, Bill. Anyone come by?"

"Not a soul. What happened?"

"I'll tell you one day. One day when we're old and retired."

"My cousin's still asleep?" I asked.

"She's either asleep or dead," Stockton said. "Oh, sorry, ma'am. I shouldn't have said that."

I stepped into my room. O'Riley was about to close my door. "Officer O'Riley, one moment before you leave. When we were sitting in that office warehouse, I'm sure I smelled—"

"Me, too," he said. "I've been around this hotel enough these last few days to recognize that odor. "The only problem is how do I tell Dixon without mentioning our night on the town? Besides, it's probably not important anyway."

As much as Officer Bud O'Riley had grown on me, I knew why at his age, he'd never advanced beyond a beat cop.

I made another pile of ruined clothes on the floor in the bathroom, filled the tub, and planned to stay there until my skin pruned. I thought about the person who'd tried to kill me. Even though Mr. Charles had been at Stingy House, I wasn't sure he was the one who tried to slash my throat. The attacker was well hidden under a trench coat, scarf, and hat. But I knew for certain Mr. Charles was involved. That casino was clearly a big-time gambling operation. If organized crime was indeed moving back to town, what better place to start the ball rolling. And if the 'boss' was to operate out of the Arlington, that provided Mr. Charles with a connection. I pulled the plug and watched the brown water swirl down the drain. First thing in the morning I'd be in the hotel manager's office—his first appointment for the day.

I was told that Mr. Charles came in early and went to the ballroom on the second floor to make sure everything was set up for a big wedding planned that afternoon. I hurried to the ballroom before I lost my nerve. The place was decorated to the hilt. The chandeliers were shining, casting tiny beams of light across the ceiling. The wedding cake, sitting in the middle of the wedding-party table, stood at least five feet tall. I pushed a chair up to the table and looked closely at the ceramic bride and groom perched on top of the cake. I almost fainted.

The bride was a head taller than the groom. She had red hair like me. On her left foot was a shoe with a silver spiked heel and on her right a green Roman sandal. Her betrothed was wearing a slick brown suit and a fedora. His coat was slightly opened and strapped to his chest was a holster and gun. Suddenly the light from the chandeliers went out and from the stage I heard three loud stomps. Reverend Smiley was shouting for sinners to repent. Then he made a plea that could only be meant for me. "Redheaded white woman, come here and beg the Lord to save your soul! If you ain't up here by the time I count to three, you going to the devil!" He raised his foot. Pound! Pound! Pound! I screamed for mercy and tumbled off the chair.

"Sydney! Sydney! Wake up."

I opened my eyes. Ruth stood over me, shaking me by my shoulders.

"Why did you sleep on the sofa?"

"What?"

"Syd? Are you okay?"

I looked around the room.

"Who's Reverend Smiley?" she said.

I pushed my sweaty hair out of my face. "Nobody. I was dreaming. I need coffee."

"It's on the way."

Ruth was already dressed. She was wearing a pink suit trimmed with black cording. It looked wonderful on her.

"You look great," I grumbled.

"It's amazing what a good night's sleep can do. Seems like both of us went to sleep early. But you don't look so hot. Hey, how did you scratch your chin?"

"Uh, a bobby pin in the wrong place. What time is it?"

"Eight-thirty."

"I slept too long," I lied, looking around for any evidence of last night's foray. I remembered my dirty clothes in the bathroom and rushed in before Ruth could find them. "I hope you ordered breakfast too," I called, as I hid my clothes in the cabinet under the sink.

"I thought those two nice officers outside might accompany us down to the dining room."

"You'd better call Dixon and clear it with him first."

"I will. Get dressed."

That was easier said than done. My new wardrobe had dwindled by one outfit.

•

I had to restrain myself from ordering everything on the menu. I must have lost five pounds on that train trestle. Ruth ordered the Denver omelet. I ordered scrambled eggs, French toast, and a bowl of fruit, small. The waiter brought our basket of baked goodies to tide us over until the real food came.

"So, how's your shoulder?" I said.

"Sore, but at least it's not throbbing anymore."

"You know you should stay with the aspirin today, but probably lay off the booze."

Ruth stuck out her lower lip. "Okay," she said.

Aspirin would probably do me some good too since every muscle in my body burned with pain. I closed my eyes. I could still feel the cold river water stinging my corneas. When I opened them, I saw a hand reaching for a muffin.

"I can't believe it," Dixon said. "You two actually managed to stay out of trouble last night." He had moved a chair up to our table, straddling the backrest. He swathed butter on my muffin.

I looked over at the Jockey Bar where O'Riley and Stockton were sitting having coffee a few feet away. O'Riley was shaking his head. He looked as if he were ready to collapse.

"Listen, how long are those two cops going to guard us. They look dead on their feet," I said.

"Got replacements coming. I'm sure they managed a few winks last night sitting in the hall. I'm surprised you didn't throw them a couple of pillows."

I wanted to throw Dixon a couple of right hooks. It was the first time I'd seen him since the kiss, not that I'd been counting the hours.

"Any new developments?" I asked.

"None that I can tell you about."

"Then tell me if you're close to solving these murders. Ruth and I are leaving as soon as possible." We weren't, but I wanted to prod him into action.

"Oh, yeah?"

"What? Did you expect us to stick around forever?"

Dixon's smug look dissipated. "No. No, I can't expect that." He ate the last of my muffin and left.

"What's wrong with him?" Ruth said.

"Who knows?"

Our food arrived and suddenly I wasn't hungry anymore.

Chapter 33

When we returned to our room, Ruth said she had to call Sophia to check in and get caught up on the life she was missing out on in Dallas. That conversation would last at least forty-five minutes—the cost of that long-distance call probably equal to my rent. This was a good time for me to grab a few winks. Two nights in the last four had been lost to my adventure with the Smalls and a night on the town, not to mention my escapades involving the Crooked J and my subsequent visit to the emergency room the night before I left. I felt punch drunk. I undressed and wrapped myself in my bathrobe, but was too jittery for a nap. I needed to get my mind off Hot Springs, Arkansas and, call home as well, when I heard a soft whisper.

"Syd. Syd. Over here."

In my half-wake, half-asleep state, I heard those baby dolls, still in their open box, calling my name. "Syd, try us on. You may be surprised."

"Surprised?" I said. "How?"

"Just try us on."

"Shut up," I said. This time they didn't answer back. I lit a cigarette. I looked around my room. It felt as though I'd lived here for a month.

I looked at the box. Well, one little try-on wouldn't hurt. I peeled away the tissue paper, held up the baby dolls, then slipped them on. I turned around in front of the mirror. Not bad.

Decorated with tiny pink blossoms on a light, green chiffon, this type of scanty sleep wear was too delicate for me. But, hey, green's my favorite color. My new green cap would match perfectly. How would my hair look in a twist? I rushed to the bathroom, grabbed my cosmetic bag, and brought it to the dresser. In the bottom, I found a few bobby pins. Ten minutes later, I was inserting the last pin when it slipped through my fingers. I got down on my hands and knees and felt around on the floor when something sharp pricked my finger. It didn't feel like a bobby pin. The object was wedged deep into the carpet fibers. I had to tug hard to remove it. As it lay in the palm of my hand, the crazy events of the last week came into focus. I understood the reason I was kidnapped, why my room was ransacked, and who stuffed Ellison James' bloody clothes in my dresser drawer.

The way he stood outside the doorway of 1119 after I'd found Ellison James in the tub flashed clearly in my mind—the nervous gestures, grabbing his tie, looking down at it, reaching into his pocket for a handkerchief that wasn't there, using the tie to mop the sweat from his forehead and then tucking it inside his shirt, an odd thing to do, but not if you wanted to hide the fact that you'd lost your tie tack.

The gold tie tack in the shape of the letters HC could only belong to one person. Mr. Hamston Charles must have dropped it when he came in to hide Ellison James' clothes. Ellison James' must have tugged it loose in his struggle with his killer. And if Metzner and his gang were responsible for my kidnappings, then Mr. Charles was the impetus behind the plan, making the hotel manager the new boss.

As I sat there on the floor and pounded my dense head with my fist, I tried to figure out why. Why did Mr. Charles kill his bookkeeper? Had Ellison James suspected the hotel manager's true identity? If James knew, then Mr. Charles had probably reasoned that Elsa knew also and she had to be silenced as well. But something wasn't ringing true. What did Myra tell me? That things are not always what they seem. Elsa was having an affair with someone, and since they were friends, everyone assumed it was Ellison James. But the autopsy indicated that because of his blood type, he couldn't have been responsible for Elsa's pregnancy. Then I remembered an edict I insisted my science students learn when trying to solve a problem. Stick with what you know, but pay attention to the small things. Elsa, looking for a sugar daddy, gets pregnant; Mr. Charles taking long lunches; Elsa giggling in the linen closet. Damn!

I phoned the front desk and asked if Donna Jennings was working today.

"Is this Miss Lockhart?" Mrs. Willis' voice pierced my ear with the intensity of a hot cattle prod. "If you need something, there's a maid on your floor."

If I hadn't been dressed in my baby dolls and confined to my room, I'd

have run down to the front desk and slapped the woman. Instead I
thanked her and hung up. Then I phoned Mrs. Lindstorm. The information she gave me wasn't good. Donna Jennings called this morning to say
she wasn't returning to work. I should have paid more attention to her the
day we talked in Muldoon/Irving's room. She knew more than she was
telling.

There were three Jennings in the Hot Springs phone book. Donna
answered on the third try. If the woman was frightened enough to quit her
job, she wouldn't be eager to talk to me, so I had to catch her off guard.

"Miss Jennings, this is Miss Lockhart. Elsa was having an affair with
Mr. Charles, wasn't she?"

Her sharp intake of breath confirmed my suspicions along with, "How
did you find out?"

"You just told me." I hung up.

That slimy, greasy bastard. If Elsa was willing to get an abortion, why
did he have to kill her? I should have called Dixon right then and there.
But I didn't. Maybe living dangerously for the last several days was
becoming the norm for me, for I had a strong desire to let Mr. Greasy
Bastard Slime-Ball know that I was on to his tricks. I thought about calling him, but a phone conversation wouldn't have the same effect. I wanted to see his eyes, read the expression on his face.

Thankfully two fresh cops, an Officer Peters and Officer Jabowitz, had
replaced O'Riley and Stockton. After last night, O'Riley would never fall
for any excuse I gave him for wanting to leave my room. My article was
finished, but my new bodyguard didn't know that, so I told him that I
needed some last-minute information.

Officer Peters was a sharp, young cop. Had he been on duty last night,
I wouldn't have gone anywhere. He refused to allow me to step one foot
outside my door without clearing it with Dixon first.

"The Lieutenant said half-an-hour." Officer Peters walked me to the
third-floor offices. I still wasn't sure exactly what I'd planned to do. I had
a few options. I could confront Mr. Charles straight away. "I saw you
(even though that was not quite true) at Stingy House last night. What
were you doing, making crime connections, Mr. Boss-man?" I'd seen too
many *Thin Man* movies. Mr. Charles would have to be a real fool to fall
for that. Or I could lay his tie tack in the middle of his desk. That wasn't
a good idea, either. He'd probably flash his switchblade right then and
there. I tried to remember what Margaret had said about Mr. Charles'

phone conversation, something about things moving slowly and not to get pushy; something about getting off his back. But that was a long time ago, and he could have been talking to anybody.

As Peters and I walked down the third floor hallway, a brilliant idea struck.

Mr. Charles was in his office, but on the phone, Miss Roberts informed me. "If you could just wait five minutes, Miss Lockhart, I'm sure he'll have time to see you. When guests come into our office, I usually ask them if they've had a pleasant stay, but somehow, that question doesn't seem appropriate in your circumstances."

"That's an understatement, Miss Roberts."

The door flew open and Charles, red-faced and jittery, barked, "Lisa, no more calls. Understand!" He looked over and saw me sitting in the chair and his mood worsened, although he tried to hide his annoyance by straightening his tie and running his fingers through his black, greasy, lime-scented hair.

"Miss Lockhart? What brings you here?" His cold, blue eyes threw daggers. All of a sudden my brilliant idea didn't seem so wonderful. I glanced in the hallway to make sure Officer Peters was standing guard. Then I threw my shoulders back and stood up.

"I'd like a word with you. It won't take long. I know you're awfully busy."

"I can spare a couple of minutes." He stepped aside for me to walk in.

The door clicked shut, causing me to jump. I turned around expecting to see a gun pointed at my back. A cold jolt of nerves shot up my spine.

"Sit down," he said, walking behind his desk and plopping into his chair.

I glanced at the cigarette box on his desk. He signed, picked it up, and offered me one. Then he leaned over with his lighter, lit mine, and then his.

I studied the cigarette as if I had all the time in the world. "Luckys, my father smokes Luckys." I ignored his offer to sit down and strolled over to the window. His office looked outover Central Avenue. "Nice view. Those magnolia trees must be lovely when they're in bloom."

"I wouldn't know. I'm too busy to gawk out the window."

"Running this hotel must not leave you any time for anything else. Maybe you could use some help."

"I'm sure you didn't come here to talk about my work schedule, Miss

Lockhart."

"No, you're right. But I do like it here . . . a lot."

"Thinking of moving in, are you?"

"I might be."

"You're joking."

"Why would I joke? I like to be where the action is."

"Well, you've certainly seen action here."

"Oh, I'm not talking about that kind of action. You see, reporting gets me around and I usually discover more than just places to stay and things do to."

He looked at me through half-closed eyes and a cloud of blue cigarette smoke. He leaned forward and rested an elbow on his desk. "I'm not sure what you're getting at, Miss Lockhart."

"Oh. I think you do. I paid a visit to Stingy House last night."

His elbow slipped off and he barely caught himself before his face slammed into the desk.

"I leave on Saturday morning. You know where I'll be until then." I walked over and stubbed out my cigarette in his ashtray. "You really should take in the view out your window. It might put you in a better mood."

As Peters walked me back to my room, I felt the sweat running down my sternum. What the hell did I do? Mr. Charles could have interpreted what I had said in several ways. One thing was for sure; he wouldn't be knocking on my door with a bottle of champagne and a box of chocolates as long as a police officer was standing by. And if he was involved with the underworld and took my offer seriously, well . . . I would soon find out.

Nothing happened the rest of the day. With Dixon's permission, Ruth and I went down to the mineral pool around three. We looked a fine pair. Her with a bandage on her shoulder and me with fresh black and blue bruises on top of old ones now turning a sickly yellow. At first I worried about Ruth noticing the recent bruises, but then I knew she couldn't tell the difference between old and new ones. The temperature had dropped into the forties after last night's front blew in and the hot water in the pool felt better than it had all week. Peters and Jabowitz sat patiently on lounge chairs near the towel cabinet. The city couldn't possibly pay these guys enough.

"How are things at home?" I asked Ruth.

"Wonderful. I don't know what I'd do without Sophia."

"Maybe you should give her a raise."

"I might do that. Mom called and she'll be back from France next week. She'll be here for the holidays and then off to Greece." Ruth blew a stream of smoke over her shoulder. "Some of those bruises look like they've just come up, especially that one right below your left clavicle."

Okay, maybe Ruth did remember her high school biology, but I ignored her comment.

"You should go with her."

"Who'd take care of you?"

I looked down at my beaten up body and shook my head. "You're not very good at your job."

"You should talk."

"We're pathetic," I sighed. "Maybe we should both go to Greece."

"I don't know about Greece. They eat squid."

"I'm sure they cook it first."

Red and pruned, Ruth and I stood out in the hall while Peters and Jabowitz checked our rooms for thugs before letting us in. I half expected to have a message from Mr. Charles pushed under my door. There wasn't one. Maybe I didn't get my meaning across. Just then the phone rang.

"Syd. How about you and Ruth joining me for dinner tonight?" Rita said. "Tomorrow night I have a banquet I have to supervise. It's either tonight or next time you come to town."

"Tonight's great."

"We'll have to make it later, around eight. Mr. Charles took off early today and the bozo left me with all his work. I've got so much paper work to do, I'll probably have to come in early in the morning to finish it."

"He left early?"

"He barged into my office around two and said he had some personal business to take care of. Said he'd be back in the morning. If I ever did that, he'd dock my pay."

I hung up the phone and before I let go of the receiver it rang again. I let it ring three more times before I answered. I read somewhere that a lady should never be too anxious to answer the phone.

"Sydney Jean Lockhart! What is going on at that hotel?"

"Mom, so glad you called."

"Don't 'so glad you called,' me, young lady. Your brother told me about the other murder. Your father knew about this, didn't he?"

"Mom, he didn't want you to worry."

"Worry! Worry! What happens if you're next?"

"Are you still in El Paso?"

"Scott and I are in Phoenix. I suppose you don't remember what happened to that woman traveling alone in the Bahamas?"

My mother had read an article in the Galveston County New about an American woman who had disappeared while vacationing on a Caribbean island. Her partially decomposed body was discovered three months later. Whenever Mom worries about me being on the road, she brings up that story.

"I'm sure Hollywood is much more dangerous than any place I travel."

"Don't get smart with me. I'm still your mother."

"Mom, why don't you go home? You and Dad can get remarried. We'll turn the anniversary celebration into a wedding celebration. It'll be fun."

"I can never show my face in Galveston again. I'm an unwed mother."

"No one has to know. It'll be our secret. You could tell your friends that you and Dad are just renewing your vows."

"God would know."

"I don't think God would really care one way or another."

"Blasphemous, just like your father. Speaking of coming home. You're the one who needs to leave that place."

"I'm not alone. Ruth's here."

"That's supposed to give me comfort? Every time you two get together, someone winds up with stitches, or broken bones, or . . . or almost drowned."

"All those things happened when we were little. We're adults now."

"Oh, for heaven's sakes! Until you're married, you're in no better shape than a teenager."

For the life of me, I never understood that reasoning. I guess a husband would make all the bad things go away.

"I'll be home on Saturday. I promise."

"That's two days from now. A lot can happen in two days."

"Actually, a day and a half. Besides, there are cops all over the hotel. Nothing's going to happen. We're being very care—"

Clink.

"You're a real pain in the ass, Mom, you know that?"

"Sydney!"

I jumped. Ruth was standing in the doorway.

"How can you talk to Aunt Mary Lou like that?"

"Easy. She hung up."

"Is she back home?"

"Nope. She and my momma's-boy brother are in Phoenix."

"Don't worry. As soon as Francie gets back, she'll talk some sense into Aunt Mary Lou."

"That'll be the day. Listen, Rita called and invited us to dinner tonight."

"Wonderful."

"Ruth, I have a phone call to make."

She folded her arms and cocked her head.

"It's personal."

She raised her eyebrow.

"I'll tell you about it later."

She stomped her foot.

"It's a surprise."

"Another surprise? Haven't I had enough of those?"

"Oh, shut up and give me just one minute of privacy."

She turned on her heel, went back into her room, and slammed the door.

I called Yancy at the newspaper office to see if my slide was ready. If he was still out with a cold, I'd have to leave my address for him to mail the woodpecker photo. No problem, I'd give it to Ruth as a Christmas present. Hopefully by then, she'd be over that incident in the woods and not faint when she saw it.

Yancy was in and we shouted at one another over the clanking and slamming of machinery in the background. The press was running full force. He apologized for Ruth's picture ending up on the front page, claiming that a reporter had lifted it from his office when he was out. I told him that since I was indisposed he could make it up to me by bringing over the enlargement. Asking Dixon's permission to leave the hotel again was pushing my luck. Besides, I wanted to save the favor for tonight when we met Rita for dinner. Yancy agreed and a messenger delivered an envelope soon after we'd hung up.

I opened the envelope and slid out two eight and a half by eleven glossies and a note.

Two?

I picked up the note. "The woodpecker shot turned out great," Yancy wrote. "I did my best with the other one, but it's still a bit fuzzy.

Other one?

The pileated woodpecker's red crest and white stripe down its neck stood out brightly against the browns and green of the forest. The second photo was a shot of the woods. Ruth must have taken it. I'd have to give her some photography lessons, unless she'd purposely tried to catch the shadows across the trail, either way, lessons were in order.

I slid the photos back into the envelope and as I was tucking them away in a dresser drawer, I heard a strange sound.

Ruth was actually knocking on our adjoining door.

"Come in."

"So, what was the surprise?" Ruth said.

"If I told you, it wouldn't be a surprise."

"It had to have something to do with your slides."

"You weren't listening at the door, were you?"

"Who? Me? I wouldn't stoop that low. You didn't enlarge that photo of me in those horrible hiking clothes."

I just smiled. "Sydney Lockhart! You didn't?!"

"It turned out great. I sent it down to the front desk to have it mailed. Maryanne Newton should get it by Monday. When your high school reunion brochure goes out next spring, your scowling face will probably be on the front cover."

She was speechless. When she finally found her voice, it came out in short-syllabled squeaks.

"I . . . will . . . ne . . ver . . . for . . . give . . . you!"

"Relax. I'm joking."

Chapter 34

Dixon's answer was a firm "No." If we wanted to have dinner with Rita, we'd have to eat in the hotel restaurant. He refused to let us out. This was the answer Officer Peters gave us after phoning the Lieutenant. Telling Officer Peters that we'd probably be safer elsewhere did no good.

The three of us were seated at a small table near the fountain in the Fountain Room. Water trickled from an urn held over the head of a whimsical nymph whose bare feet rested on a serpent. I suppose the effect was meant to relax diners, but after my splash in Lake Hamilton, I'd much prefer a dining room with a desert motif.

"Too bad we couldn't go to Mario's," Rita said. "He has the best Italian food I've ever eaten." She leaned back as the waiter snapped the napkin open and laid it in her lap. He did the same for Ruth and me. "But I understand Dixon's concern for your safety." The waiter handed her the wine list. "We'll order wine later, right now bring us three martinis. A twist for me and olives for my friends."

"I'm starved," Ruth said. "What do you recommend?"

"The special on Thursday night is prime rib. It's wonderful," Rita said. "I can't believe you two are leaving on Saturday. We're just getting to know one another. I hope you won't let these recent murders keep you from coming back. Hot Springs is a wonderful little vacation spot."

For the next two hours we forgot about murders, men, and mishaps. We talked about ourselves, our families, our interests—goals, dreams, and plans for the future. Three single, independent women, making our way in a married men's world.

The meal was probably one of the best I'd ever eaten. We lingered over wine, then lingered over dessert and coffee, then lingered over glasses of sherry. Finally up to our eyeballs in food and drink, the only thing left to do was linger over cigarettes. Ruth pulled out her ebony cigarette hold-ers. "I only have two, but I'm sure Syd won't mind if you use hers." She wedged in a cigarette and offered it to Rita.

"No, thanks, I've given it up. I'm restricting my indulgent habits to alcohol. I read a newspaper article that said cigarette smoking might cause health problems."

For some strange reason the desire for an after-dinner smoke did not evoke the usual craving. I'd heard those bad health claims myself. Was the power of suggestion assaulting my olfactory nerves as a warning? No, that wasn't it. Something in the back on my mind tried to swim forward. Something important that had gotten lost among the puddle of useless facts in my brain had surfaced momentarily, but was swallowed up and going down for the third time. I tried to grab hold and rescue the memo-ry, but just as quickly as it had surfaced, it sank.

"Don't believe everything you read," Ruth said. "These are menthol. Everyone knows menthol is healthy. It cleans the lungs and makes for easier breathing. That's why they put menthol in Mentholatum." Ruth handed me the holder. "Besides, the last time I tried to do something healthy," Ruth shot me a dirty look, "like go for a hike in the woods, I got shot."

"Thanks," I said, feeling a bit irksome, as if the incident were my fault. I told myself to snap out of it. I had no reason to feel anything but absolutely wonderful. I had propositioned a gangster and kissed a cop. Way to go, Syd. "Ah."

"What?" Ruth and Rita said.

I hadn't realized I'd spoken my annoyance out loud. "I mean, you hear all sorts of things and no one knows what to believe." To show I had faith in my convictions I took a sip of sherry and inhaled some healthy men-thol-laced smoke.

"Sydney's been cranky lately," Ruth said. "I think she's in love."

It was a good thing we'd finished eating because I spit my sherry across the table.

"Oh?" Rita smiled. She graciously took her napkin and mopped up my mess.

"Don't listen to her, it's the aspirin and alcohol, it makes her say weird things." Before my darling cousin could respond, the toe of my shoe made hard contact with her shin.

Rita had the good sense to not pursue the subject. Instead she selected

a topic agreeable to any woman. "You did good, Sydney. It takes me forever to find what I'm looking for when I shop. That blouse is beautiful on
you. It looks like something you'd find in a boutique in Paris. You have
an eye for style."

Like a drowning victim that refused to die, that shadowy memory bolt-
ed up once more and slammed against my skull, scattering the useless
facts that had been floating on the surface. I had just taken another swallow of sherry, but had the foresight to grab my napkins before spitting it
across the table a second time. "Can't we talk about something else?" I
coughed.

"Cranky, cranky," Ruth said. She expeditiously swung her legs from
under the table, causing me to kick air.

Rita threw her head back and let out a hearty laugh. "You two are a
hoot. I'm really going to miss you."

The waiter brought the check and Rita snatched it up.

"Rita, you've been too generous," I said.

"Don't be silly. I invited you to dinner. Beside, my friends are dull compared to Ruth Echland and Sydney Lockhart." She raised her glass in a
toast. "To new friends, and . . . healthier hikes in the future."

Rita said goodnight and made us promise to stop by her office on
Saturday for a final goodbye. After that talk with my mother, I decided to
give up on the idea of finding the wedding picture. It wasn't worth dying
for. Our bodyguards rode with us in the elevator to the tenth floor.

"What was wrong with you at dinner tonight?" Ruth hissed. "Why have
you been so moody lately?"

The last question was so ridiculous it didn't deserve an answer. I could
have given her a string of reasons why my mood was less than bright. But
I didn't feel like bickering with my cousin.

Back in our rooms, I once again used the excuse of a headache. Ruth
brought me some of her aspirin and told me not to bother her; she had to
give some serious thought to packing for the trip home. I had to give serious thought to the crazy idea that was swirling around in my head. I had
to call Dixon and tell him about the tie tack. I had to stop checking into
hotels where murderers lurked.

O'Riley knocked on my door to tell me that he and Stockton were on
duty for the night. I ordered them a pot of coffee. I wanted our bodyguards wide-awake.

·

The night passed without incident. I slept fitfully and woke up later than usual and crankier than the night before. I bathed and tackled my hair. It was punishing me for tossing and turning and was more unruly than ever. I had almost given up and was looking through my cosmetic kit for a rubber band to put my hair into a ponytail when Ruth waltzed in.

"Have you room in your suitcase?"

"Forget to knock?"

"Knock? I knocked yesterday. Besides, this is one big room with a little door."

"No, Ruth, it's not one big room! There's your room and my room, divided by said little door."

"Listen, Miss Snotty. I'm getting pretty sick of your moodiness." Ruth plopped down on my sofa. "You were acting so stuck up last night at dinner. What's going on?"

"Do I really have to answer that question with all that's happened this week? Never mind." I held up my hands like a shield. "I don't want to talk about it. You're packing now? We don't leave until tomorrow."

"I know we don't leave until tomorrow, but I don't throw my clothes into a suitcase and slam it shut like you. I like to take my time. Anyway, I bought too much stuff. It won't all fit."

"Well, I certainly won't have room in my one little suitcase. You brought more luggage than a traveling Broadway show. You should hire a porter. Besides, I'm not going to your apartment with you. We part ways once we hit Dallas."

"Why?"

"Why?" I didn't bother to remind her that I was going to the airport. Instead, I said, "I might decide to drive all the way home. Maybe take a slow cruise through the Piney Woods of East Texas."

"Spare me! I've had enough of the woods for the rest of my life!"

"Good, 'cause you're not invited. Go down to the millinery shop. They have luggage. You can buy another piece."

"Good idea. Officer Jabowitz's on duty. I like him. He's not snotty. I'm sure he'll enjoy helping me pick out luggage."

"Take the rest of the morning, will you? In fact, take the entire Hot Springs Police Department. If you look long enough maybe you'll find a nice yellow piece that matches your gloves."

"Thanks for the idea. I'll take the gloves with me to get a perfect match." Ruth stormed into her room. I kicked the door shut.

As soon as I heard Ruth and Officer Jabowitz leave, I pulled the phone to my lap to call Dixon. I couldn't waste any more time. I had to tell him about the tie tack and my suspicions, no matter how farfetched. And I had to tell him about my near murder at Stingy House. Suddenly a sense of foreboding washed over me and I put the phone down. I ran over and jerked open the drawer where I had the envelope with the enlargements. I had placed the tie tack for safe keeping inside. When I saw that it was still there, I breathed a sigh of relief. Keeping it in my room last night was a stupid thing to do. The way people waltzed in and out of here, it could have disappeared. As I slid the photos back in, the shot that Ruth had taken caught my eye. I took a closer look and suddenly felt deathly ill. It wasn't Ruth who had taken the picture, it was me. Could it possibly be? I didn't want to believe it, but the truth was staring me in the face. My suspicions turned to hard, cold facts.

I phoned Dixon. He was out. I left a message. I didn't know how to locate Irving. For the first time since I found Ellison James' body, I felt a genuine fear for my own life.

Chapter 35

I was well into pacing a rut in the carpet when Officer Peters tapped on my door. "Note for you, Miss Lockhart." He handed me a small brown envelope. I thanked him and waited for him to leave. Somehow I knew the news wasn't good. I was right. The note was simple. The object that accompanied it twisted my insides and caused my heart to stop.

I told myself not to panic. But I had to act now. I had no choice. Remembering one of Mickey's connections and taking Ruth's advice from a few days ago, I thumbed through the phone book, found the number, and made the call before I could talk myself out of it. Then I called Dixon again, but my reason for needing to speak to him had changed. I couldn't tell him about the tie tack. I couldn't tell him about the photo. He answered with his usual bark. He was busy; what did I want. Damn him. I did something I hated to do. I whined, pleaded, and yapped like a woman. After three minutes of listening to me snivel, he told me to put Officer Peters on the line.

"Yes sir, I understand. No sir. I will. Yes sir."

This time it was much easier, having practiced the night before. I stuck the last bobby pin into my hair. A few ringlets hung down the side of my face. I placed the green cap on my head and pulled down the net veil. The effect was just what I hoped for, a slight sheltering of my eyes. I was out the door in a flash.

Not a lunchtime hot spot, the Ohio Club was almost empty. I took a seat at the bar. I was early, but I'd planned it that way. Officer Peters stood at the door with one eye on me and the other on the street. Somehow his vigilance did nothing to ease my trepidation. As far as he knew this was an innocent lunch date. I purposely kept him in the dark. When he turned his glance to me, I pointed to the lady's room down the hall and he nodded. Once in the hall, I looked back at my bodyguard. His head was bent over his cupped hands as he lit a cigarette. I dashed out the back door.

Danny Mueller had my purchase ready when I walked into his news-stand/pawn shop. He handed me the package and I handed over fifty bucks. I ran back to the Ohio Club, ducked into the lady's room, prepared everything, and walked back to the bar, patting the back of my French twist. The entire transaction, including travel time, took less than six minutes. Officer Peters smiled when he saw me, and then he turned his attention back to the door. He held it open and my lunch date walked in—right on time.

"Well, don't you look stunning," she said. "I wasn't sure you liked that cap. I knew when I saw it, that you'd look like a million bucks wearing it." She ordered two martinis, an olive for me and a lemon twist for herself.

She was dressed in her usual business suit and heels. White pearls draped over her red silk blouse. Her hair and makeup were perfect, her poise and demeanor confident. The only thing that marred her appearance was the pencil she'd forgotten to remove from her twist. Despite her normal camouflage, Rita looked different.

"Where's Ruth?" I laid her yellow glove on the bar.

"Safe for now."

"You better not harm a hair on—"

"You're in no position to make demands, Syd." She laid a hand on her clutch and moved it closer to her.

"Even you wouldn't try anything with a cop standing a few feet away," I said.

She looked over my shoulder at Peters. "Cops don't worry me."

"Evidently not."

"Listen, Syd, by the time we finish lunch, I can arrange for you and Ruth can be on your way home."

"You expect me to believe that?"

Rita placed her red-nailed hand over her heart. "Of course. You're not involved in any of this."

"Then why did you try to slit my throat at the casino? And why did you take Ruth?"

"I could have killed you if I'd wanted to. Think of it as a warning. As

far as Ruth goes, I needed some leverage to get you out of town. I saw
that look on your face at dinner last night. You'd never make it as a poker
player. You figured something out. I'm not sure what, but whatever you
know is only conjecture."

"So this is just another warning. You're going to let me and Ruth leave
Hot Springs and forget we were ever here."

"That's your only choice."

"Please, Rita, don't take me for a fool. You killed four people and I'm
supposed to look the other way?"

"Go on. Go to the cops with your suspicions. If you do, your life will
become a nightmare, and for me . . . well, let's just say it'll be business
as usual.

"I have more than suspicions."

She picked up her martini.

"You should have taken this cap when you stole the rest of my clothes."

Her lips froze on the rim of the glass, her eyes locked with mine. "I like
the way you've pulled down the veil. It makes you look . . . sly."

I picked up my cigarettes and handed her one. "Oh, I forgot. You quit.
I've heard it's hard to do."

"I've managed."

"Ever have one . . . you know . . . in a weak moment."Never. I'm afraid
I'd start again."

"Too bad."

"Why?" she said. "I don't miss it."

"No. I mean too bad it wasn't you—"

"What?"

"—smoking in the cupola that morning we found Elsa's body. I thought
it was you smoking a cigarette while I made my way across the plank."

Her hand gripped her clutch. She looked around the room as if hoping
to find a reasonable response carved somewhere in the grain of dark wood
paneling, or maybe in the faces of other customers, or in my cigarette
smoke swirling toward the ceiling.

I slipped my hand into my skirt pocket. The comfort I'd felt earlier
when I bought the gun was no longer there. The piece felt cold and hard.

"I don't know what you mean," Rita said.

"I smelled cigarette smoke while I edged my way across the plank.
There were two people in the cupola, you and Elsa, but since Elsa was
dead, you had to have been the one smoking, unless . . ."

She turned her face away and stared at her reflection in the bar mirror. The bartender looked over at us and smiled. He sat three lemons on a towel and started cutting them into thin slices.

I lowered my voice. "But if it wasn't you smoking, it had to have been Elsa, which meant she was alive, enjoying her work break. You work fast, Rita. The blast of the fire-truck siren, the scarf blown over my eyes, the darkness inside the cupola, all provided a perfect opportunity, great cover . . . and an alibi. You should have taken the cap when you took the rest of my clothes. I might never have figured it out."

Using her thumb, she flicked open the clasp of the clutch.

"I wouldn't if I were you. We don't want to make a scene."

Her hand remained where it was.

"I underestimated you, Syd. How stupid of me."

She held out her other hand to the bartender and he placed a lemon slice in her palm. She twisted it, adding a few drops to her martini. She took a sip. "The smell of cigarette smoke, a gift that wasn't stolen, come on, Syd, that sounds too farfetched." She turned to look at me. "So you see? None of this means anything. And I don't have a switchblade in my purse." She laughed.

"The FBI might find all of this very curious though. And they'd be on your trail. You're the link they need to tie all of this together."

"I don't think so. My trail's pretty well protected."

"Maybe. But what if I handed them a piece of hard evidence?"

The bartender walked over to take the order of a man who sat a couple of stools away from Rita.

"What might that be?"

"A photo. Remember? The day you followed Ruth and me into the woods. I had my camera around my neck. After you shot Ruth, I turned to run after her. I tripped at the same time you fired at me. I thought the flash was from your gun, but it was my flashbulb. My camera snapped accidentally and I got a great picture of you." It was not quite the truth. The person in the photo was barley visible, but it was Rita nonetheless. "Why didn't you come after us? You could have finished us off right then and there."

"I almost did. But you weren't the only ones on the trail. Someone was coming up behind me. I couldn't chance it. I don't like witnesses. Stupid hikers."

I noticed a slight crack in her veneer. She tucked an invisible stray hair behind her ear.

"Where's Ruth?" I asked again. I had this horrible thought that if I didn't play this right, I'd never see my cousin again. I was ready to make a trade—the photo and negative for Ruth, but I never got that far. Rita took another sip of her martini. She smoothed out her bar napkin and sat her glass directly in the center. "I like things to be neat." She ran her finger around the rim of the glass. "But sometimes that's not possible. You don't leave me much choice." Then in one fluid, well-practiced motion, she shoved her clutch across the bar, knocking over our glasses. She grabbed the bartender's knife and slashed at my face catching the blade in the cap's veil before I could grab the gun from my pocket. I fumbled with it as I fought to grab her wrist. She swung down for another swipe. Suddenly an explosion sounded and Rita fell backward over the barstool. I looked down and saw a dark stain spread across her chest. My gun rested on the floor next to her body. My eyes darted from the gun back to Rita in disbelief.

"Don't worry, hon. It wasn't you."

I turned to see Dixon and several police officers standing in the doorway. He slipped his gun into its holster. He walked over and brushed my hair from my face, then picked up a bar napkin and pressed it to my forehead. Rita hadn't exactly missed in her attempt to scalp me.

"They have Ruth," I choked back a sob.

"What are you talking about?" Dixon said. "Ruth's at the hotel giving Grady a raft of shit."

"What?"

"Someone stole her yellow gloves and she's having a conniption."

I slumped back on the barstool. Dixon put his arm around me. "Too bad your green sandals were stolen. They'd look nice with that cap." My cap rested on the floor between my gun and Rita's body.

All I could do was stare.

"I think you need stitches again," he said.

Tears trailed down my cheeks. "That's okay. I'm used to stitches."

He pulled me to his chest and held me until I stopped shaking.

Chapter 36

"It wasn't your fault," Grady said to me. "Mr. Charles had botched so many jobs already, Rita was waiting for the right moment to get rid of him as well."

Our waiter came by with two martinis, two bourbons on the rocks, and a Royal Crown Cola. We were sitting in the lounge at the Park Hotel— Grady, Mickey, the off-duty O'Riley, and Ruth and I. After the discovery of Mr. Charles' body, the Arlington was crawling with police once again. When we passed through the lobby on the way out, there was a line at the front desk that snaked back to the valet area. Except for the cops and the wedding celebration going on in the second floor ballroom, I feared that Rita Fredricks' murders would render the hotel empty by the afternoon. One body was fodder for good gossip; two bodies struck fear into people's hearts; but the third produced a swarm of hotel guests impatiently waiting to check out and get the hell home, the Asian family among them. As I walked by, I saw the father grab his son by his ankles, turned him upside down, and shake him like a potato sack. I heard a clink and a tiny gold object popped out of the boy's mouth. The mother retrieved it, dried it off, and slipped it onto her ring finger where it belonged.

"It's a good thing they found Mr. Charles' body when they did or you might be in the morgue with the other poor SOBs," Mickey said.

"It would serve her right for slipping away from me again," Ruth huffed, swirling her olive and giving me a dirty look.

"I don't think the punishment fits the crime, my dear cousin. Besides, I thought she had kidnapped you."

Ruth was having none of my excuses. She folded her arms and pouted.

"I have the office secretary, Lisa Roberts, to thank for calling Dixon," I said. "I hope the poor girl's okay."

"Fainted dead way," O'Riley said, "after one look at that puddle of blood seeping from underneath the closet door in Mr. Charles' office."

"Did you first suspect Charles from the night we were at Stingy House?" Grady ask.

"What's Stingy House?" Ruth said.

"He was always in the back of my mind," I said. "But after finding the tie tack, I was sure he had to be involved. I just didn't know the specifics."

"What tie-tack?" Ruth's voice rose.

"Mr. Charles told Rita about Miss Lockhart's visit to his office," O'Riley said. "She must have realized it was only a matter of time before Miss Lockhart put two and two together. Besides, Rita didn't trust Mr. Charles and needed him silenced. Just like she silenced Metzner and Chester Morani. But, like Grady said, it was something she'd planned to do all along, even before you got here, Miss Lockhart."

"What visit to Mr. Charles' office?" Ruth shouted.

"Actually, when I suspected Mr. Charles, I had no idea about Rita. It wasn't until we had dinner Thursday night that everything came together. Her stealing my clothes and leaving the gift she'd bought me, her no longer smoking but me smelling cigarette smoke in the cupola, and finally that photo."

"What photo?" Ruth stood up and stomped her size-five foot. "How do you know all this?"

"Rita Fredricks came out of surgery and began singing like a canary," O'Riley said. "She ain't no fool. A clean confession buys her some time and maybe a little protection from the mob."

"Maybe we should back up and clue in Miss Echland," Grady said.

Seeing that Ruth was about to blow her stack, I had to agree with Grady. Although that meant I'd have to admit that I'd broken my promise to Ruth about not lying to her anymore. Thinking back, I might be able to use the excuse that I hadn't lied, that keeping mute about my shenanigans during the last couple of days was my way of protecting her.

I reached over and plucked Ruth's olive from her martini so she wouldn't be tempted to spear out my eyes with the toothpick.

"If you sit down and shut up, we'll tell you what happened," I said.

"Well, I should think so." She seated herself and straightened the hem of her skirt. She affixed her holder with a menthol cigarette. "After what I've been through, I shouldn't have to throw a tantrum to find out what's going on. Now, tell me the rest of it."

I knew Ruth would never allow me to forget that she took that bullet in the shoulder. And to make sure it never happened again, I gave my newly purchased gun to Grady as a departing gift.

After I finished my story, I added, "those are the facts so far. "What exactly happened with Ellison James and Elsa Dubois, we can only piece together. I figured Ellison found out about Mr. Charles' involvement, and, since Ellison's hands were dirty involving horseracing, he probably wanted a piece of the mob action as well."

"You're right, Sydney. Ellison was no innocent," Grady continued. "He'd been hanging around bookies and the likes of them for a while. Who knows how he found out about Rita and Charles' connection with the mob, but he did. That's when Mr. Charles cooked up that story about his bookkeeper disappearing with the office cash. The only problem was Ellison came back."

"He feared for Elsa," I said. "They were friends, not lovers. Since Elsa told him the stork was on the way, she probably confided in him about her affair with Mr. Charles. Ellison came back to the hotel to tell Elsa he'd found a doctor and had arranged everything in Little Rock for the next morning. Mr. Charles must have seen him, and having been given orders by Rita to get rid of him, did just that."

"Eleven nineteen is a good place for murder," Mickey added. "Well hidden. When I become hotel manager, I'll put mirrors on the walls in that part of the hall."

Ruth dismissed Mickey's future plans with a wave of her hand. "But why kill Elsa?" she said.

"It's my guess that Rita couldn't be sure Mr. Charles didn't talk in his sleep," I said.

"That was a risky move." Grady rattled his bourbon-empty glass, at the passing waiter. "Killing Elsa in the cupola with you right there, and then pretending to faint."

"Rita's no amateur." I felt the bandage over my eye. "She saw an opportunity and she took it. She also suspected that Muldoon, I mean Irving, was a cop, otherwise why steal his gun to kill Metzner? Muldoon's lucky he didn't end up on her death list."

"All this killing going on right under our noses, imagine that," Mickey opined.

"That reminds me of that Dorothy Sayers' Lord Wimsey mystery," Ruth said. "The one where a guy is murdered while playing bridge. No one sees it happen, but it had to have been one of the four bridge players at the table."

That was Agatha Christies's Hercule Poirot mystery *Cards on the Table*, but I refrained from correcting Ruth. Like the pleated woodpecker, it wasn't important.

The valet drove up with my rental car and handed over the keys. I sat my suitcase in the trunk and as I was about to slam it shut, a shadow darkened my right shoulder. I turned with a start.

"Just me." Dixon handed me a paper sack.

"What's this?"

"Two things: a wedding photo. Why you travel around with your parents' wedding photo is none of my business. Unless perhaps you lifted it from the wall in that long-forgotten dining room on the second floor, in which case I might have to arrest you." The dimple was back, causing my knees to soften like butter.

"You found my things? What else? You said two."

"Your sandals." He actually smiled.

"At Rita's place, right?"

"Right. The Feds have to keep the rest of your stuff, at least for a while. Part of the investigation. I managed to slip these out when Irving wasn't looking."

"Won't he notice?"

"Probably. But what's he going to do, launch a full-scale investigation for an old photo and a pair of green shoes?"

"Thanks. They're my favorite shoes."

"Mine, too. Hey, maybe I could come see you sometimes. Don't get down to Texas much."

I put the sack in the trunk. Before I could talk myself out of it, I grabbed him by the lapels of his snappy suit, pressed my lips against his, and gave him a kiss I hoped he'd never forget. "Now you have a damn good reason to get down my way."

"You bet, number #7, Tarrytown Terrace Apartments at 817 Enfield Road. Phone number TA-3899. Sometimes I do a little private detecting." He returned my kiss, crushing my ribs. Then he let go, turned, and left.

I was giving serious thought to removing my sandals and photo from the paper sack and putting it over my head to keep from hyperventilating when Ruth walked up.

"What's the matter with you? You look as if you're overheating."

"I'm fine. It's your overactive imagination." I slammed the trunk shut. "Follow me to Texarkana. We'll stop for lunch."

"Why don't we drop your rental car off at the airport here in Hot Springs? We'll ride together in my car."

That was a damned good idea, but I didn't want to spend the next eight hours in the car with her. I needed time to think. So I said, "There's a hefty fee for one-way rentals."

"I'll pay it," she said.

"No, you won't. You've shelled out enough already."

"It doesn't matter."

"It does."

"You're getting stubborn in your old age."

"I'm not yet thirty."

"Why do you have to make this so hard?" She stomped her foot and handed over the keys to her new Styline. "Here, I'll take the rental car back to the airport in Dallas. You can drive the Styline back to Austin."

"That makes absolutely no sense at all, Ruth. Why in the hell would I do that?"

"Because it's in your name." She handed me the pink slip. "It's yours. Have that wreck of yours towed from the airport before it blows up in the parking lot." She pulled her handkerchief from her purse and wiped away something from my mouth. "Maybe one day you'll tell me about how your lipstick became smeared, standing here in the parking garage."

Chapter 37

I put on my new pajamas (not the baby dolls; I'd bought some practical ones), poured myself a glass of Burgundy, and moved my typewriter onto a table in the living room. I had a nice cozy fire blazing in the fireplace. Things had returned to normal rather quickly. Mom was back home terrorizing my father and Scott was home doing the same to Jeremiah. My pets were with me. Mealworm sat patiently on the windowsill eyeing the bird feeder, probably strategizing how she planned to catch a mockingbird in the morning. Monroe strolled over and rested her sweet little head on my foot. How could I have envied Margaret Rochester and her big home? What I had here was pretty nice.

I'd turned in my Hot Springs travel article this morning. It turned out well, even if I say so myself. I stared into the fire and listened to the logs crackle, trying to rid my mind of murder, gangsters, and people who I thought were friends, only to wind up being killers. Putting Rita Fredricks behind bars would hopefully keep the "good citizens," as Margaret so adequately stated, of Hot Springs safe for a while longer.

I rolled a fresh sheet of paper over the cartridge. I took a sip of wine. When I have a good first line to a piece, the rest flows without much effort. Driving away from the Arlington Hotel two days ago was bittersweet. A couple of times, I almost turned around and went back, for what I wasn't sure. Then the line echoed in my head and my focus shifted to the reason I had gone to Hot Springs in the first place—to get fodder for an article. I didn't expect to come away with a second story. When I told Ernest what had happened in Hot Springs, a smile spread across his ugly face; an exposé on murder was too good to ignore. But first I had something more pressing I need to write:

When you're not looking, that's when you usually find something worth finding. The real citizens in Hot Springs, Arkansas aren't standing on the street waving banners and tooting their horns, they're not chatting over coffee at the country club, or trying to make a difference by making a name for themselves. If you keep your eyes and ears alert; if you're willing to get your shoes dirty, or even lose them (for many places are located in the boonies), you'll find these folks, and you'll be glad you did.

I thought of Tooths Filsome—his bright smile and flashy dance steps. I pictured him in his white dentist smock, humming some snappy tune while filling the cavity of a child who would otherwise have gone without. Then Hot Momma in her marshmallow outfit pushed the dentist aside and came into view. She might not win citizen of the year, especially in her line of work, but at least she gave respect where respect was due. I had to admire her for standing up for her waitress, even if it meant flinging a couple of disrespectful customers into the lake. Reverend Smilin' Joe's unique method of fundraising might land him in jail one day, and that would be a real shame. You'd never see these people at the Hot Springs Garden Club or running for some state office, but they had their priorities straight and you knew where they stood.

My mind drifted to the red and silver bigamy twins. I wondered if they'd kept my saddle shoe as a remembrance of the crazy unmarried redhead. Except for the tale of the shared husband, I never got around to hearing their story. I'd have to return to Stingy House one night to discover who these two women really were—teachers at the colored high school, owners of a fabulous restaurant, or maybe even fashion models—they had the bodies for it. The phone rang, jarring me out of my ruminations.

Mealworm's tail twitched. She shot an irritating look at the phone, then turned her attention back to the feeder. I looked down at Monroe, who was whimpering because of a doggy dream, which caused her to drool on my slipper.

The clock chimed ten.

"Who'd be calling at this hour?" I asked Mealworm. She knew the call wasn't for her, so she ignored my question. It could be my mother calling to thank me for saving her marriage, or Red Newsome, inviting me to return to the Crooked J for an encore, or, maybe . . . Lieutenant Ralph Dixon. I wasn't willing to take the chance.

Much to my cat's annoyance, I just let the phone ring.

Printed in the United States
136498LV00002B/38/P